ARCHIE COMIC [...]

dedicated to the memory [...] [...]
president and co-publish[...] [...]T
RICHARD H. GOLDWATE[...]
1936-2007

vp/editor-in-chief
VICTOR GORELICK

vp/director of circulation
FRED MAUSSER

managing editor
MIKE PELLERITO

art director
JOE PEP

cover
PAT SPAZIANTE

production
STEPHEN OSWALD
PAUL KAMINSKI
ADAM SAMTUR

archiecomics.com   sega.com

SONIC THE HEDGEHOG ARCHIVES, Volume 8. Printed in Canada. Published by
Archie Comic Publications, Inc., 325 Fayette Avenue, Mamaroneck, NY 10543-2318.
Richard H. Goldwater, President and Co-Publisher, Michael I. Silberkleit, Chairman
and Co-Publisher. Sega is registered in the U.S. Patent and Trademark Office. SEGA,
Sonic The Hedgehog, and all related characters and indicia are either registered
trademarks or trademarks of SEGA CORPORATION © 1991-2008. SEGA CORPORA-
TION and SONICTEAM, LTD./SEGA CORPORATION © 2001-2008. All Rights
Reserved. The product is manufactured under license from Sega of America, Inc.,
650 Townsend St., Ste. 650, San Francisco, CA 94103 www.sega.com. Any similari-
ties between characters, names, persons, and/or institutions in this book and any
living, dead or fictional characters, names, persons, and/or institutions are not
intended and if they exist, are purely coincidental. Nothing may be reprinted in
whole or part without written permission from Archie Comic Publications, Inc.
ISBN-13: 978-1-879794-32-0   ISBN-10: 1-879794-32-2

TABLE OF CONTENTS

Sonic the Hedgehog #31:
"A Robot Rides the Rails"
The return of Rebel Underground leader Geoffrey St. John leaves
Sally's heart torn between two loves...If the rest of her isn't torn
apart by Robotnik's deadly mech-monster: Dynamac 3000!

"Lost...And Found!"
Knuckles searches the Floating Island for the missing Chaotix...not realizing
that while he is watching out for them, someone else is watching him...

"Tundra Road, Part 1"
In this, the first Rotor solo-story, a distress call from the Frozen North Seas
brings our wily walrus around the world to search for his family.

Sonic the Hedgehog #32:
"Blast from the Past"
For once, Antoine's slipups end in something useful, as the Freedom Fighters
discover an enormous Mobian Cavebear frozen in ice. But they get more
than they bargained for when they unthaw the wild beast!

"Prisoners!"
The mystery identity of Archimedes is revealed...
not to us, but to his captives, the Chaotix!

"Tundra Road, Part 2"
Having been saved from an icy grave by the Arctic Freedom Fighters,
Rotor attempts to take down Robotnik's world-chilling factory.
The only thing standing in his way is...his family?!

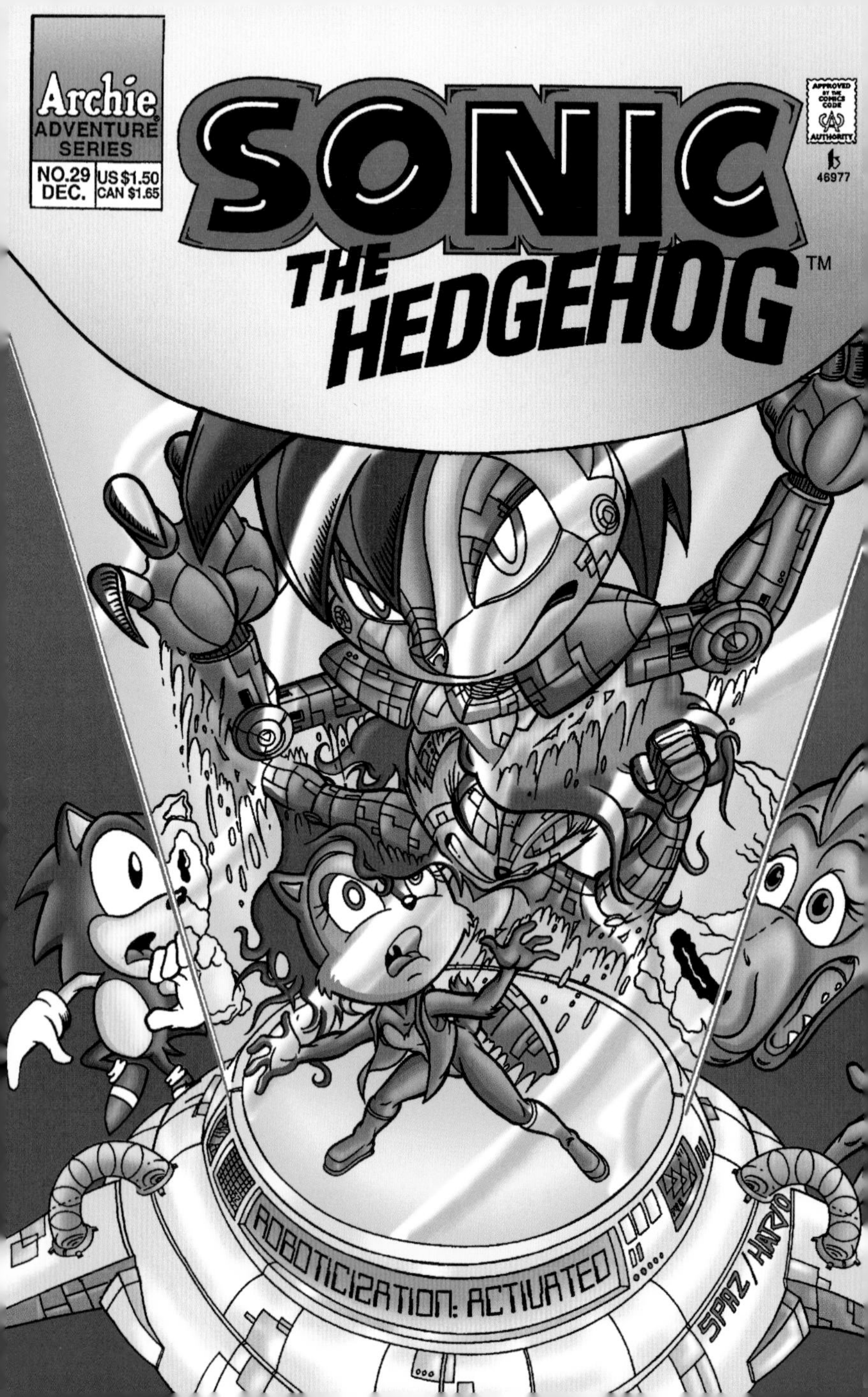
Archie
ADVENTURE SERIES
NO.29 DEC.
US $1.50
CAN $1.65
SONIC THE HEDGEHOG™
APPROVED BY THE COMICS CODE AUTHORITY
46977
ROBOTICIZATION: ACTIVATED
SPAZ / HARVEY

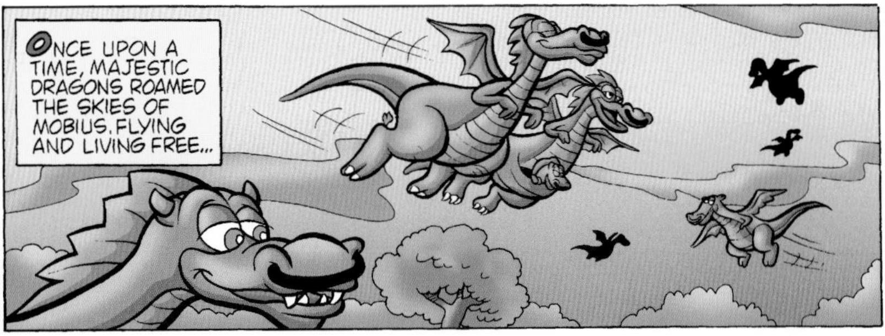
ONCE UPON A TIME, MAJESTIC DRAGONS ROAMED THE SKIES OF MOBIUS, FLYING AND LIVING FREE...

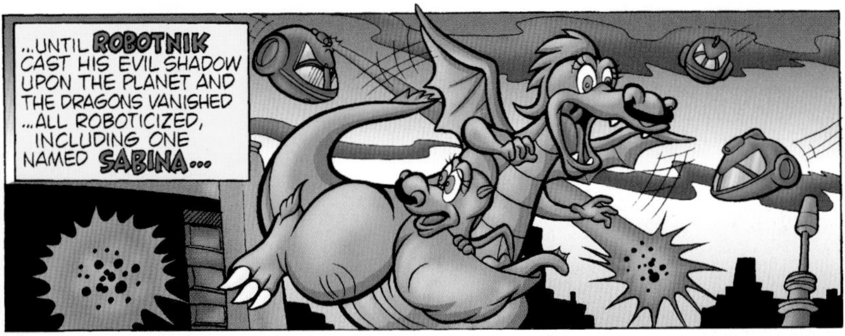
...UNTIL ROBOTNIK CAST HIS EVIL SHADOW UPON THE PLANET AND THE DRAGONS VANISHED ...ALL ROBOTICIZED, INCLUDING ONE NAMED SABINA...

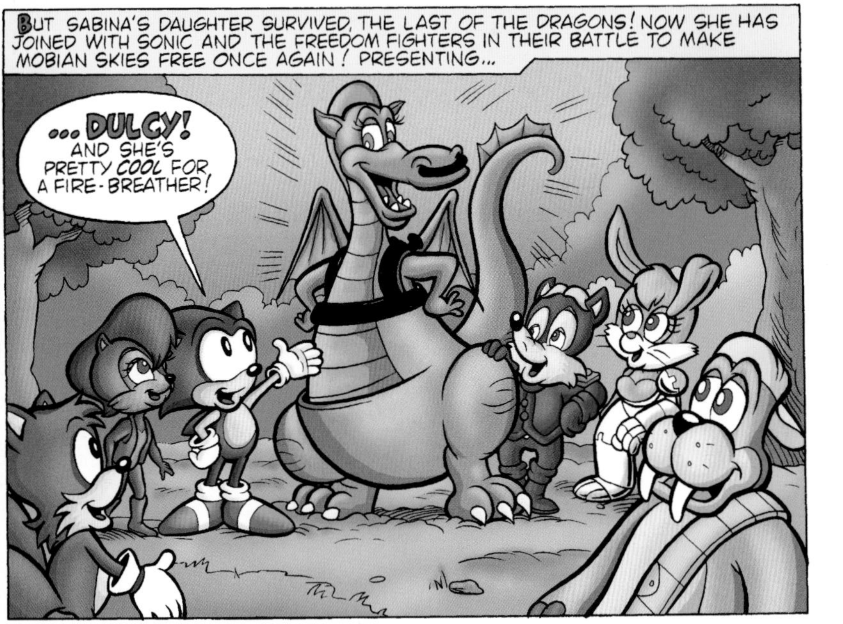
BUT SABINA'S DAUGHTER SURVIVED, THE LAST OF THE DRAGONS! NOW SHE HAS JOINED WITH SONIC AND THE FREEDOM FIGHTERS IN THEIR BATTLE TO MAKE MOBIAN SKIES FREE ONCE AGAIN! PRESENTING...
...DULCY! AND SHE'S PRETTY COOL FOR A FIRE-BREATHER!

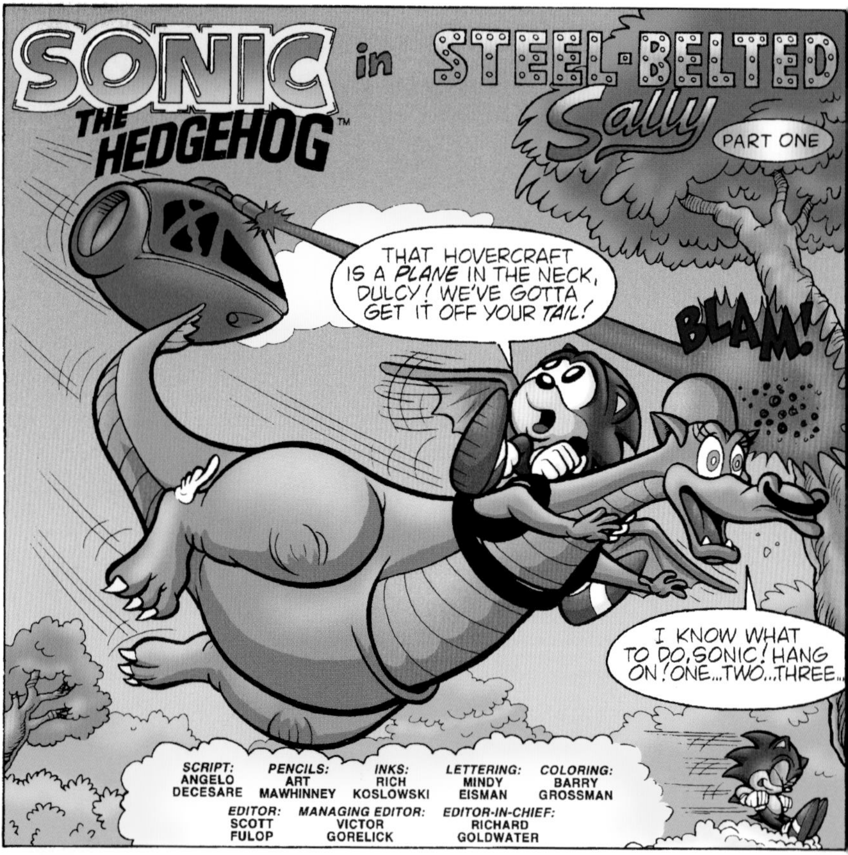
SONIC THE HEDGEHOG™ in STEEL-BELTED Sally
PART ONE
THAT HOVERCRAFT IS A PLANE IN THE NECK, DULCY! WE'VE GOTTA GET IT OFF YOUR TAIL!
BLAM!
I KNOW WHAT TO DO, SONIC! HANG ON! ONE...TWO...THREE...
SCRIPT: ANGELO DECESARE
PENCILS: ART MAWHINNEY
INKS: RICH KOSLOWSKI
LETTERING: MINDY EISMAN
COLORING: BARRY GROSSMAN
EDITOR: SCOTT FULOP
MANAGING EDITOR: VICTOR GORELICK
EDITOR-IN-CHIEF: RICHARD GOLDWATER

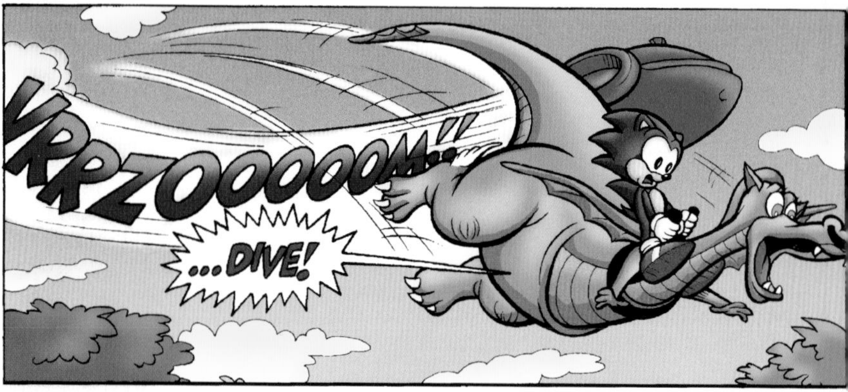
VRRZOOOOOM..!!
...DIVE!

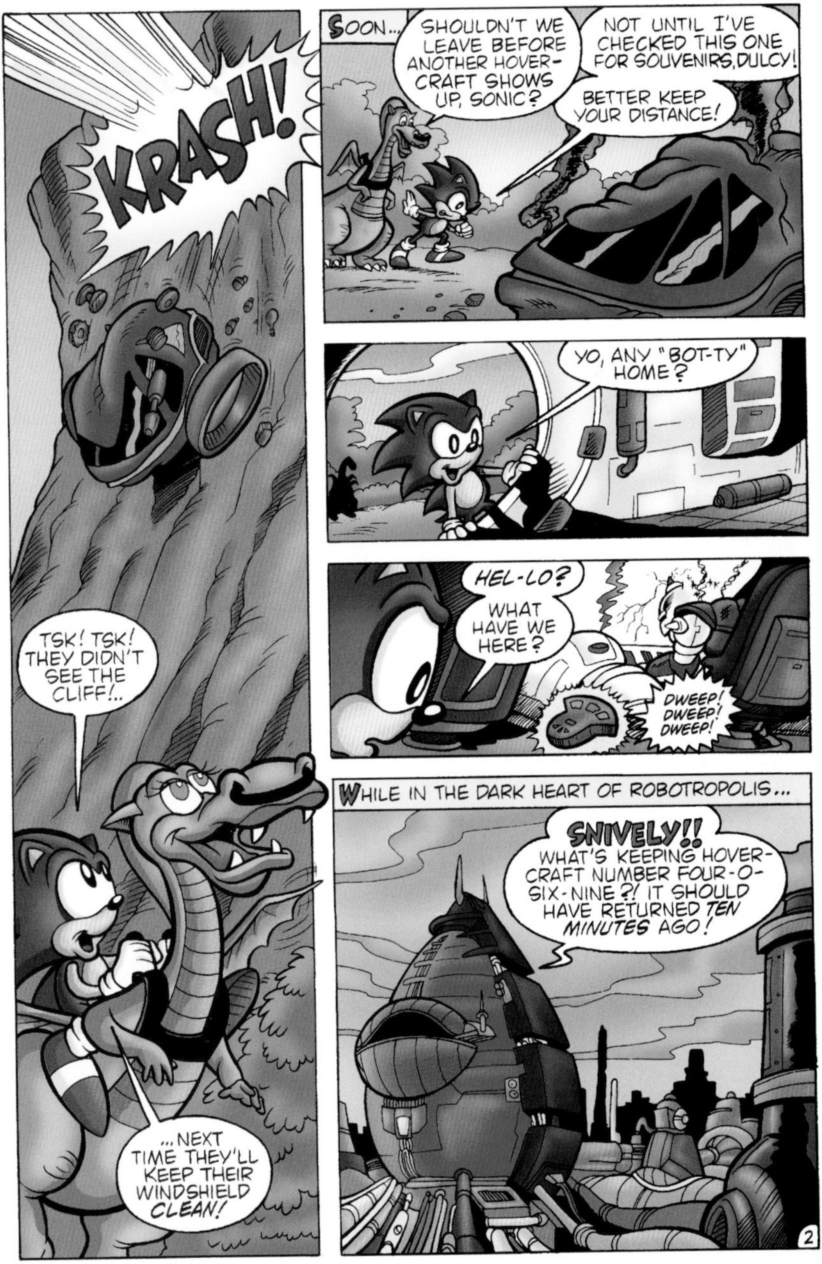
KRASH!
TSK! TSK! THEY DIDN'T SEE THE CLIFF!..
...NEXT TIME THEY'LL KEEP THEIR WINDSHIELD CLEAN!
SOON...
SHOULDN'T WE LEAVE BEFORE ANOTHER HOVER-CRAFT SHOWS UP, SONIC?
NOT UNTIL I'VE CHECKED THIS ONE FOR SOUVENIRS, DULCY!
BETTER KEEP YOUR DISTANCE!
YO, ANY "BOT-TY" HOME?
HEL-LO?
WHAT HAVE WE HERE?
DWEEP! DWEEP! DWEEP!
WHILE IN THE DARK HEART OF ROBOTROPOLIS...
SNIVELY!! WHAT'S KEEPING HOVER-CRAFT NUMBER FOUR-O-SIX-NINE?! IT SHOULD HAVE RETURNED TEN MINUTES AGO!

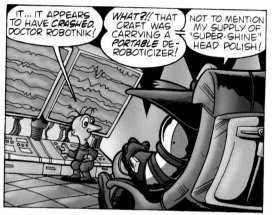

IT... IT APPEARS TO HAVE *CRASHED*, DOCTOR ROBOTNIK!

WHAT?!! THAT CRAFT WAS CARRYING A *PORTABLE* DE-ROBOTICIZER!

NOT TO MENTION MY SUPPLY OF "SUPER-SHINE" HEAD POLISH!

IF THAT DEVICE FALLS INTO THE WRONG HANDS, IT COULD HAVE *GRAVE CONSEQUENCES*... ESPECIALLY FOR *YOU!*

ACTIVATE THE SELF-DESTRUCT MECHANISM AND BLOW THE CRAFT UP, SNIVELY... *NOW!!*

Y-Y-YES, SIR!

BEEP! BEEP! BEEP!

UH-OH!

SOMETHING TELLS ME I'D BETTER JUICE!

HMMMMMMM

DESTRUCT ACTIVATED

SEE YOU LATER, DETONATOR!

LET'S GET THIS TOY BACK TO KNOTHOLE AND HAVE ROTOR LOOK IT OVER, DULCY!

BA-DOOM!!

VRROOOM!

3

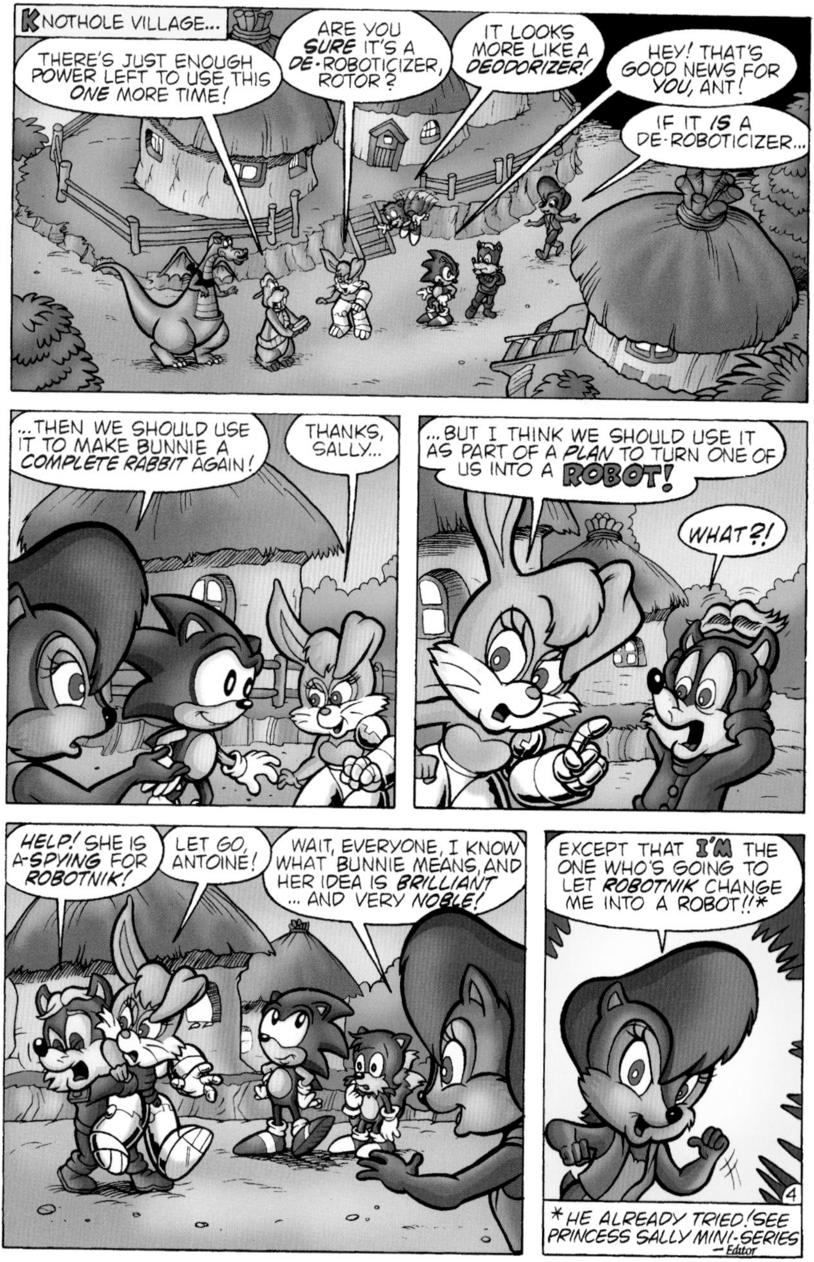
KNOTHOLE VILLAGE...
THERE'S JUST ENOUGH POWER LEFT TO USE THIS ONE MORE TIME!
ARE YOU SURE IT'S A DE-ROBOTICIZER, ROTOR?
IT LOOKS MORE LIKE A DEODORIZER!
HEY! THAT'S GOOD NEWS FOR YOU, ANT!
IF IT IS A DE-ROBOTICIZER...
...THEN WE SHOULD USE IT TO MAKE BUNNIE A COMPLETE RABBIT AGAIN!
THANKS, SALLY...
...BUT I THINK WE SHOULD USE IT AS PART OF A PLAN TO TURN ONE OF US INTO A ROBOT!
WHAT?!
HELP! SHE IS A-SPYING FOR ROBOTNIK!
LET GO, ANTOINE!
WAIT, EVERYONE, I KNOW WHAT BUNNIE MEANS, AND HER IDEA IS BRILLIANT ... AND VERY NOBLE!
EXCEPT THAT I'M THE ONE WHO'S GOING TO LET ROBOTNIK CHANGE ME INTO A ROBOT!!*
4
*HE ALREADY TRIED! SEE PRINCESS SALLY MINI-SERIES —Editor

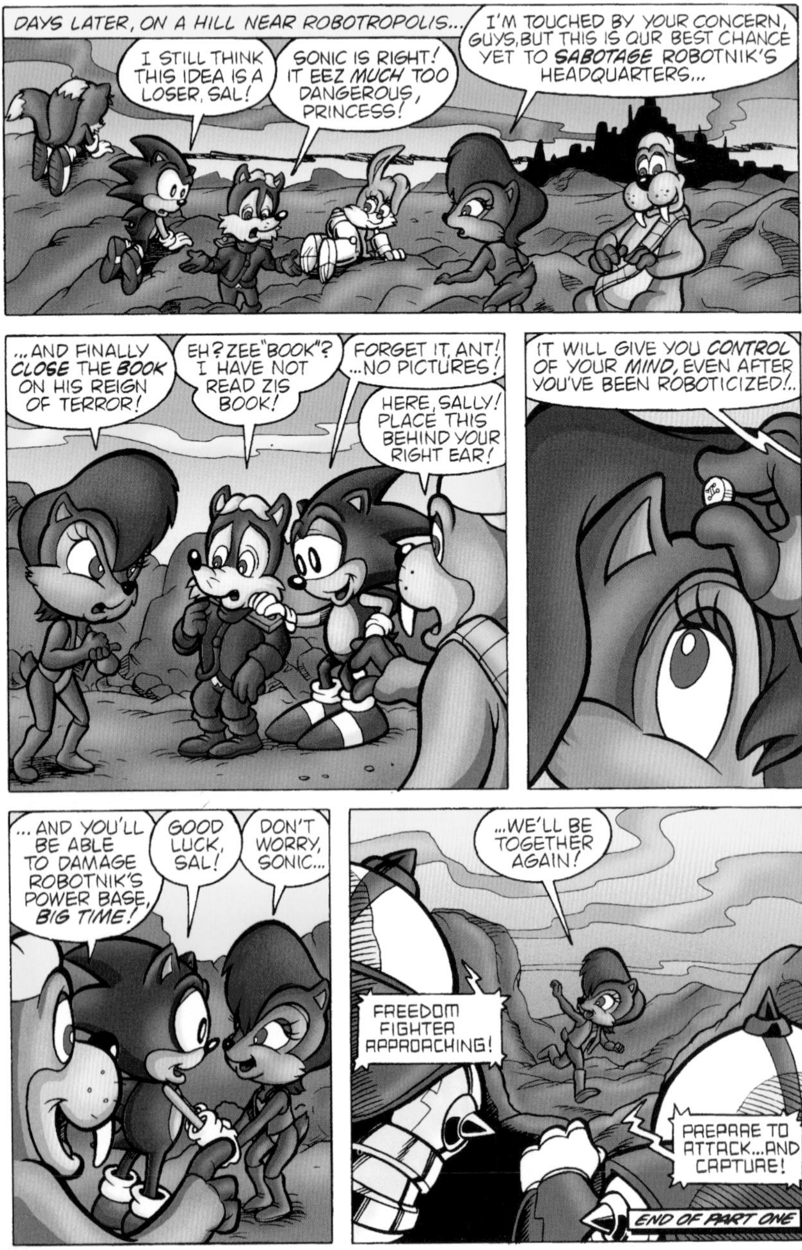
DAYS LATER, ON A HILL NEAR ROBOTROPOLIS...
I STILL THINK THIS IDEA IS A LOSER, SAL!
SONIC IS RIGHT! IT EEZ MUCH TOO DANGEROUS, PRINCESS!
I'M TOUCHED BY YOUR CONCERN, GUYS, BUT THIS IS OUR BEST CHANCE YET TO SABOTAGE ROBOTNIK'S HEADQUARTERS...
...AND FINALLY CLOSE THE BOOK ON HIS REIGN OF TERROR!
EH? ZEE "BOOK"? I HAVE NOT READ ZIS BOOK!
FORGET IT, ANT! ...NO PICTURES!
HERE, SALLY! PLACE THIS BEHIND YOUR RIGHT EAR!
IT WILL GIVE YOU CONTROL OF YOUR MIND, EVEN AFTER YOU'VE BEEN ROBOTICIZED!..
...AND YOU'LL BE ABLE TO DAMAGE ROBOTNIK'S POWER BASE, BIG TIME!
GOOD LUCK, SAL!
DON'T WORRY, SONIC...
...WE'LL BE TOGETHER AGAIN!
FREEDOM FIGHTER APPROACHING!
PREPARE TO ATTACK...AND CAPTURE!
END OF PART ONE

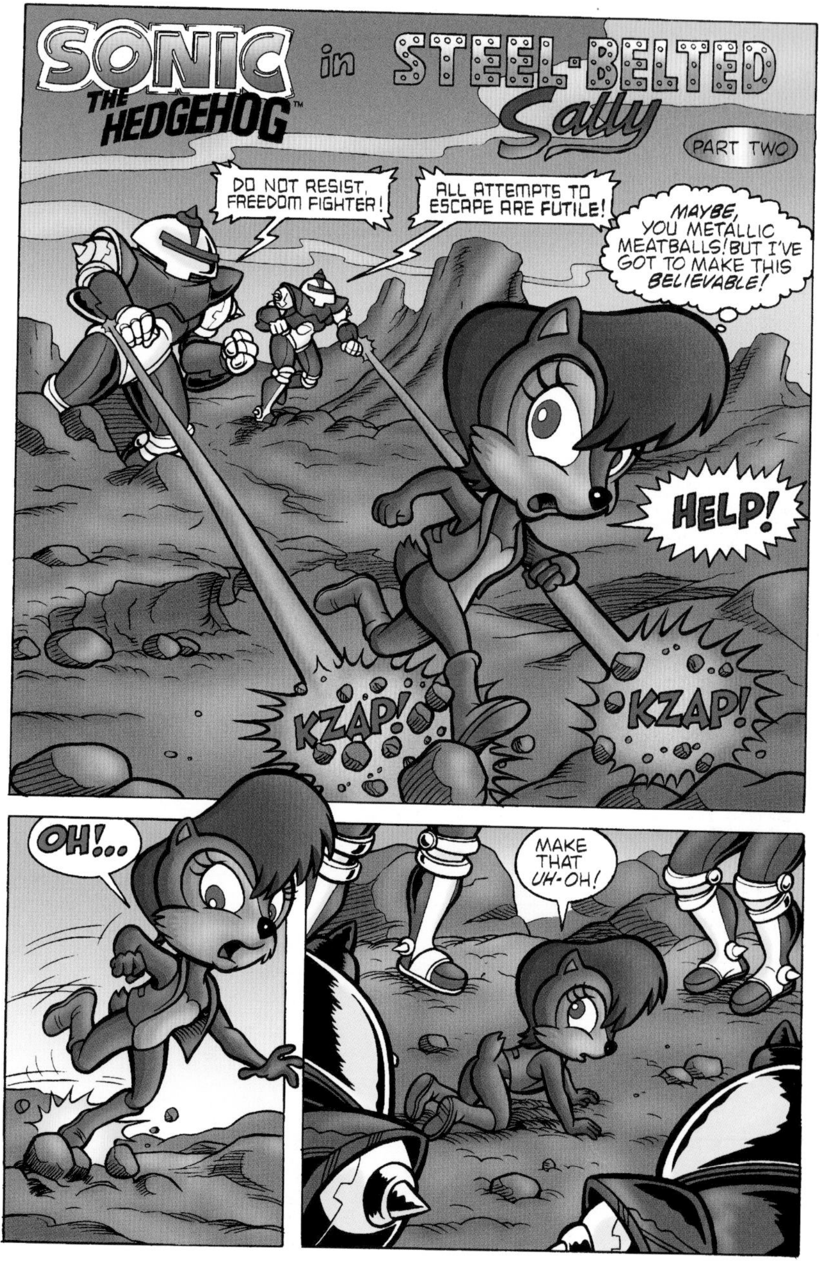
SONIC THE HEDGEHOG™ in STEEL-BELTED Sally
PART TWO
DO NOT RESIST, FREEDOM FIGHTER!
ALL ATTEMPTS TO ESCAPE ARE FUTILE!
MAYBE, YOU METALLIC MEATBALLS! BUT I'VE GOT TO MAKE THIS BELIEVABLE!
HELP!
KZAP!
KZAP!
OH!...
MAKE THAT UH-OH!

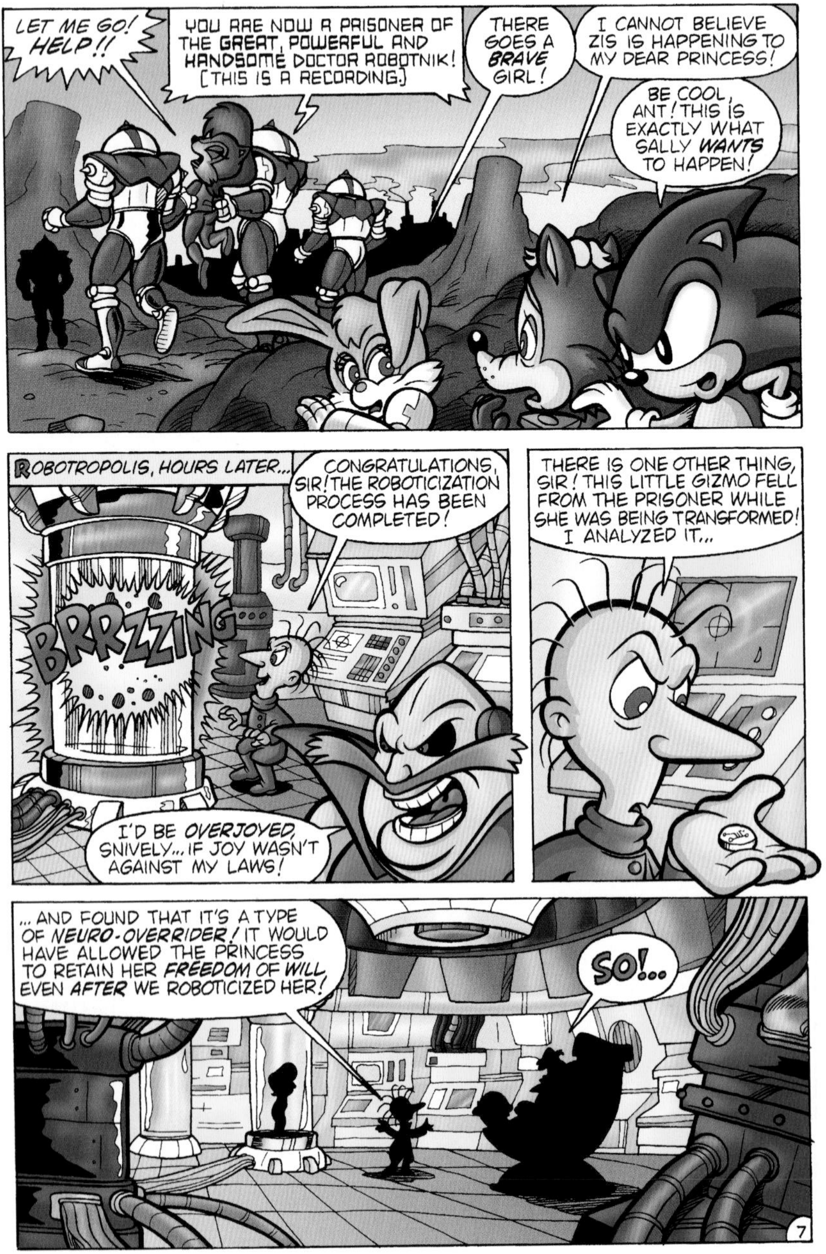
LET ME GO! HELP!!
YOU ARE NOW A PRISONER OF THE GREAT, POWERFUL AND HANDSOME DOCTOR ROBOTNIK! [THIS IS A RECORDING.]
THERE GOES A BRAVE GIRL!
I CANNOT BELIEVE ZIS IS HAPPENING TO MY DEAR PRINCESS!
BE COOL, ANT! THIS IS EXACTLY WHAT SALLY WANTS TO HAPPEN!
ROBOTROPOLIS, HOURS LATER...
CONGRATULATIONS, SIR! THE ROBOTICIZATION PROCESS HAS BEEN COMPLETED!
BRRZZING
I'D BE OVERJOYED, SNIVELY... IF JOY WASN'T AGAINST MY LAWS!
THERE IS ONE OTHER THING, SIR! THIS LITTLE GIZMO FELL FROM THE PRISONER WHILE SHE WAS BEING TRANSFORMED! I ANALYZED IT...
... AND FOUND THAT IT'S A TYPE OF NEURO-OVERRIDER! IT WOULD HAVE ALLOWED THE PRINCESS TO RETAIN HER FREEDOM OF WILL EVEN AFTER WE ROBOTICIZED HER!
SO!...
7

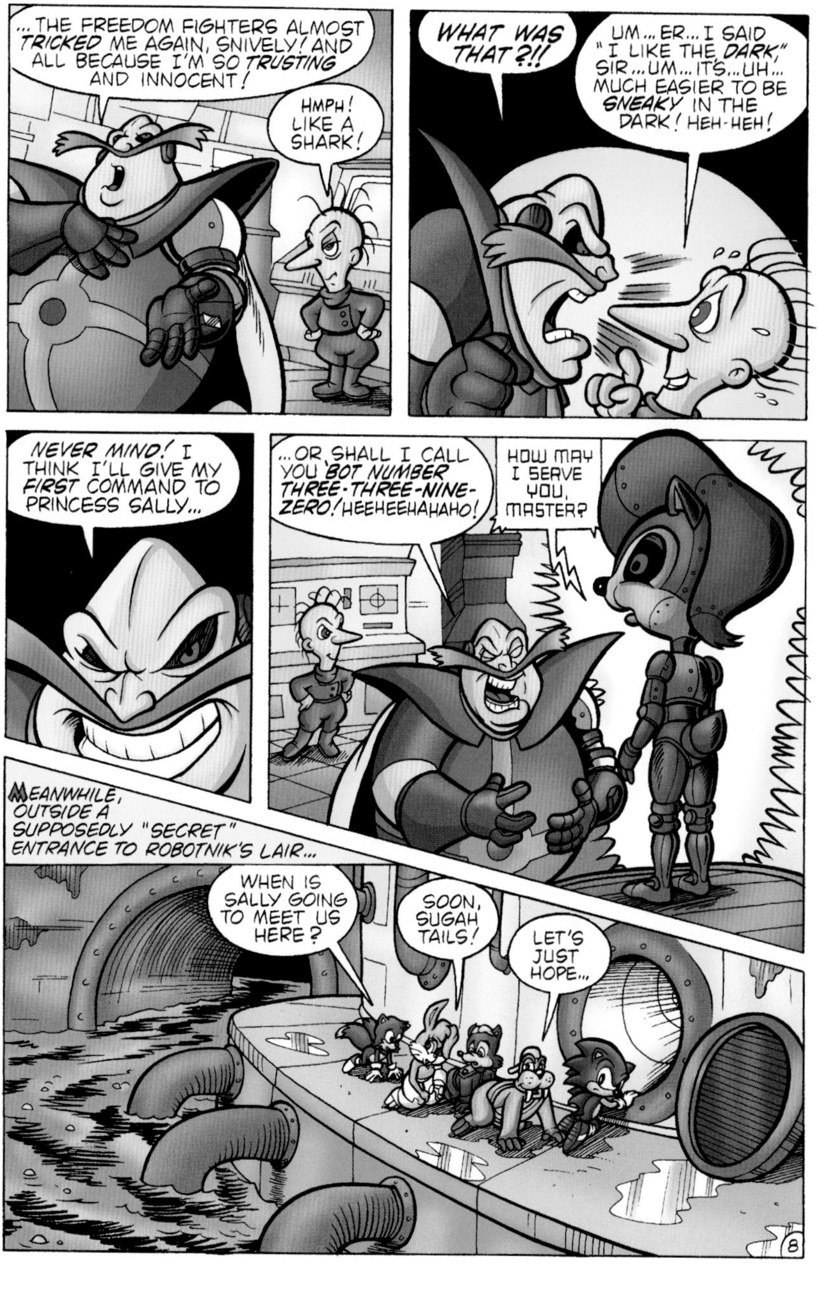
...THE FREEDOM FIGHTERS ALMOST TRICKED ME AGAIN, SNIVELY! AND ALL BECAUSE I'M SO TRUSTING AND INNOCENT!
HMPH! LIKE A SHARK!
WHAT WAS THAT?!!
UM... ER... I SAID "I LIKE THE DARK," SIR... UM... IT'S... UH... MUCH EASIER TO BE SNEAKY IN THE DARK! HEH-HEH!
NEVER MIND! I THINK I'LL GIVE MY FIRST COMMAND TO PRINCESS SALLY...
...OR, SHALL I CALL YOU 'BOT NUMBER THREE-THREE-NINE-ZERO! HEEHEEHAHAHO!
HOW MAY I SERVE YOU, MASTER?
MEANWHILE, OUTSIDE A SUPPOSEDLY "SECRET" ENTRANCE TO ROBOTNIK'S LAIR...
WHEN IS SALLY GOING TO MEET US HERE?
SOON, SUGAH TAILS!
LET'S JUST HOPE...
8

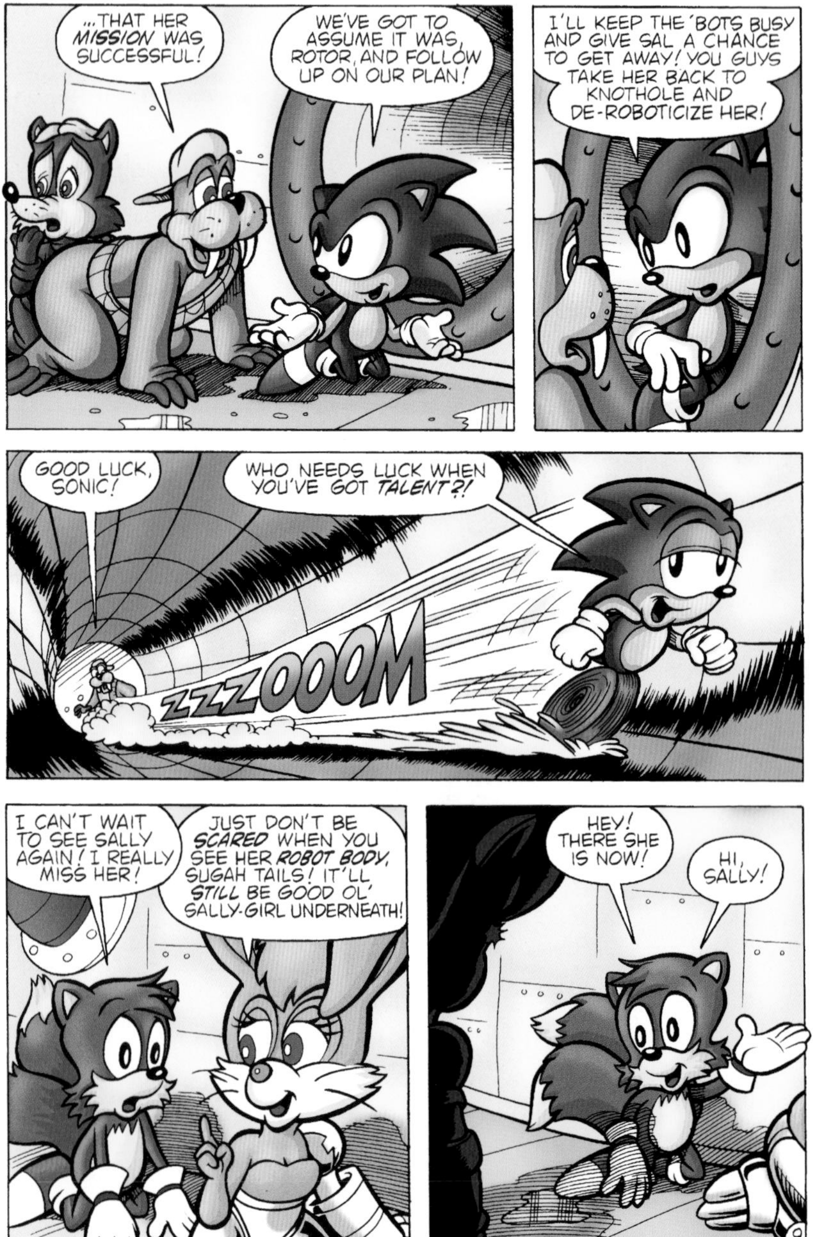
...THAT HER MISSION WAS SUCCESSFUL!
WE'VE GOT TO ASSUME IT WAS, ROTOR, AND FOLLOW UP ON OUR PLAN!
I'LL KEEP THE 'BOTS BUSY AND GIVE SAL A CHANCE TO GET AWAY! YOU GUYS TAKE HER BACK TO KNOTHOLE AND DE-ROBOTICIZE HER!
GOOD LUCK, SONIC!
WHO NEEDS LUCK WHEN YOU'VE GOT TALENT?!
ZZZOOOM
I CAN'T WAIT TO SEE SALLY AGAIN! I REALLY MISS HER!
JUST DON'T BE SCARED WHEN YOU SEE HER ROBOT BODY, SUGAH TAILS! IT'LL STILL BE GOOD OL' SALLY-GIRL UNDERNEATH!
HEY! THERE SHE IS NOW!
HI, SALLY!
9

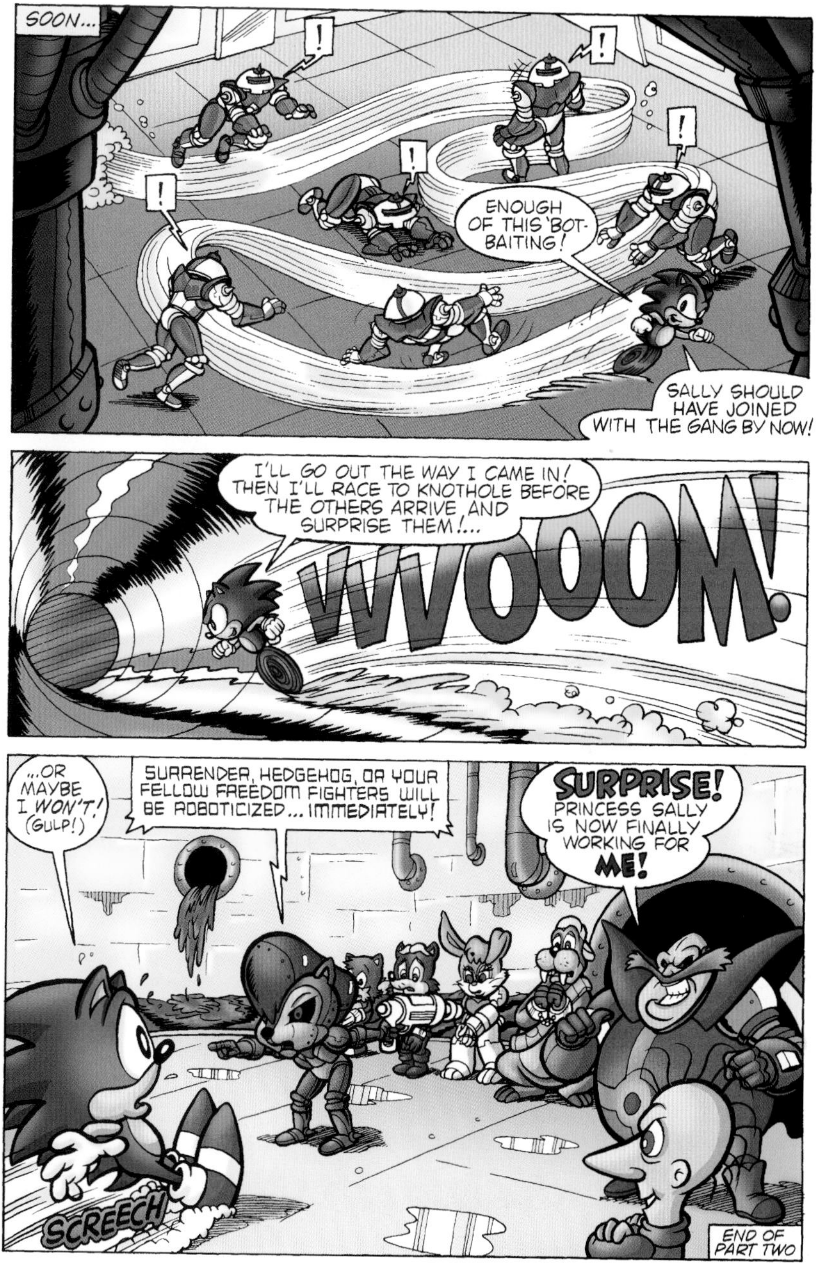
SOON...
!
!
!
!
!
ENOUGH OF THIS 'BOT-BAITING!
SALLY SHOULD HAVE JOINED WITH THE GANG BY NOW!
I'LL GO OUT THE WAY I CAME IN! THEN I'LL RACE TO KNOTHOLE BEFORE THE OTHERS ARRIVE AND SURPRISE THEM!...
VVVOOOOM!
...OR MAYBE I WON'T! (GULP!)
SURRENDER, HEDGEHOG, OR YOUR FELLOW FREEDOM FIGHTERS WILL BE ROBOTICIZED... IMMEDIATELY!
SURPRISE! PRINCESS SALLY IS NOW FINALLY WORKING FOR ME!
SCREECH
END OF PART TWO

SONIC THE HEDGEHOG™ in STEEL BELTED Sally

PART THREE

THERE! THE *DEVICE* YOU *ATTEMPTED* TO USE TO KEEP THE PRINCESS' MIND *FREE* IS CRUSHED--

...AND SO IS YOUR *REBELLION!*

THE ONLY REASON WE HAVEN'T ROBOTICIZED THE LOT OF YOU IS THAT WE *KNOW* YOU HAVE ONE OF OUR *DE-ROBOTICIZERS!*

KRUNCH!

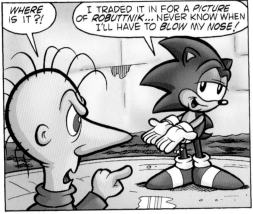

WHERE IS IT?!

I TRADED IT IN FOR A *PICTURE* OF *ROBUTTNIK*... NEVER KNOW WHEN I'LL HAVE TO *BLOW* MY *NOSE!*

(chuckle!) ...UM, I MEAN... *FOOL!!* YOU'LL TELL ME WHAT I WANT TO KNOW WHEN YOU'RE STANDING *INSIDE* A *ROBOTICIZER!*

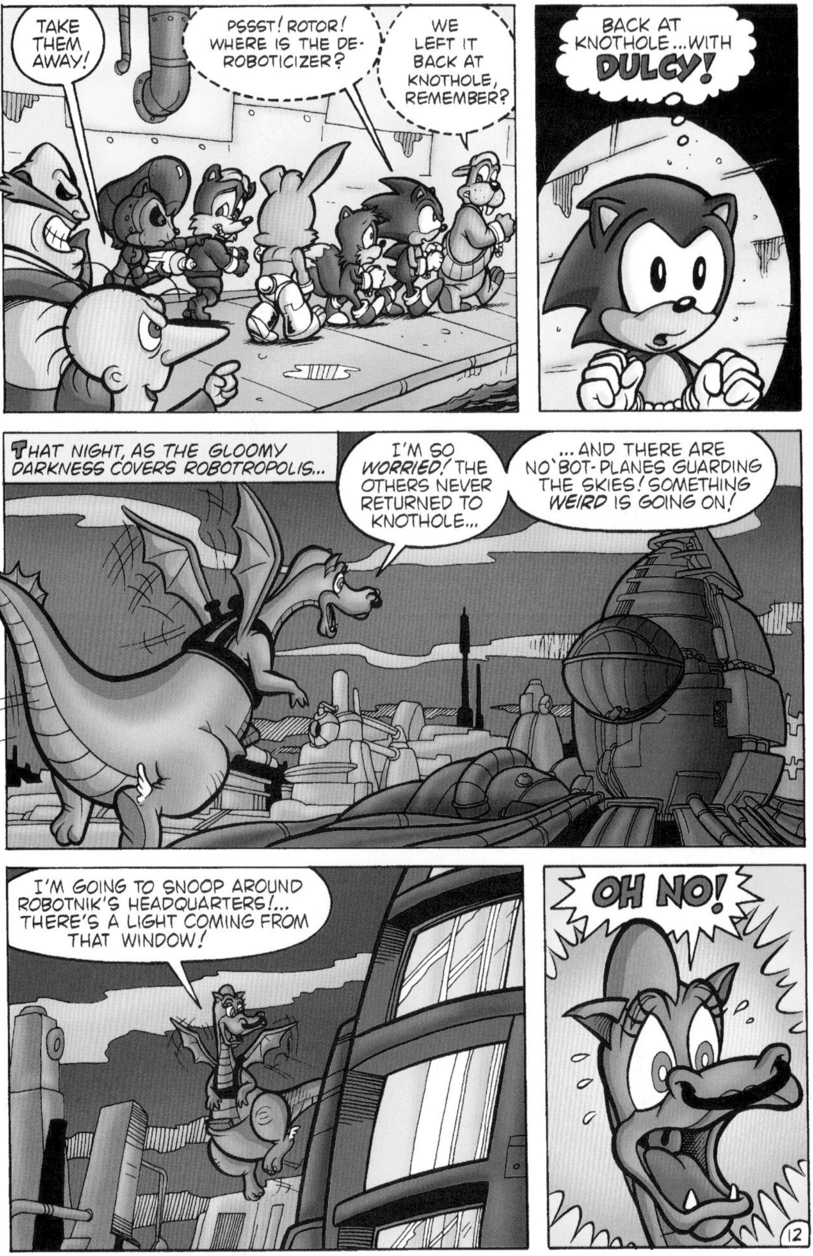
TAKE THEM AWAY!
PSSST! ROTOR! WHERE IS THE DE-ROBOTICIZER?
WE LEFT IT BACK AT KNOTHOLE, REMEMBER?
BACK AT KNOTHOLE...WITH DULCY!
THAT NIGHT, AS THE GLOOMY DARKNESS COVERS ROBOTROPOLIS...
I'M SO WORRIED! THE OTHERS NEVER RETURNED TO KNOTHOLE...
...AND THERE ARE NO 'BOT-PLANES GUARDING THE SKIES! SOMETHING WEIRD IS GOING ON!
I'M GOING TO SNOOP AROUND ROBOTNIK'S HEADQUARTERS!... THERE'S A LIGHT COMING FROM THAT WINDOW!
OH NO!
12

I'VE DECIDED TO FORGET ABOUT THE DE-ROBOTICIZER! AFTER ALL, ONCE YOU'VE ALL BEEN ROBOTICIZED, NO ONE WILL BE ABLE TO STOP ME!

THAT'S RIGHT! AND AS A SYMBOL OF DOCTOR ROBOTNIK'S VICTORY...

...THE ROBOTICIZER WILL BE ACTIVATED BY YOUR FORMER COLLEAGUE... ROBOT THREE-THREE-NINE-ZERO!

I AM READY, MASTER!

I BROUGHT THE DE-ROBOTICIZER-- JUST IN CASE OUR PLAN FAILED-- BUT I'M NOT SURE HOW TO USE IT!

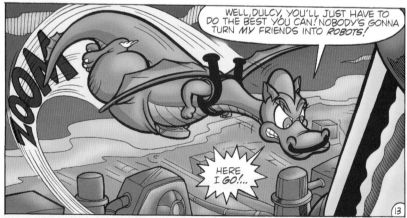

WELL, DULCY, YOU'LL JUST HAVE TO DO THE BEST YOU CAN! NOBODY'S GONNA TURN MY FRIENDS INTO ROBOTS!

ZOOM

HERE I GO!...

13

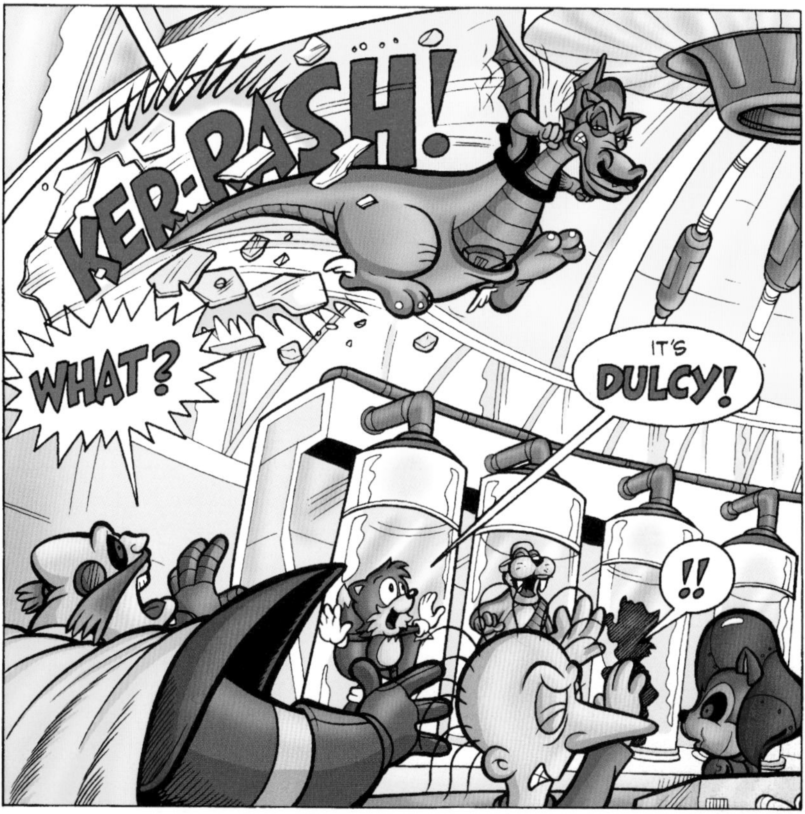
KER-RASH!
WHAT?
IT'S DULCY!
!!

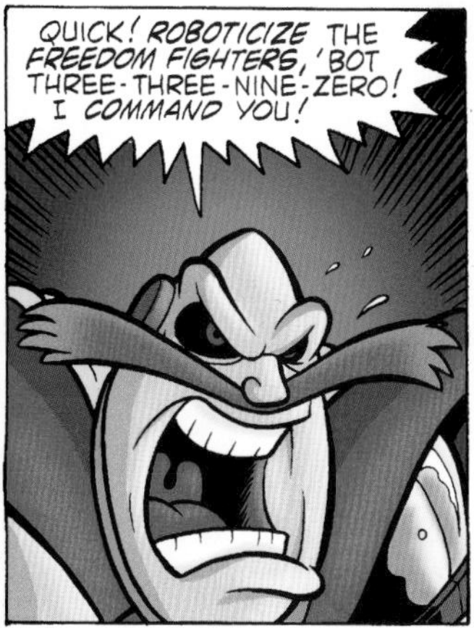
QUICK! ROBOTICIZE THE FREEDOM FIGHTERS, 'BOT THREE-THREE-NINE-ZERO! I COMMAND YOU!

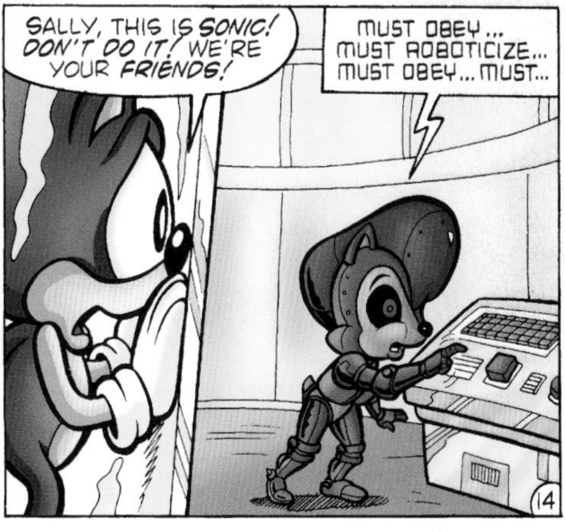
SALLY, THIS IS SONIC! DON'T DO IT! WE'RE YOUR FRIENDS!
MUST OBEY... MUST ROBOTICIZE... MUST OBEY... MUST...

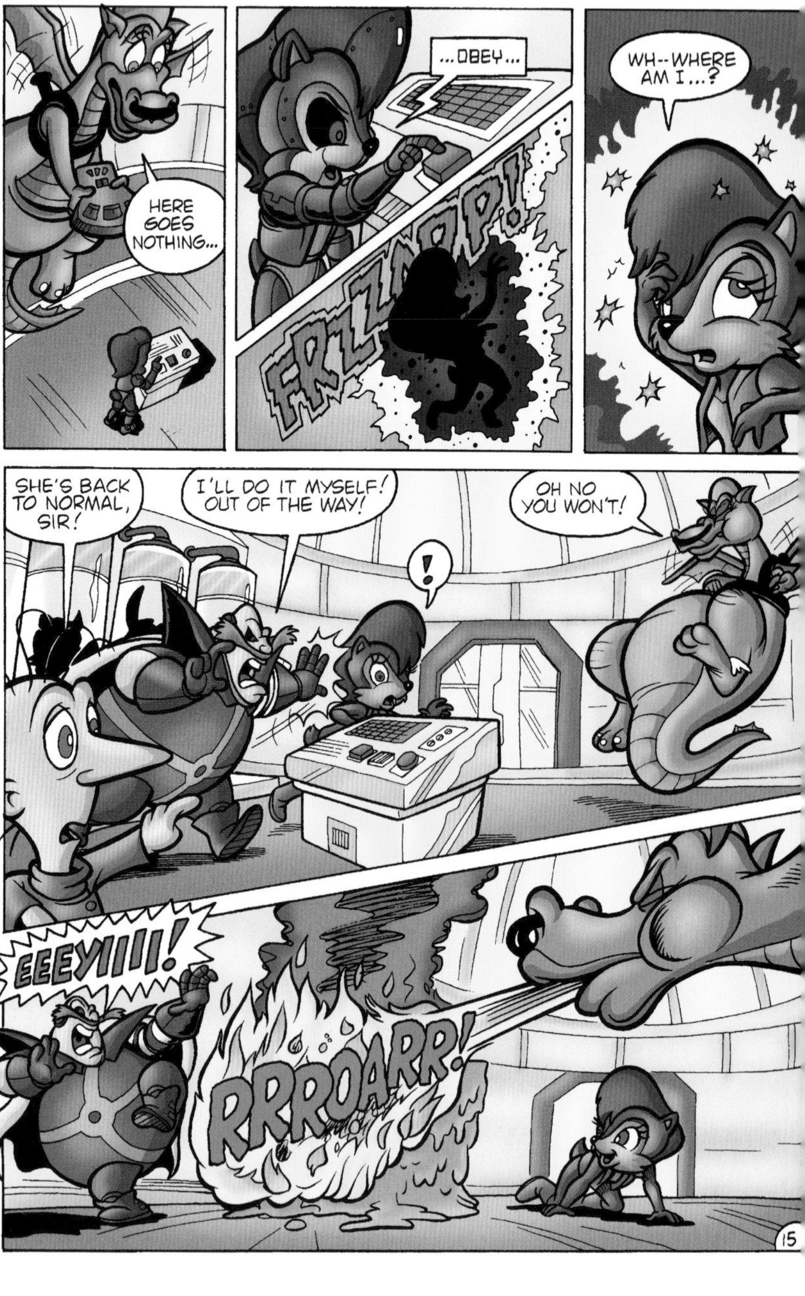
HERE GOES NOTHING...
...OBEY...
FRZZAPP!
WH--WHERE AM I...?
SHE'S BACK TO NORMAL, SIR!
I'LL DO IT MYSELF! OUT OF THE WAY!
!
OH NO YOU WON'T!
EEEYIIII!
RRROARR!

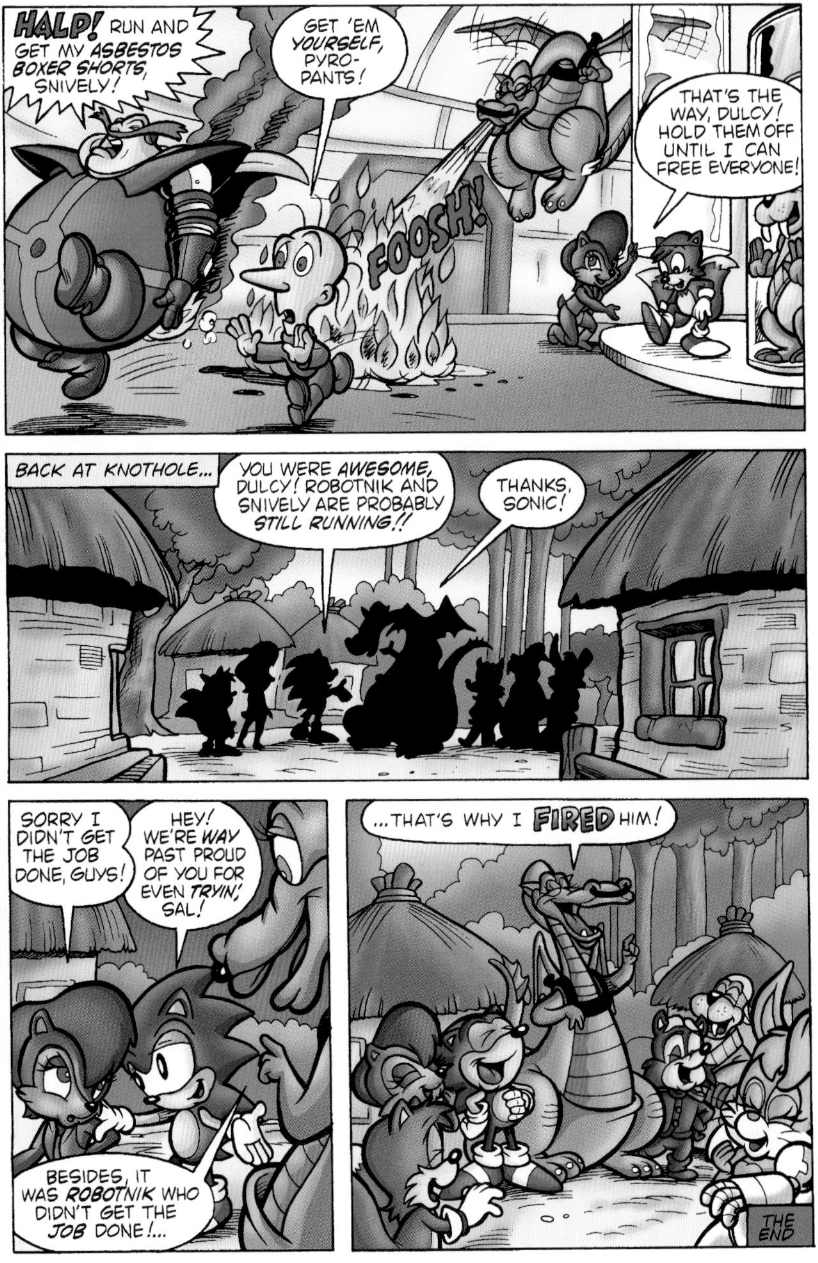
HALP! RUN AND GET MY ASBESTOS BOXER SHORTS, SNIVELY!
GET 'EM YOURSELF, PYRO-PANTS!
FOOSH!
THAT'S THE WAY, DULCY! HOLD THEM OFF UNTIL I CAN FREE EVERYONE!
BACK AT KNOTHOLE...
YOU WERE AWESOME, DULCY! ROBOTNIK AND SNIVELY ARE PROBABLY STILL RUNNING!!
THANKS, SONIC!
SORRY I DIDN'T GET THE JOB DONE, GUYS!
HEY! WE'RE WAY PAST PROUD OF YOU FOR EVEN TRYIN', SAL!
BESIDES, IT WAS ROBOTNIK WHO DIDN'T GET THE JOB DONE!...
...THAT'S WHY I FIRED HIM!
THE END

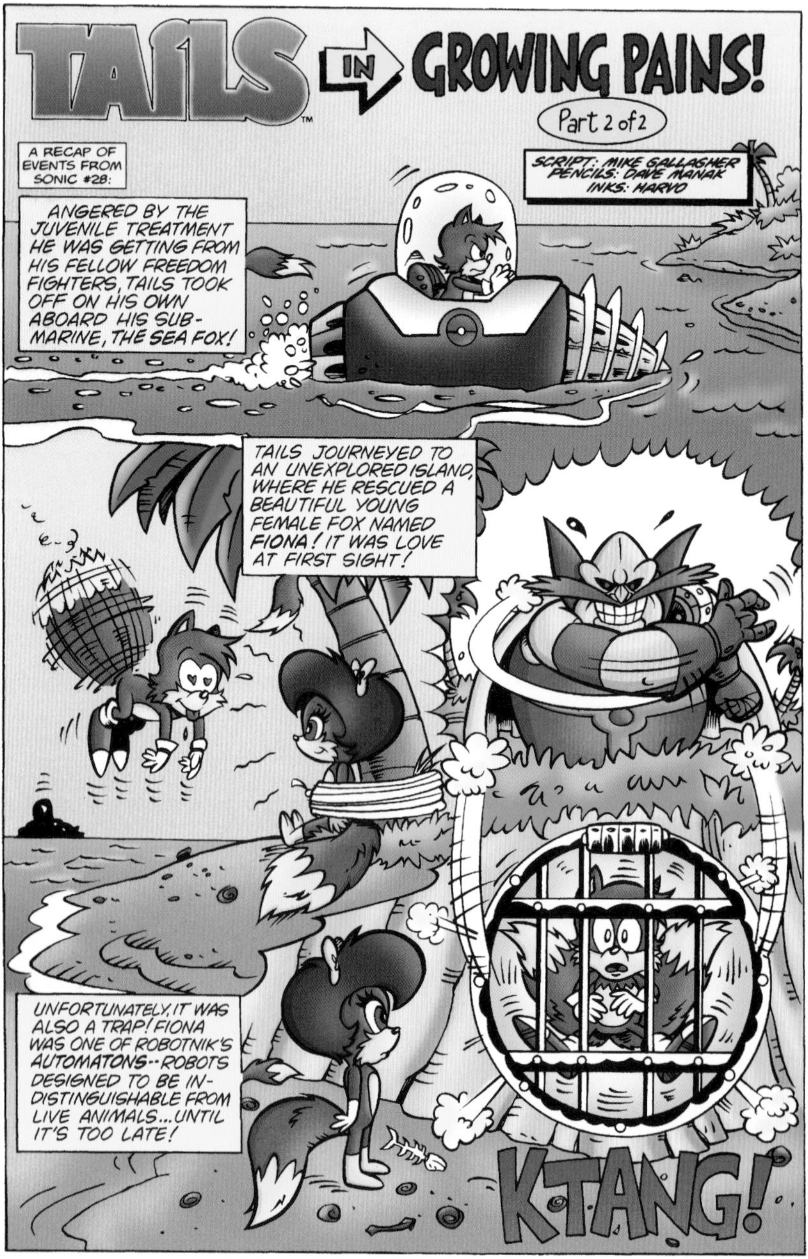
TAILS
IN
GROWING PAINS!
Part 2 of 2
A RECAP OF EVENTS FROM SONIC #28:
SCRIPT: MIKE GALLAGHER
PENCILS: DAVE MANAK
INKS: HARVO
ANGERED BY THE JUVENILE TREATMENT HE WAS GETTING FROM HIS FELLOW FREEDOM FIGHTERS, TAILS TOOK OFF ON HIS OWN ABOARD HIS SUB-MARINE, THE SEA FOX!
TAILS JOURNEYED TO AN UNEXPLORED ISLAND, WHERE HE RESCUED A BEAUTIFUL YOUNG FEMALE FOX NAMED FIONA! IT WAS LOVE AT FIRST SIGHT!
UNFORTUNATELY, IT WAS ALSO A TRAP! FIONA WAS ONE OF ROBOTNIK'S AUTOMATONS--ROBOTS DESIGNED TO BE IN-DISTINGUISHABLE FROM LIVE ANIMALS...UNTIL IT'S TOO LATE!
KTANG!

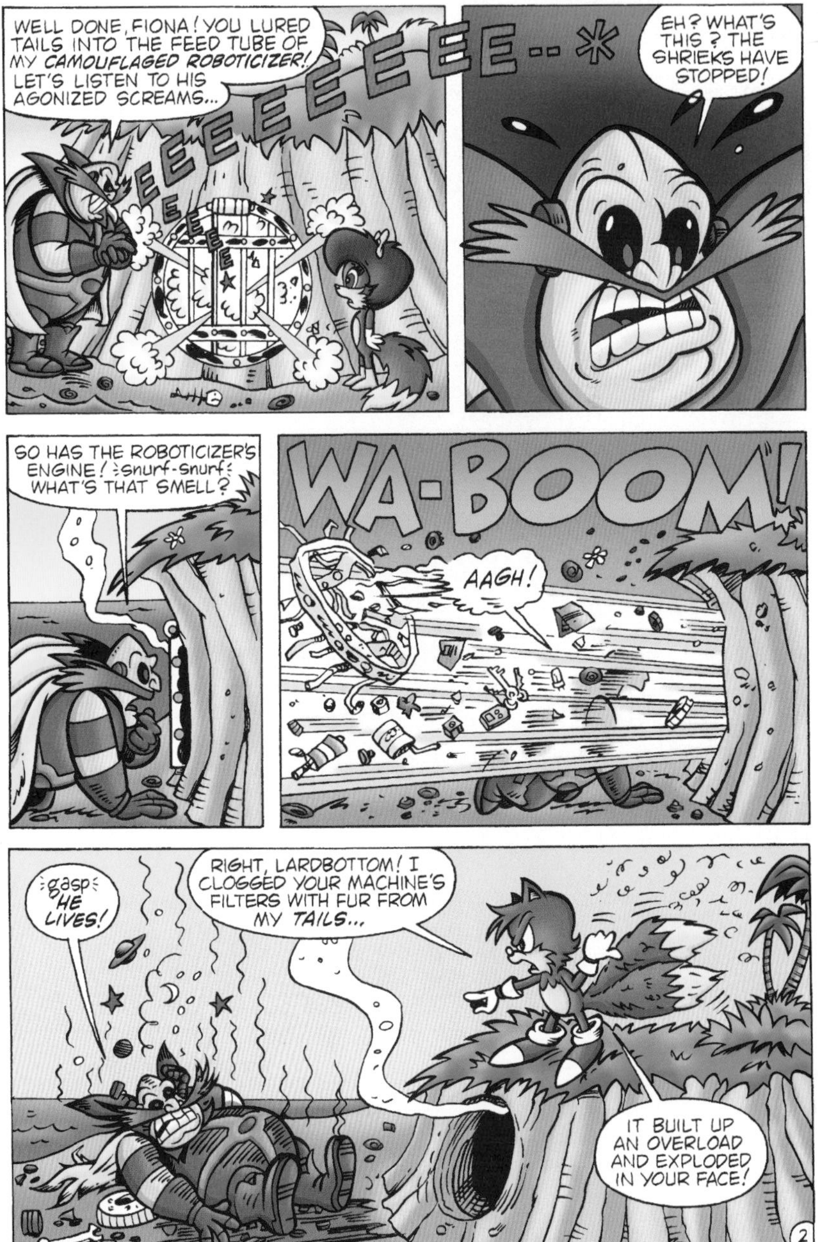
WELL DONE, FIONA! YOU LURED TAILS INTO THE FEED TUBE OF MY CAMOUFLAGED ROBOTICIZER! LET'S LISTEN TO HIS AGONIZED SCREAMS...
EEEEEEEEEEEE..*
EH? WHAT'S THIS? THE SHRIEKS HAVE STOPPED!
SO HAS THE ROBOTICIZER'S ENGINE! snurf-snurf WHAT'S THAT SMELL?
WA-BOOM!
AAGH!
gasp HE LIVES!
RIGHT, LARDBOTTOM! I CLOGGED YOUR MACHINE'S FILTERS WITH FUR FROM MY TAILS...
IT BUILT UP AN OVERLOAD AND EXPLODED IN YOUR FACE!

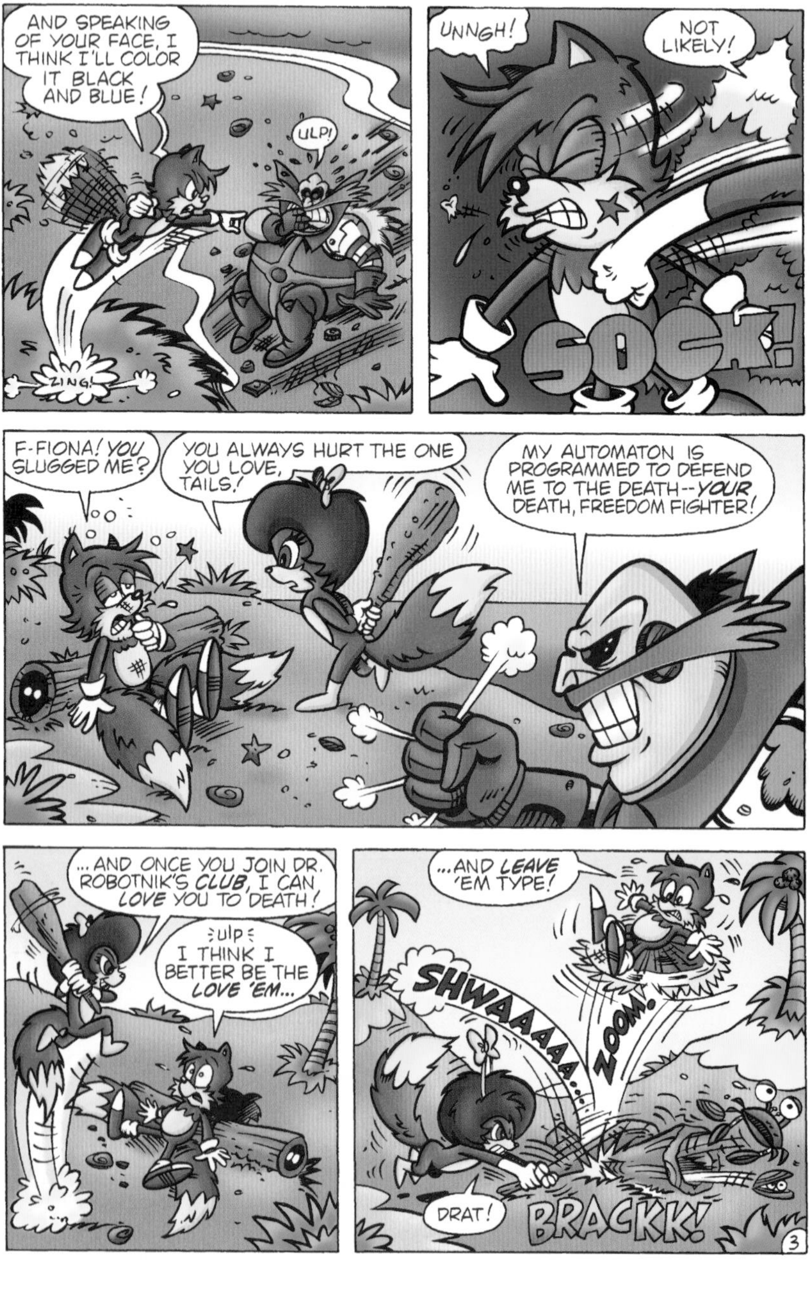

AND SPEAKING OF YOUR FACE, I THINK I'LL COLOR IT BLACK AND BLUE!
ULP!
ZING!
UNNGH!
NOT LIKELY!
SOCK!
F-FIONA! YOU SLUGGED ME?
YOU ALWAYS HURT THE ONE YOU LOVE, TAILS!
MY AUTOMATON IS PROGRAMMED TO DEFEND ME TO THE DEATH--YOUR DEATH, FREEDOM FIGHTER!
...AND ONCE YOU JOIN DR. ROBOTNIK'S CLUB, I CAN LOVE YOU TO DEATH!
ulp
I THINK I BETTER BE THE LOVE 'EM...
...AND LEAVE 'EM TYPE!
SHWAAAAAA...
ZOOM!
DRAT!
BRACKK!

SWOP

GRAB!

HURRGHK!

HAW! HAVE YOU FORGOTTEN THAT *EVERYTHING* ON THIS ISLAND IS *MECHANICAL*?..INCLUDING THE *TREES!*

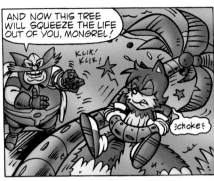

AND NOW THIS TREE WILL SQUEEZE THE LIFE OUT OF YOU, MONGREL!

KLIK! KLIK!

≷choke≷

NOT IF I UPROOT IT, BLUBBERBOLTS!

Whrrrrrrrrrrrrrrr....

SSSS

KRUNSK!

Bzzzt

GADZOOKS!

NOW I'M REALLY *TEED* OFF... **FORE!**

OH! HE'S INTO THE *WATER HAZARD!*

OOF!

OUCH!

EECH!

OOOCH!

SWOT!

4

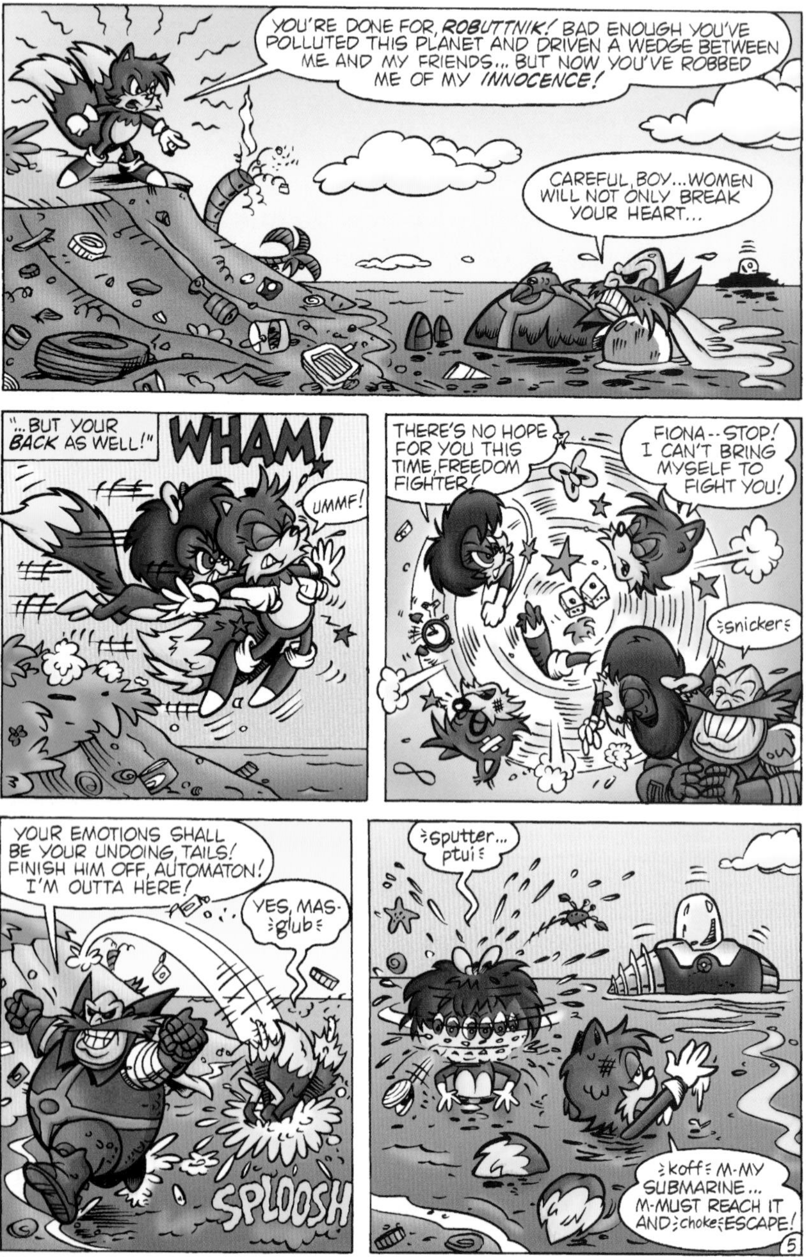

YOU'RE DONE FOR, ROBUTTNIK! BAD ENOUGH YOU'VE POLLUTED THIS PLANET AND DRIVEN A WEDGE BETWEEN ME AND MY FRIENDS... BUT NOW YOU'VE ROBBED ME OF MY INNOCENCE!
CAREFUL, BOY... WOMEN WILL NOT ONLY BREAK YOUR HEART...
"...BUT YOUR BACK AS WELL!"
WHAM!
UMMF!
THERE'S NO HOPE FOR YOU THIS TIME, FREEDOM FIGHTER!
FIONA--STOP! I CAN'T BRING MYSELF TO FIGHT YOU!
snicker
YOUR EMOTIONS SHALL BE YOUR UNDOING, TAILS! FINISH HIM OFF, AUTOMATON! I'M OUTTA HERE!
YES, MAS- glub
SPLOOSH
sputter... ptui
koff M-MY SUBMARINE... M-MUST REACH IT AND choke ESCAPE!

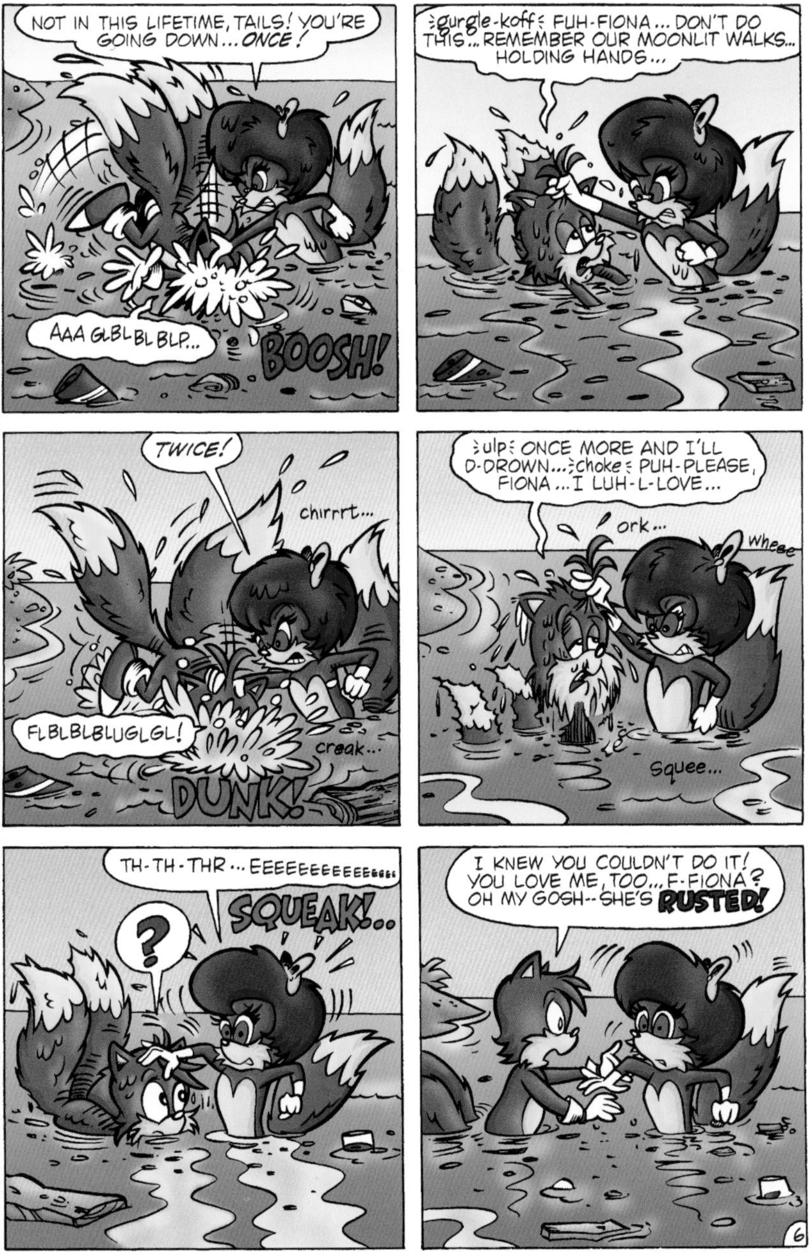
NOT IN THIS LIFETIME, TAILS! YOU'RE GOING DOWN... ONCE!
AAA GLBLBL BLBLP...
BOOSH!
gurgle-koff FUH-FIONA... DON'T DO THIS... REMEMBER OUR MOONLIT WALKS... HOLDING HANDS...
TWICE!
chirrrt...
FLBLBLBLUGLGL!
creak...
DUNK!
ulp ONCE MORE AND I'LL D-DROWN... choke PUH-PLEASE, FIONA... I LUH-L-LOVE...
ork...
wheee
Squee...
TH-TH-THR... EEEEEEEEEEEEEE
SQUEAK!..
?
I KNEW YOU COULDN'T DO IT! YOU LOVE ME, TOO... F-FIONA? OH MY GOSH--SHE'S RUSTED!
6

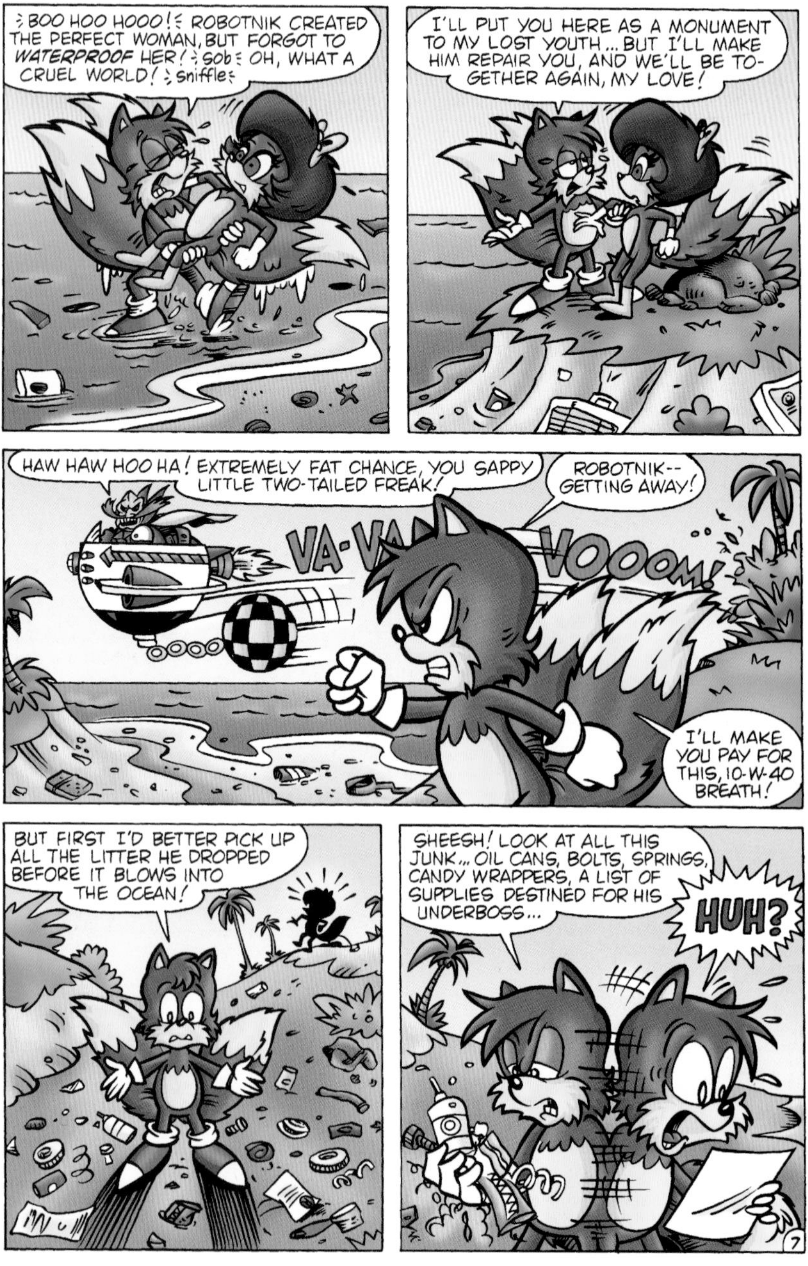
⁏BOO HOO HOOO!⁏ ROBOTNIK CREATED THE PERFECT WOMAN, BUT FORGOT TO WATERPROOF HER! ⁏Sob⁏ OH, WHAT A CRUEL WORLD! ⁏sniffle⁏
I'LL PUT YOU HERE AS A MONUMENT TO MY LOST YOUTH... BUT I'LL MAKE HIM REPAIR YOU, AND WE'LL BE TOGETHER AGAIN, MY LOVE!
HAW HAW HOO HA! EXTREMELY FAT CHANCE, YOU SAPPY LITTLE TWO-TAILED FREAK!
ROBOTNIK-- GETTING AWAY!
VA-VA... VOOOM!
I'LL MAKE YOU PAY FOR THIS, 10-W-40 BREATH!
BUT FIRST I'D BETTER PICK UP ALL THE LITTER HE DROPPED BEFORE IT BLOWS INTO THE OCEAN!
SHEESH! LOOK AT ALL THIS JUNK... OIL CANS, BOLTS, SPRINGS, CANDY WRAPPERS, A LIST OF SUPPLIES DESTINED FOR HIS UNDERBOSS...
HUH?

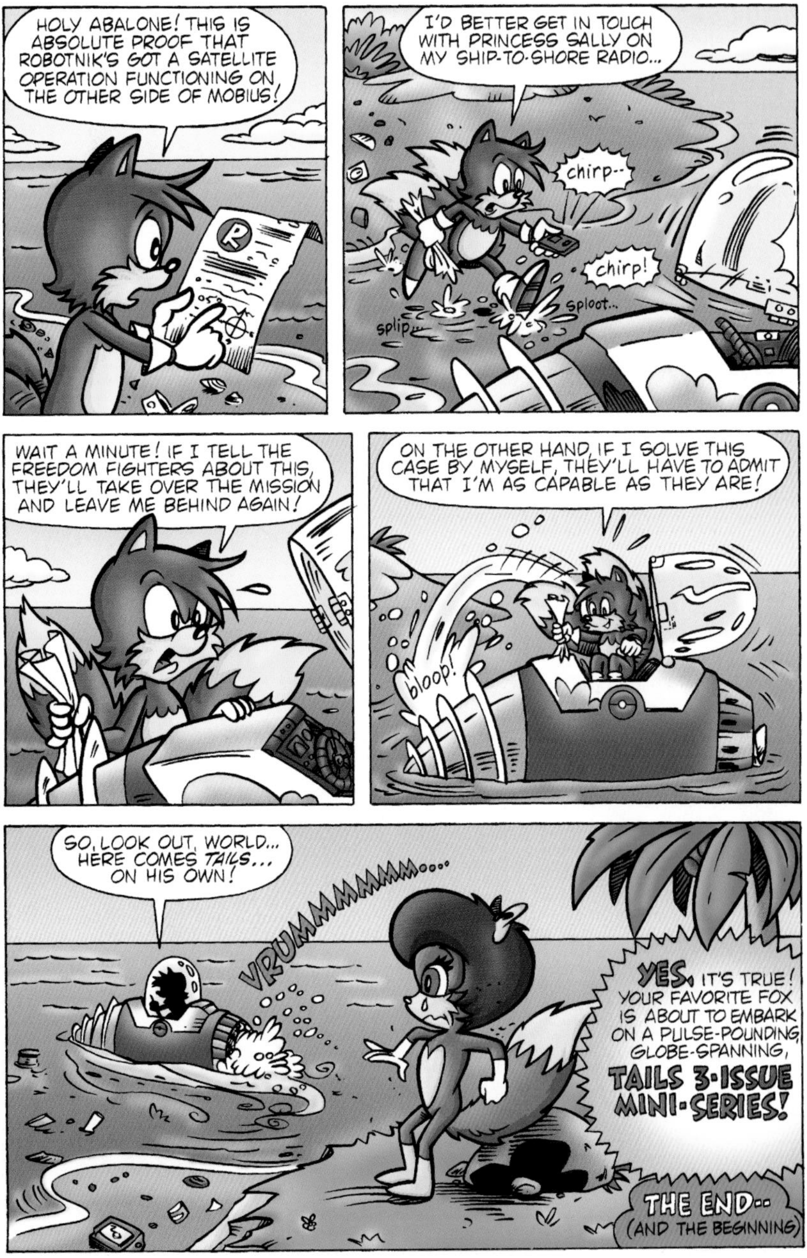
HOLY ABALONE! THIS IS ABSOLUTE PROOF THAT ROBOTNIK'S GOT A SATELLITE OPERATION FUNCTIONING ON THE OTHER SIDE OF MOBIUS!
I'D BETTER GET IN TOUCH WITH PRINCESS SALLY ON MY SHIP-TO-SHORE RADIO...
chirp--
chirp!
sploot...
splip...
WAIT A MINUTE! IF I TELL THE FREEDOM FIGHTERS ABOUT THIS, THEY'LL TAKE OVER THE MISSION AND LEAVE ME BEHIND AGAIN!
ON THE OTHER HAND, IF I SOLVE THIS CASE BY MYSELF, THEY'LL HAVE TO ADMIT THAT I'M AS CAPABLE AS THEY ARE!
bloop!
SO, LOOK OUT, WORLD... HERE COMES TAILS... ON HIS OWN!
VRUMMMMMMMooo
YES, IT'S TRUE! YOUR FAVORITE FOX IS ABOUT TO EMBARK ON A PULSE-POUNDING, GLOBE-SPANNING, TAILS 3-ISSUE MINI-SERIES!
THE END.. (AND THE BEGINNING)

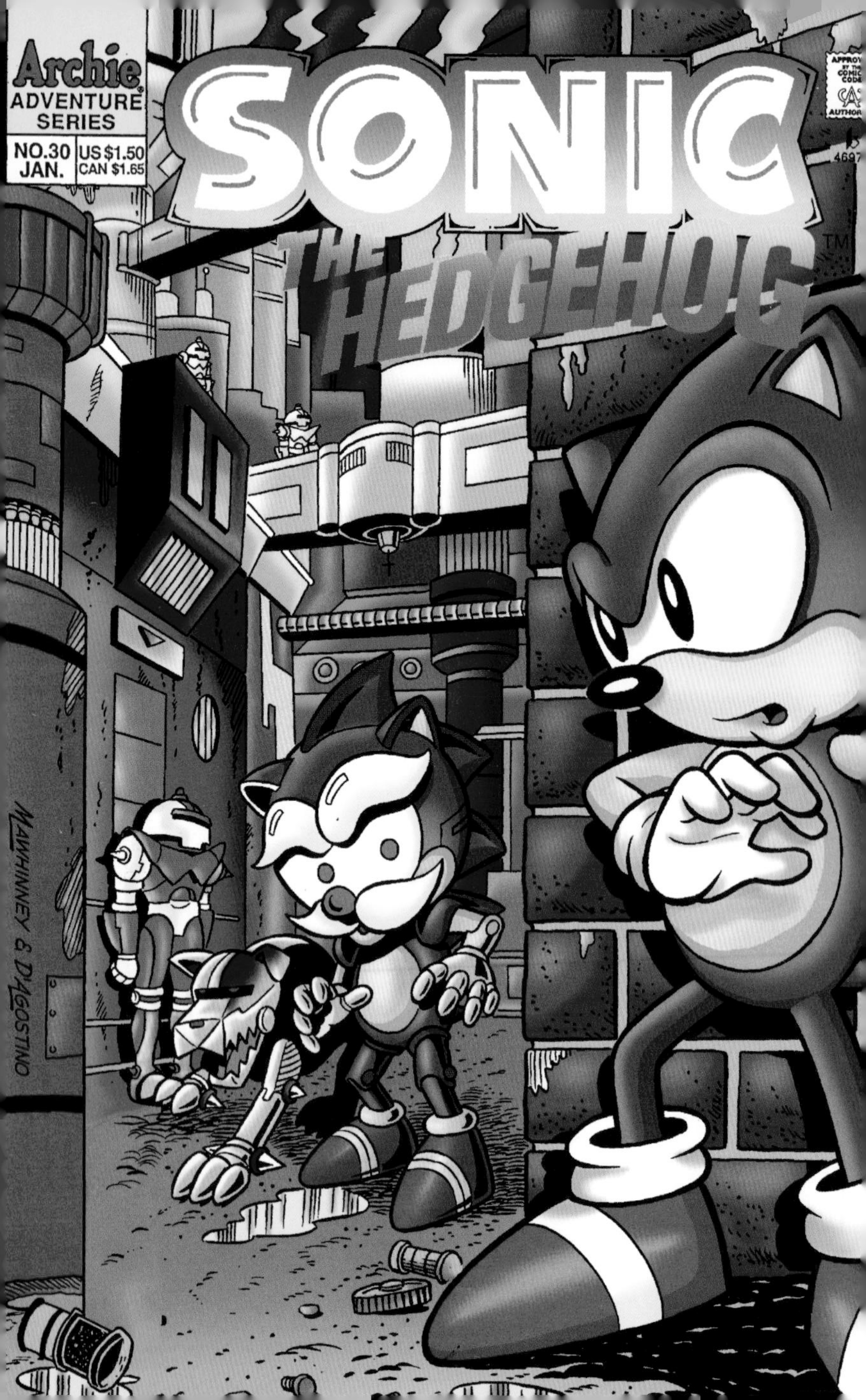
Archie
ADVENTURE SERIES
NO.30 JAN.
US $1.50 CAN $1.65
SONIC
THE HEDGEHOG
TM
MAWHINNEY & D'AGOSTINO

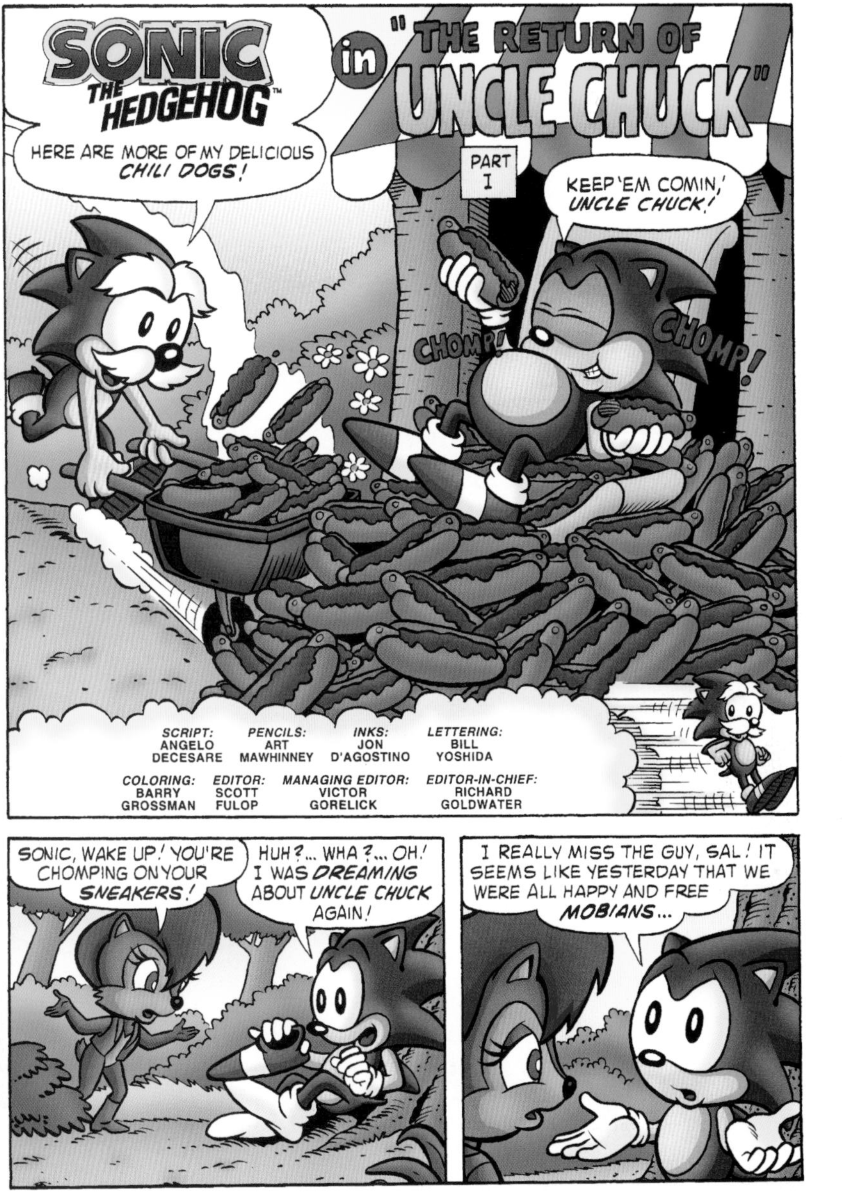
SONIC THE HEDGEHOG™
in "THE RETURN OF UNCLE CHUCK"
HERE ARE MORE OF MY DELICIOUS CHILI DOGS!
PART I
KEEP 'EM COMIN,' UNCLE CHUCK!
CHOMP!
CHOMP!
SCRIPT: ANGELO DECESARE
PENCILS: ART MAWHINNEY
INKS: JON D'AGOSTINO
LETTERING: BILL YOSHIDA
COLORING: BARRY GROSSMAN
EDITOR: SCOTT FULOP
MANAGING EDITOR: VICTOR GORELICK
EDITOR-IN-CHIEF: RICHARD GOLDWATER
SONIC, WAKE UP! YOU'RE CHOMPING ON YOUR SNEAKERS!
HUH?... WHA?... OH! I WAS DREAMING ABOUT UNCLE CHUCK AGAIN!
I REALLY MISS THE GUY, SAL! IT SEEMS LIKE YESTERDAY THAT WE WERE ALL HAPPY AND FREE MOBIANS...

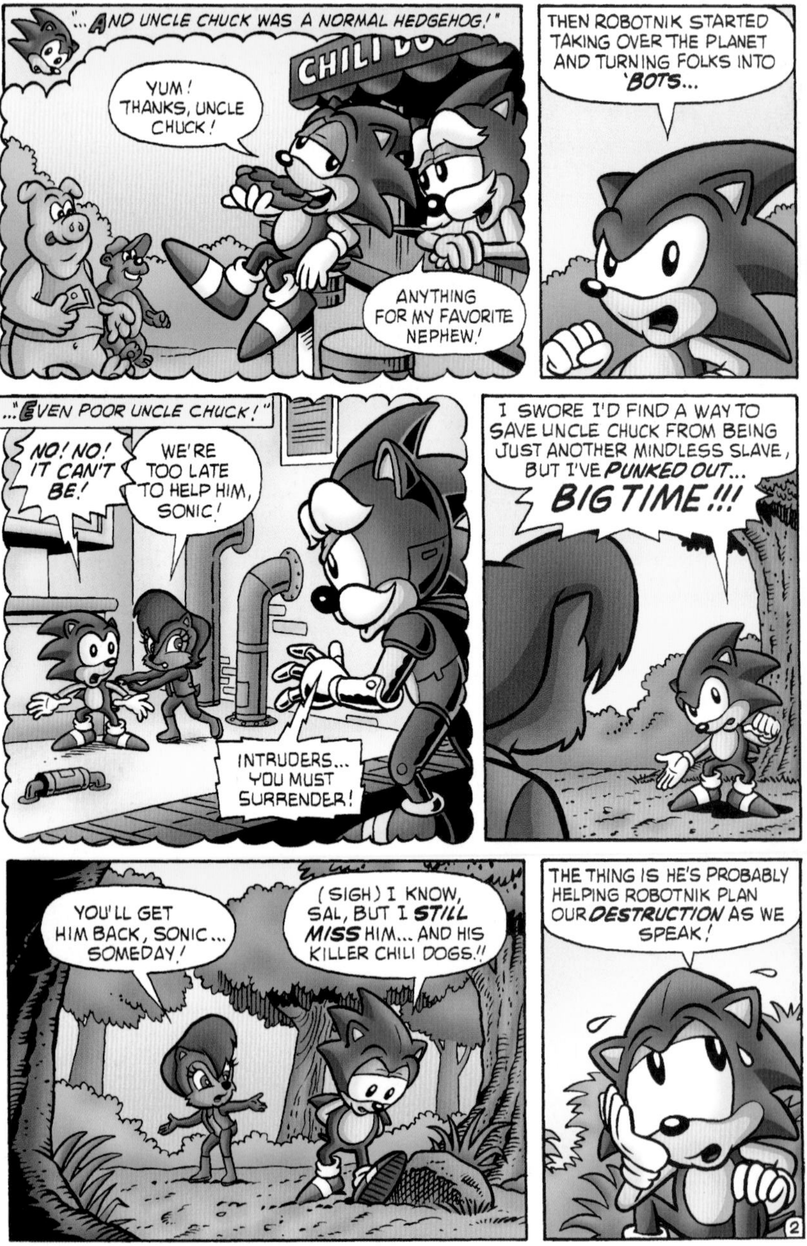
"...AND UNCLE CHUCK WAS A NORMAL HEDGEHOG!"
CHILI DO
YUM! THANKS, UNCLE CHUCK!
ANYTHING FOR MY FAVORITE NEPHEW!
THEN ROBOTNIK STARTED TAKING OVER THE PLANET AND TURNING FOLKS INTO 'BOTS...
..."EVEN POOR UNCLE CHUCK!"
NO! NO! IT CAN'T BE!
WE'RE TOO LATE TO HELP HIM, SONIC!
INTRUDERS... YOU MUST SURRENDER!
I SWORE I'D FIND A WAY TO SAVE UNCLE CHUCK FROM BEING JUST ANOTHER MINDLESS SLAVE, BUT I'VE PUNKED OUT... BIG TIME!!!
YOU'LL GET HIM BACK, SONIC... SOMEDAY!
(SIGH) I KNOW, SAL, BUT I STILL MISS HIM... AND HIS KILLER CHILI DOGS!!
THE THING IS HE'S PROBABLY HELPING ROBOTNIK PLAN OUR DESTRUCTION AS WE SPEAK!

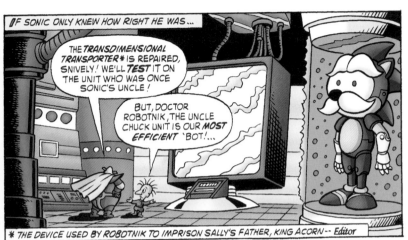

IF SONIC ONLY KNEW HOW RIGHT HE WAS...

THE *TRANSDIMENSIONAL TRANSPORTER* * IS REPAIRED, SNIVELY! WE'LL *TEST* IT ON THE UNIT WHO WAS ONCE SONIC'S UNCLE!

BUT, DOCTOR ROBOTNIK, THE UNCLE CHUCK UNIT IS OUR *MOST EFFICIENT* 'BOT!...

* THE DEVICE USED BY ROBOTNIK TO IMPRISON SALLY'S FATHER, KING ACORN -- *Editor*

IDIOT! IF THE TEST PROVES SUCCESSFUL, WE CAN BRING HIM *BACK!!*

...AND IF IT'S *NOT,* I'LL ROBOTICIZE *YOU,* AND YOU CAN *TAKE* HIS *PLACE!* NOW *GET GOING!!*

AS YOU WISH, SIR! HEH! HEH! YOU'RE IN CHARGE!

BUT *HOW* YOU GOT TO BE IN CHARGE IS A *MYSTERY!*

WHAT WAS *THAT?!*

UH... I SAID... YOU'LL GO DOWN IN *HISTORY!*

... I'LL START THE TEST, SIR...

3

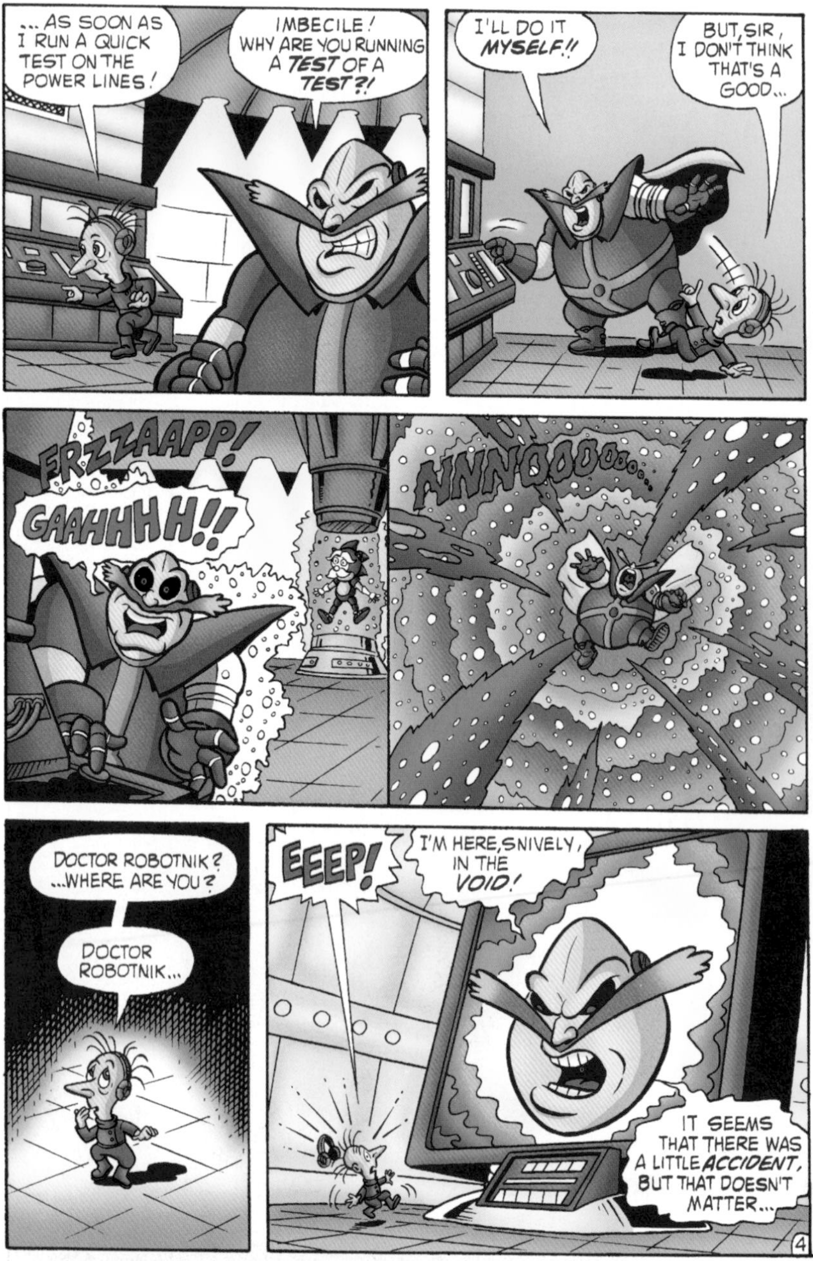
...AS SOON AS I RUN A QUICK TEST ON THE POWER LINES!
IMBECILE! WHY ARE YOU RUNNING A TEST OF A TEST?!
I'LL DO IT MYSELF!!
BUT, SIR, I DON'T THINK THAT'S A GOOD...
FRZZZAAPP!
GAAHHHH!!
NNNOOOOooo...
DOCTOR ROBOTNIK? ...WHERE ARE YOU?
DOCTOR ROBOTNIK...
EEEP!
I'M HERE, SNIVELY, IN THE VOID!
IT SEEMS THAT THERE WAS A LITTLE ACCIDENT, BUT THAT DOESN'T MATTER...

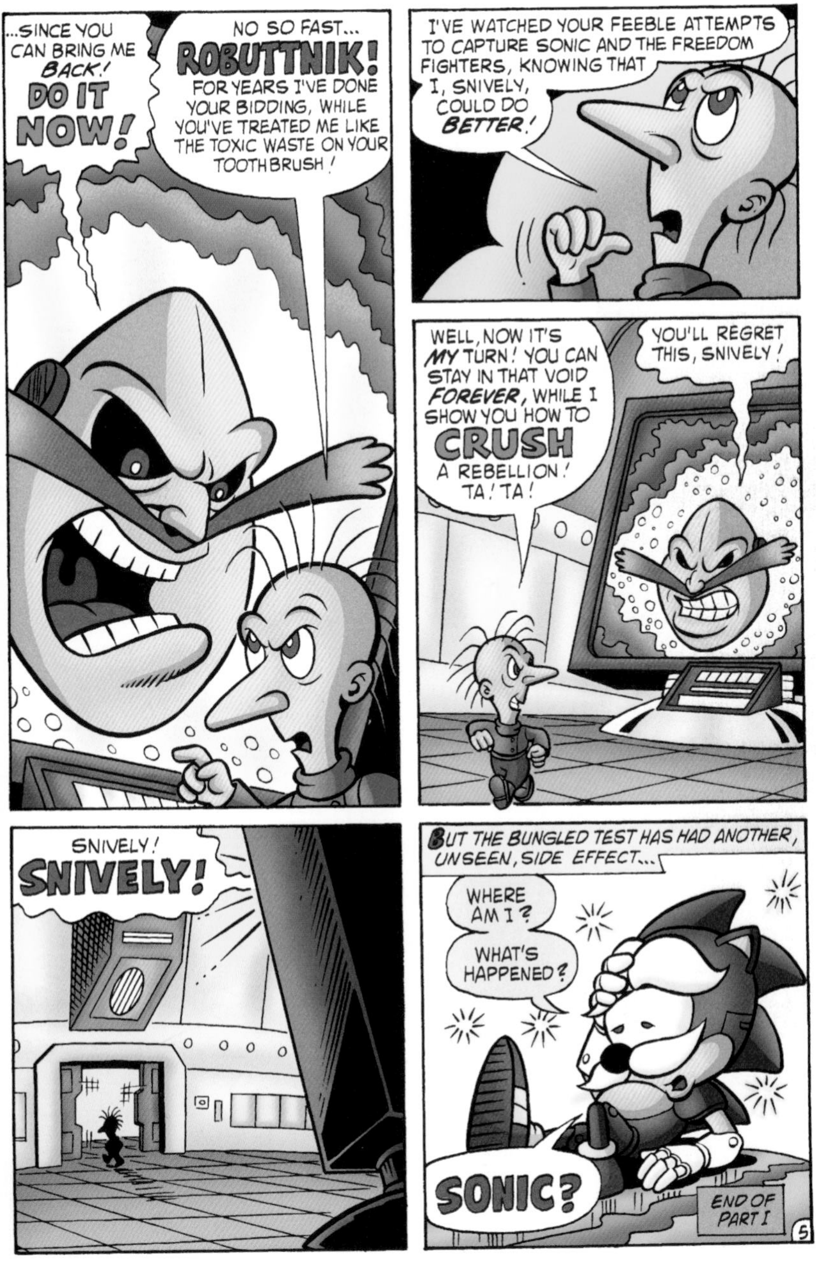
...SINCE YOU CAN BRING ME BACK! DO IT NOW!
NO SO FAST... ROBUTTNIK! FOR YEARS I'VE DONE YOUR BIDDING, WHILE YOU'VE TREATED ME LIKE THE TOXIC WASTE ON YOUR TOOTHBRUSH!
I'VE WATCHED YOUR FEEBLE ATTEMPTS TO CAPTURE SONIC AND THE FREEDOM FIGHTERS, KNOWING THAT I, SNIVELY, COULD DO BETTER!
WELL, NOW IT'S MY TURN! YOU CAN STAY IN THAT VOID FOREVER, WHILE I SHOW YOU HOW TO CRUSH A REBELLION! TA! TA!
YOU'LL REGRET THIS, SNIVELY!
SNIVELY! SNIVELY!
BUT THE BUNGLED TEST HAS HAD ANOTHER, UNSEEN, SIDE EFFECT...
WHERE AM I?
WHAT'S HAPPENED?
SONIC?
END OF PART I
5

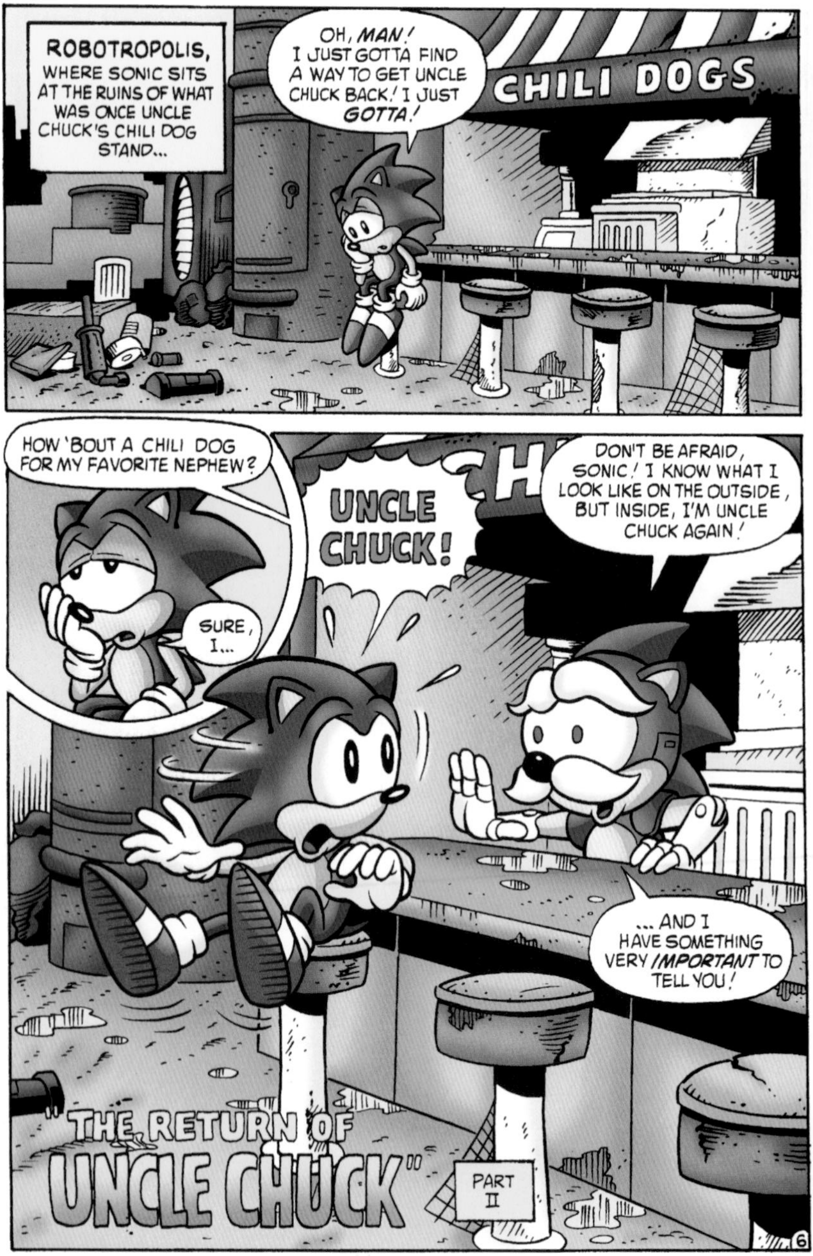

ROBOTROPOLIS, WHERE SONIC SITS AT THE RUINS OF WHAT WAS ONCE UNCLE CHUCK'S CHILI DOG STAND...
OH, MAN! I JUST GOTTA FIND A WAY TO GET UNCLE CHUCK BACK! I JUST GOTTA!
CHILI DOGS
HOW 'BOUT A CHILI DOG FOR MY FAVORITE NEPHEW?
SURE, I...
UNCLE CHUCK!
DON'T BE AFRAID, SONIC! I KNOW WHAT I LOOK LIKE ON THE OUTSIDE, BUT INSIDE, I'M UNCLE CHUCK AGAIN!
... AND I HAVE SOMETHING VERY IMPORTANT TO TELL YOU!
"THE RETURN OF UNCLE CHUCK"
PART II
6

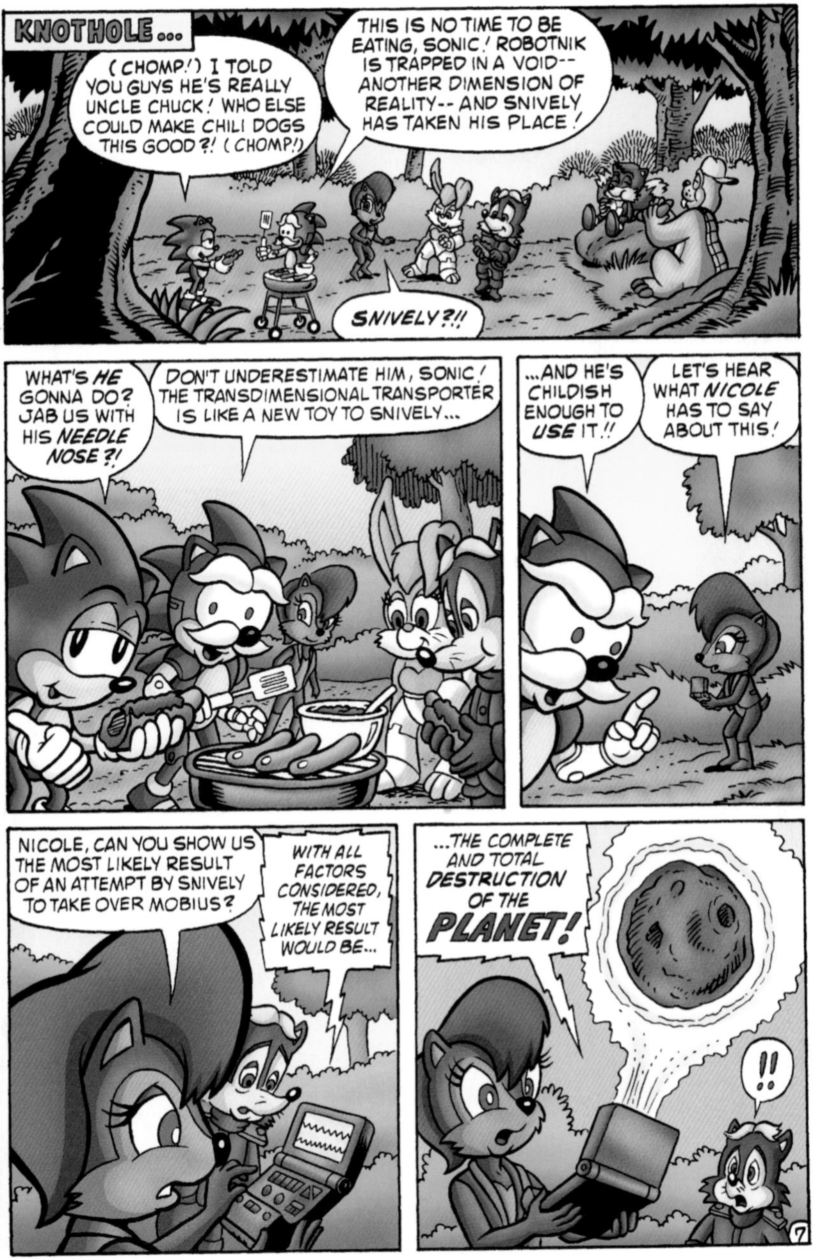
KNOTHOLE...
(CHOMP!) I TOLD YOU GUYS HE'S REALLY UNCLE CHUCK! WHO ELSE COULD MAKE CHILI DOGS THIS GOOD?! (CHOMP!)
THIS IS NO TIME TO BE EATING, SONIC! ROBOTNIK IS TRAPPED IN A VOID-- ANOTHER DIMENSION OF REALITY-- AND SNIVELY HAS TAKEN HIS PLACE!
SNIVELY?!!
WHAT'S HE GONNA DO? JAB US WITH HIS NEEDLE NOSE?!
DON'T UNDERESTIMATE HIM, SONIC! THE TRANSDIMENSIONAL TRANSPORTER IS LIKE A NEW TOY TO SNIVELY...
...AND HE'S CHILDISH ENOUGH TO USE IT!!
LET'S HEAR WHAT NICOLE HAS TO SAY ABOUT THIS!
NICOLE, CAN YOU SHOW US THE MOST LIKELY RESULT OF AN ATTEMPT BY SNIVELY TO TAKE OVER MOBIUS?
WITH ALL FACTORS CONSIDERED, THE MOST LIKELY RESULT WOULD BE...
...THE COMPLETE AND TOTAL DESTRUCTION OF THE PLANET!
!!
7

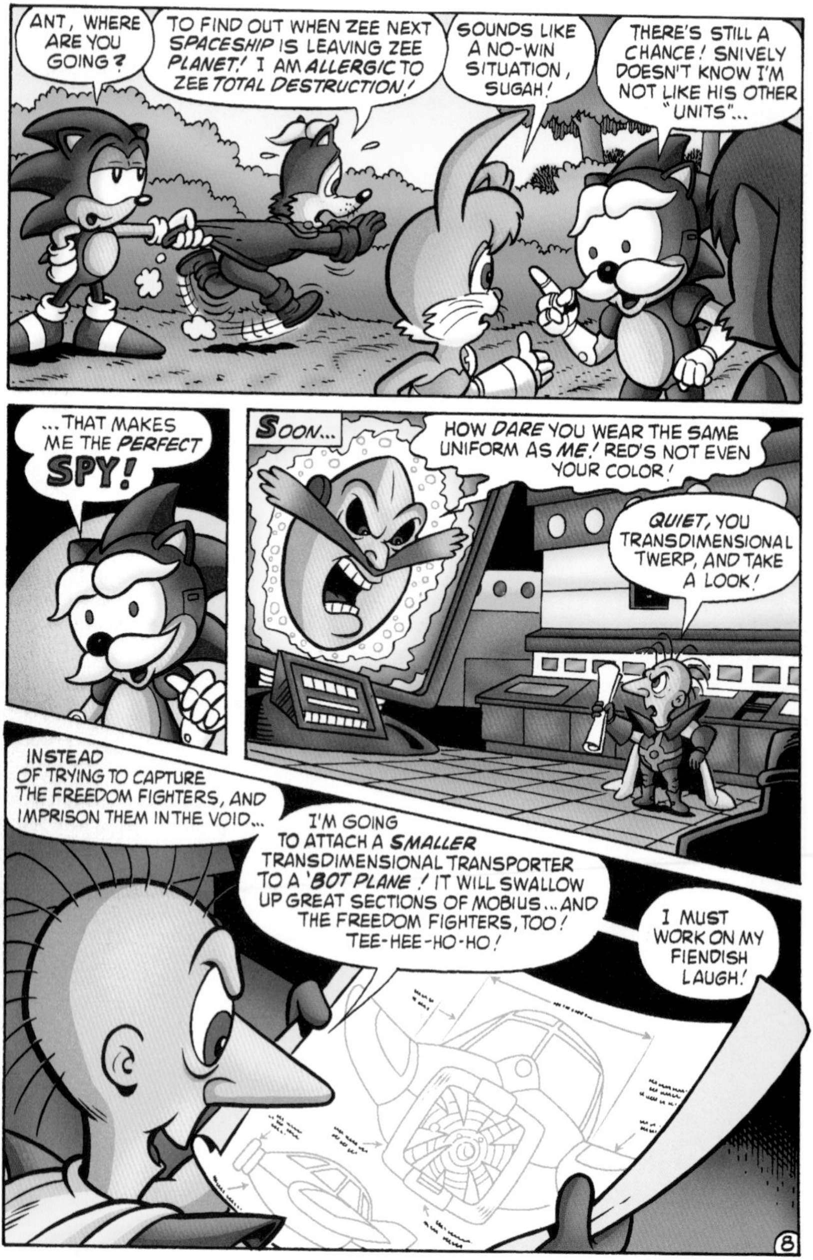

ANT, WHERE ARE YOU GOING?
TO FIND OUT WHEN ZEE NEXT SPACESHIP IS LEAVING ZEE PLANET! I AM ALLERGIC TO ZEE TOTAL DESTRUCTION!
SOUNDS LIKE A NO-WIN SITUATION, SUGAH!
THERE'S STILL A CHANCE! SNIVELY DOESN'T KNOW I'M NOT LIKE HIS OTHER "UNITS"...
...THAT MAKES ME THE PERFECT SPY!
SOON...
HOW DARE YOU WEAR THE SAME UNIFORM AS ME! RED'S NOT EVEN YOUR COLOR!
QUIET, YOU TRANSDIMENSIONAL TWERP, AND TAKE A LOOK!
INSTEAD OF TRYING TO CAPTURE THE FREEDOM FIGHTERS, AND IMPRISON THEM IN THE VOID...
I'M GOING TO ATTACH A SMALLER TRANSDIMENSIONAL TRANSPORTER TO A 'BOT PLANE! IT WILL SWALLOW UP GREAT SECTIONS OF MOBIUS...AND THE FREEDOM FIGHTERS, TOO! TEE-HEE-HO-HO!
I MUST WORK ON MY FIENDISH LAUGH!
8

HAVE YOU LOST YOUR MICROSCOPIC MIND, SNIVELY? THAT DEVICE IS *TOO POWERFUL* TO TURN LOOSE ON THE PLANET! IT COULD DESTROY *EVERYTHING*.!!

YOU'VE BECOME TOO CHICKEN, ROCLUCKNIK! I'M NOT AFRAID TO TAKE *BIG* RISKS...

...THAT'S WHY I'LL *SUCCEED!*

WHO'S *THAT?*

CLANK!

OH, IT'S *YOU!* WHERE HAVE YOU BEEN? I'VE GOT A *JOB* FOR YOU!

INSTRUCT ALL UNITS TO CONSTRUCT THIS PLANE ACCORDING TO MY DESIGN! ...AND I WANT IT DONE *QUICKLY*, UNDERSTAND?!

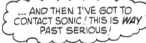

AS YOU COMMAND, MASTER!

... AND THEN I'VE GOT TO CONTACT SONIC! THIS IS *WAY* PAST SERIOUS!

9

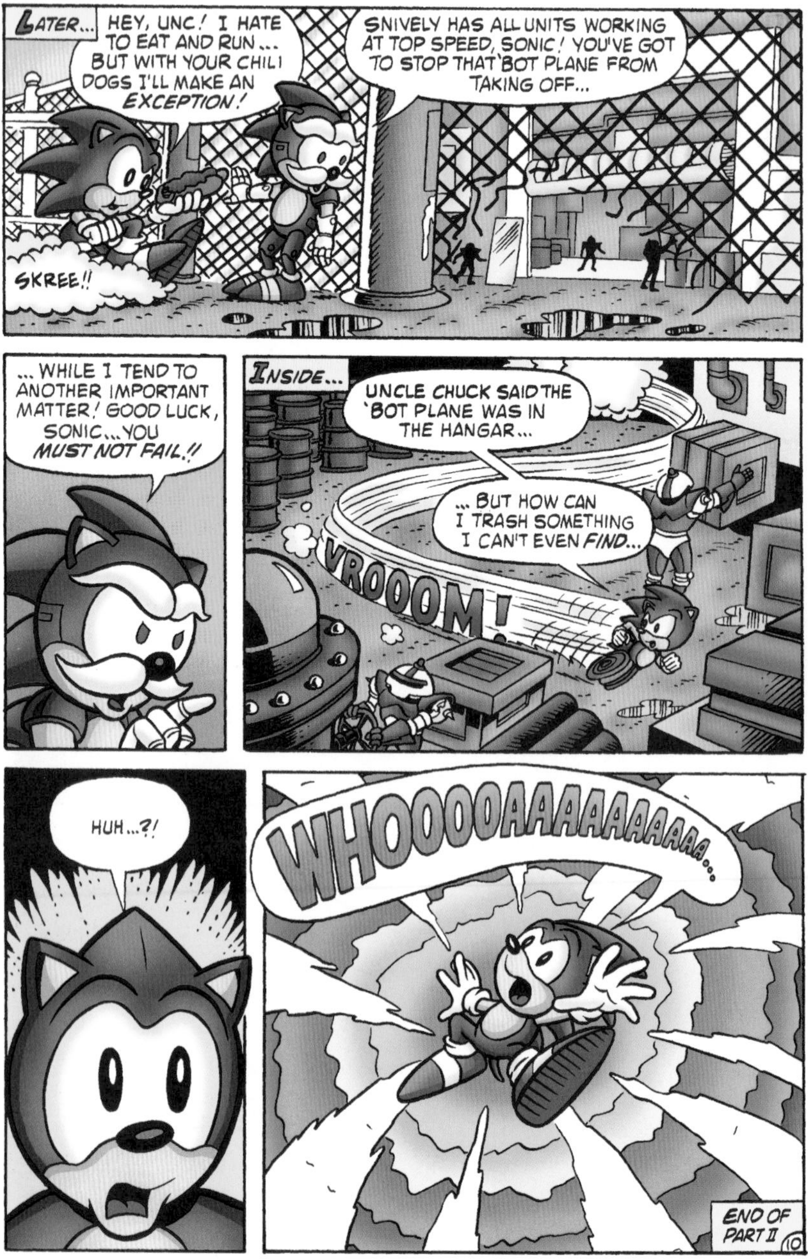
LATER...
HEY, UNC! I HATE TO EAT AND RUN... BUT WITH YOUR CHILI DOGS I'LL MAKE AN EXCEPTION!
SNIVELY HAS ALL UNITS WORKING AT TOP SPEED, SONIC! YOU'VE GOT TO STOP THAT 'BOT PLANE FROM TAKING OFF...
SKREE!!
... WHILE I TEND TO ANOTHER IMPORTANT MATTER! GOOD LUCK, SONIC... YOU MUST NOT FAIL!!
INSIDE...
UNCLE CHUCK SAID THE 'BOT PLANE WAS IN THE HANGAR...
... BUT HOW CAN I TRASH SOMETHING I CAN'T EVEN FIND...
VROOOOM!
HUH...?!
WHOOOOAAAAAAAAAa...
END OF PART II

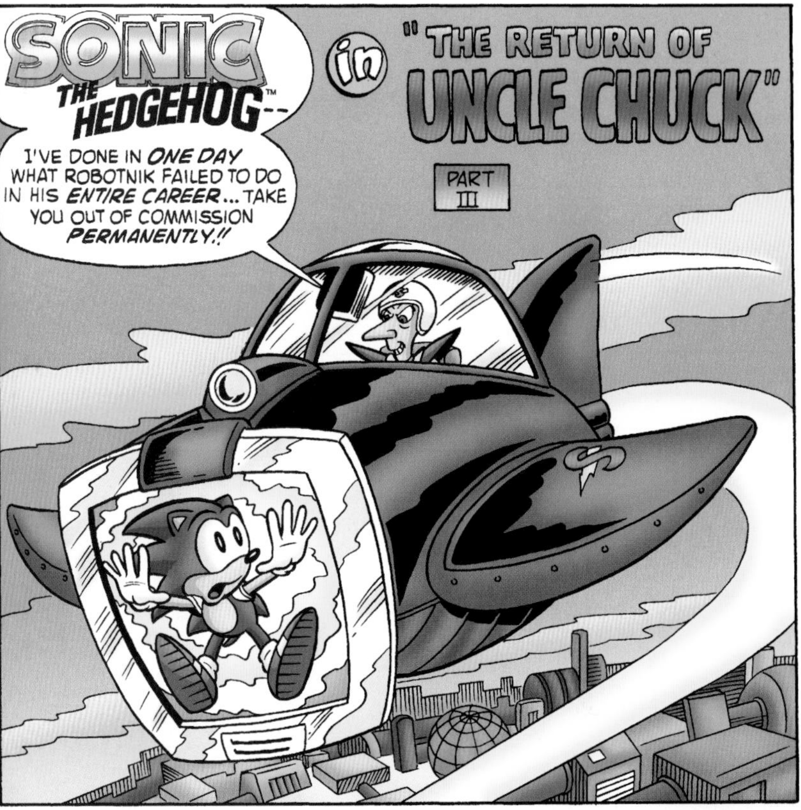
SONIC THE HEDGEHOG™--
in "THE RETURN OF UNCLE CHUCK"
PART III
I'VE DONE IN *ONE DAY* WHAT ROBOTNIK FAILED TO DO IN HIS *ENTIRE CAREER*... TAKE YOU OUT OF COMMISSION *PERMANENTLY*!!

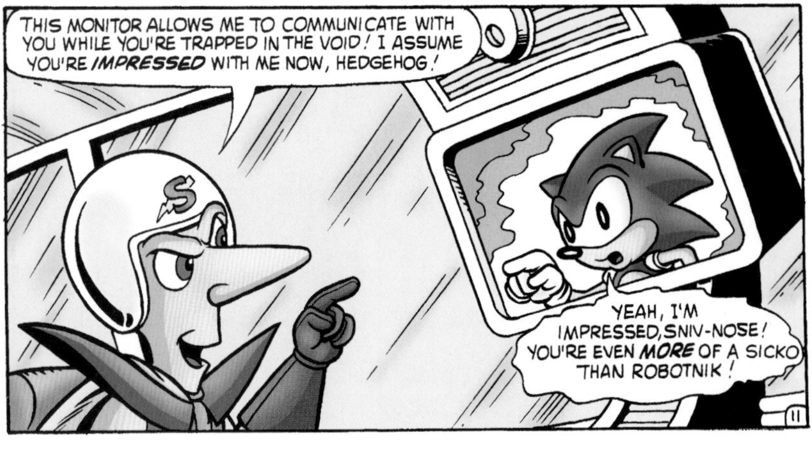
THIS MONITOR ALLOWS ME TO COMMUNICATE WITH YOU WHILE YOU'RE TRAPPED IN THE VOID! I ASSUME YOU'RE *IMPRESSED* WITH ME NOW, HEDGEHOG!
YEAH, I'M IMPRESSED, SNIV-NOSE! YOU'RE EVEN *MORE* OF A SICKO THAN ROBOTNIK!

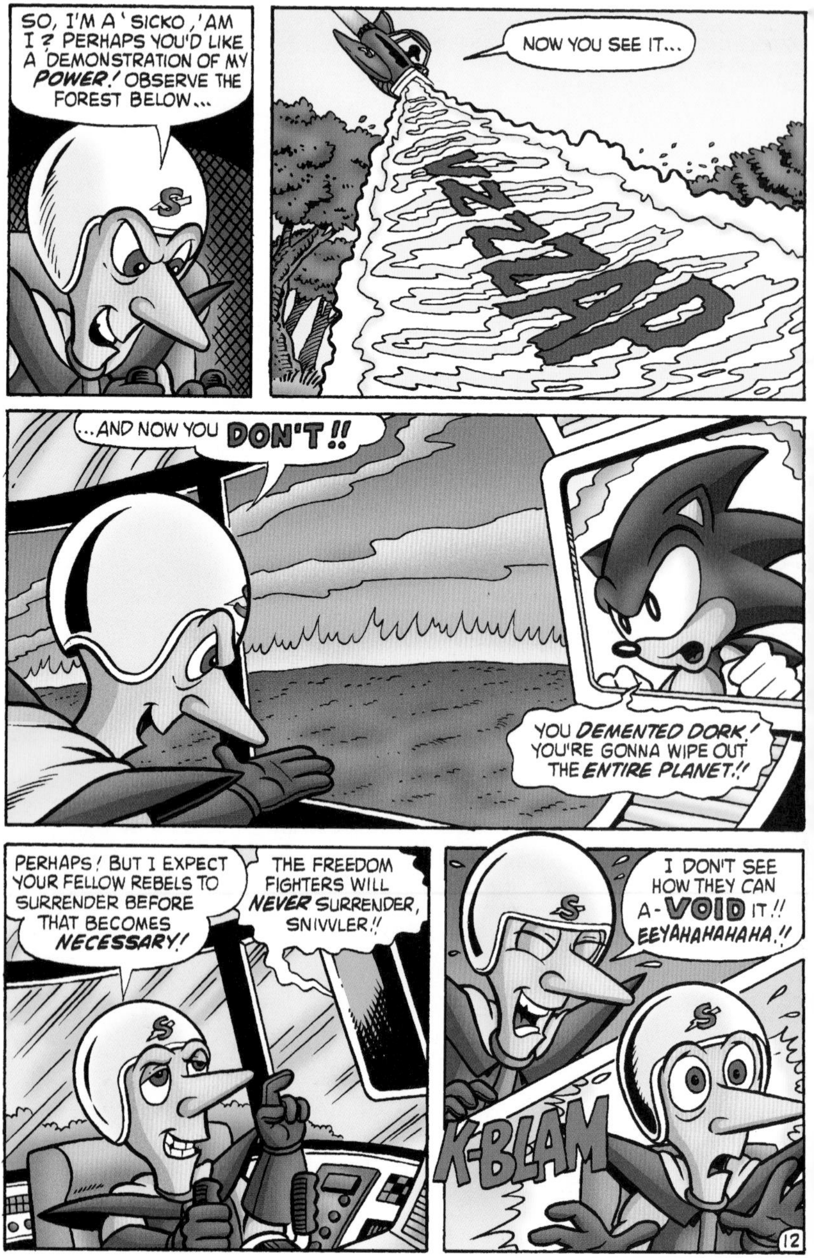
SO, I'M A 'SICKO,' AM I ? PERHAPS YOU'D LIKE A DEMONSTRATION OF MY POWER! OBSERVE THE FOREST BELOW...
NOW YOU SEE IT...
VZZAP
...AND NOW YOU DON'T!!
YOU DEMENTED DORK! YOU'RE GONNA WIPE OUT THE ENTIRE PLANET!!
PERHAPS! BUT I EXPECT YOUR FELLOW REBELS TO SURRENDER BEFORE THAT BECOMES NECESSARY!
THE FREEDOM FIGHTERS WILL NEVER SURRENDER, SNIVVLER!!
I DON'T SEE HOW THEY CAN A-VOID IT!! EEYAHAHAHAHAHA!!
K-BLAM
12

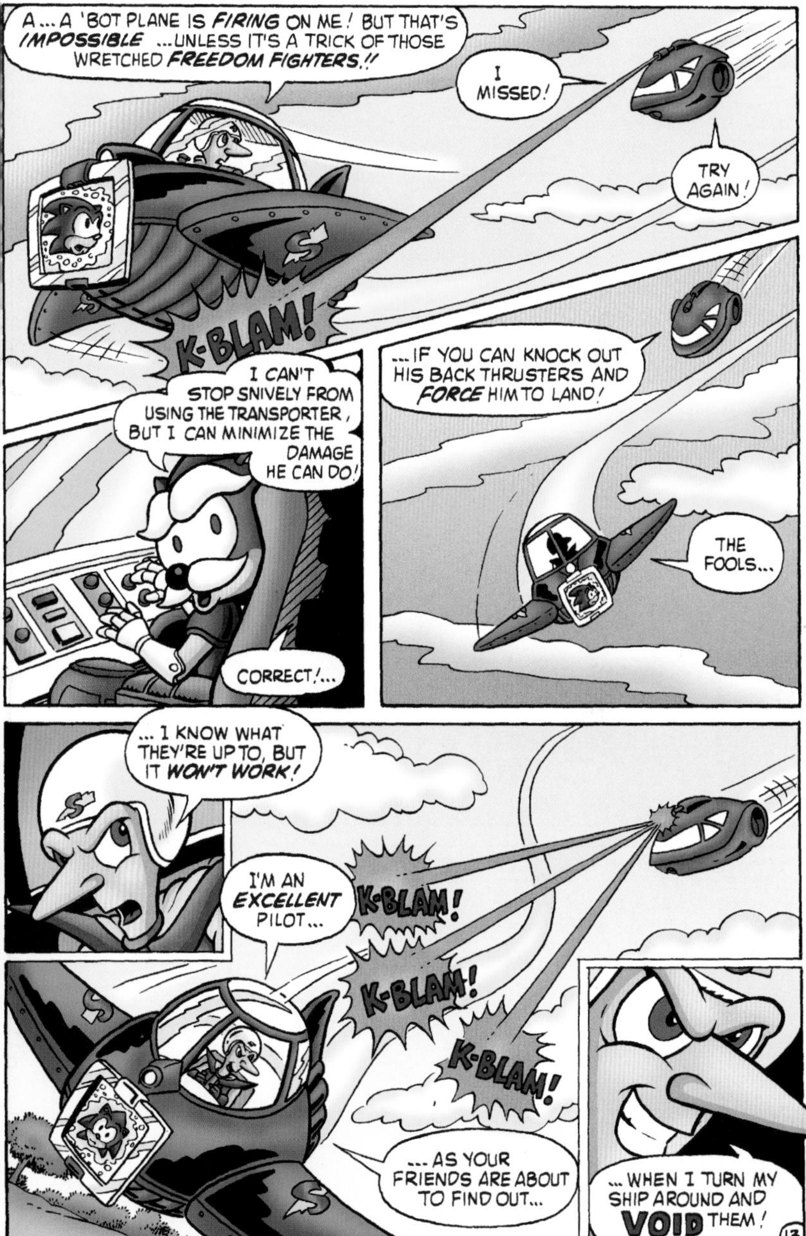
A... A 'BOT PLANE IS FIRING ON ME! BUT THAT'S IMPOSSIBLE ...UNLESS IT'S A TRICK OF THOSE WRETCHED FREEDOM FIGHTERS!!
I MISSED!
TRY AGAIN!
K-BLAM!
I CAN'T STOP SNIVELY FROM USING THE TRANSPORTER, BUT I CAN MINIMIZE THE DAMAGE HE CAN DO!
CORRECT!...
...IF YOU CAN KNOCK OUT HIS BACK THRUSTERS AND FORCE HIM TO LAND!
THE FOOLS...
... I KNOW WHAT THEY'RE UP TO, BUT IT WON'T WORK!
I'M AN EXCELLENT PILOT...
K-BLAM!
K-BLAM!
K-BLAM!
... AS YOUR FRIENDS ARE ABOUT TO FIND OUT...
... WHEN I TURN MY SHIP AROUND AND VOID THEM!
13

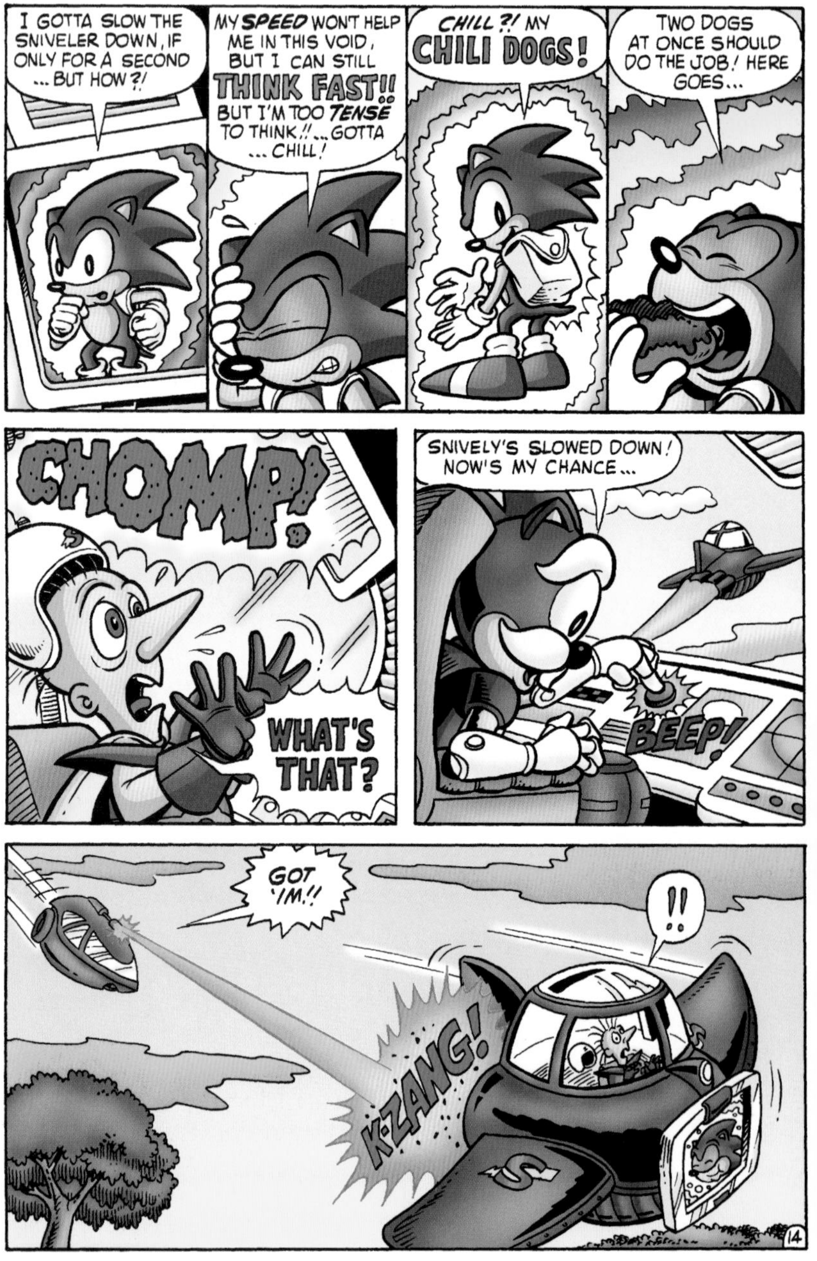
I GOTTA SLOW THE SNIVELER DOWN, IF ONLY FOR A SECOND ... BUT HOW ?!
MY SPEED WON'T HELP ME IN THIS VOID, BUT I CAN STILL THINK FAST!! BUT I'M TOO TENSE TO THINK!! ... GOTTA ... CHILL!
CHILL ?! MY CHILI DOGS!
TWO DOGS AT ONCE SHOULD DO THE JOB! HERE GOES...
CHOMP!
WHAT'S THAT?
SNIVELY'S SLOWED DOWN! NOW'S MY CHANCE...
BEEP!
GOT 'IM!!
!!
K-ZANG!
14

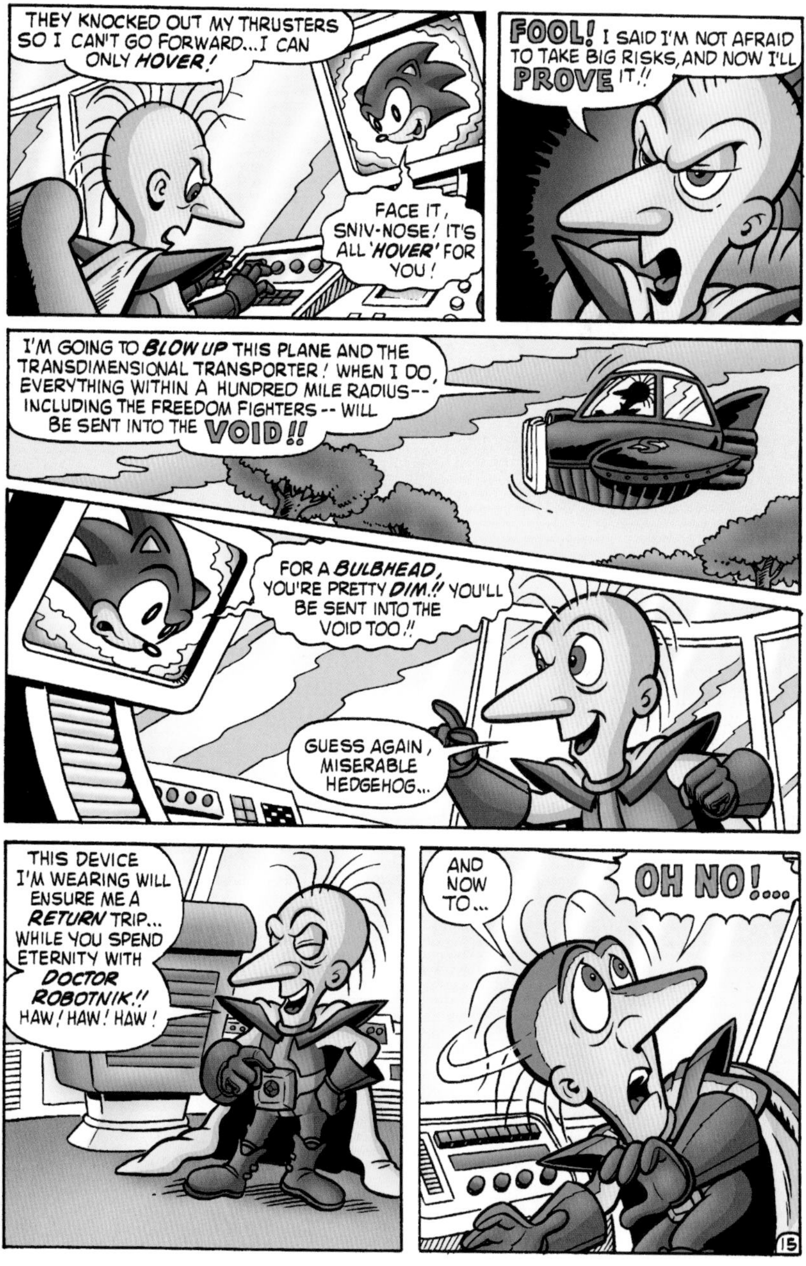
THEY KNOCKED OUT MY THRUSTERS SO I CAN'T GO FORWARD...I CAN ONLY HOVER!
FACE IT, SNIV-NOSE! IT'S ALL 'HOVER' FOR YOU!
FOOL! I SAID I'M NOT AFRAID TO TAKE BIG RISKS, AND NOW I'LL PROVE IT!!
I'M GOING TO BLOW UP THIS PLANE AND THE TRANSDIMENSIONAL TRANSPORTER! WHEN I DO, EVERYTHING WITHIN A HUNDRED MILE RADIUS-- INCLUDING THE FREEDOM FIGHTERS -- WILL BE SENT INTO THE VOID!!
FOR A BULBHEAD, YOU'RE PRETTY DIM!! YOU'LL BE SENT INTO THE VOID TOO!!
GUESS AGAIN, MISERABLE HEDGEHOG...
THIS DEVICE I'M WEARING WILL ENSURE ME A RETURN TRIP... WHILE YOU SPEND ETERNITY WITH DOCTOR ROBOTNIK!! HAW! HAW! HAW!
AND NOW TO...
OH NO!...

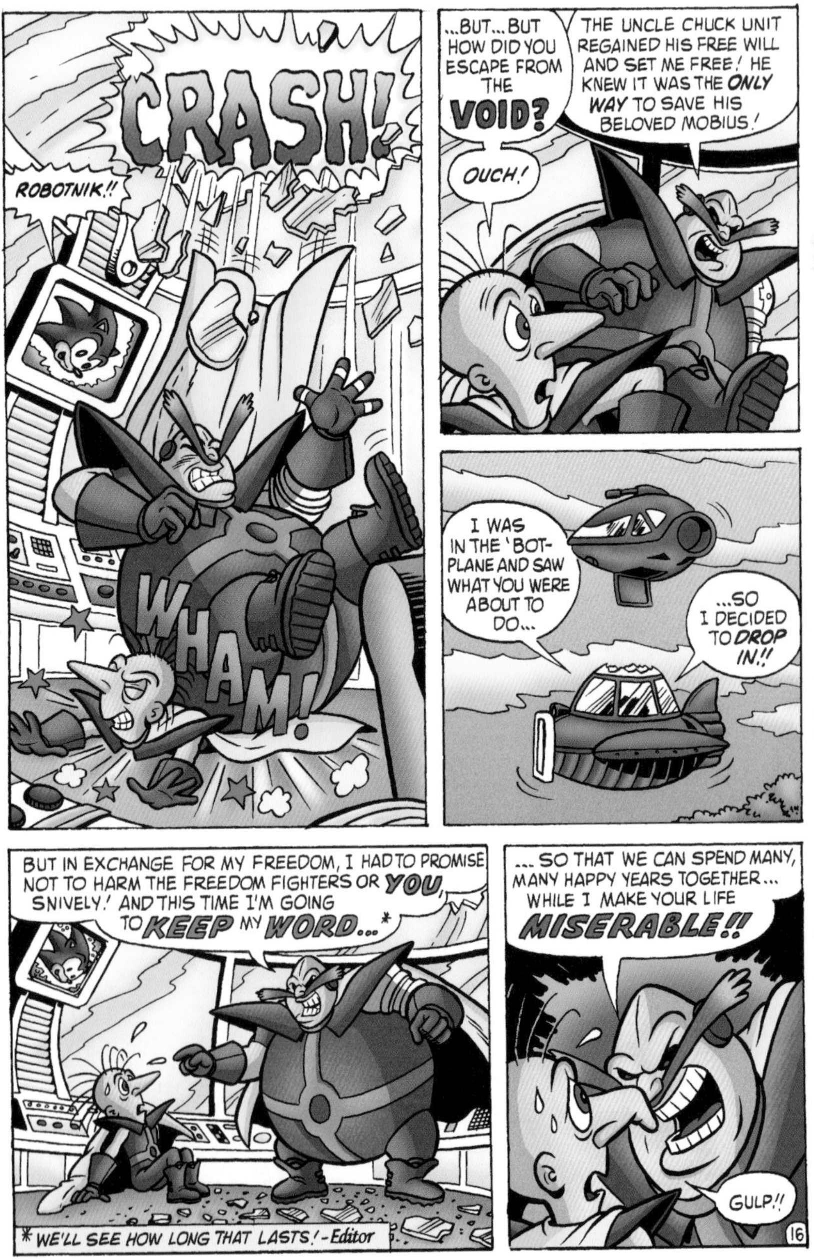
CRASH!
ROBOTNIK!!
WHAM!
...BUT...BUT HOW DID YOU ESCAPE FROM THE VOID?
THE UNCLE CHUCK UNIT REGAINED HIS FREE WILL AND SET ME FREE! HE KNEW IT WAS THE ONLY WAY TO SAVE HIS BELOVED MOBIUS!
OUCH!
I WAS IN THE 'BOT-PLANE AND SAW WHAT YOU WERE ABOUT TO DO...
...SO I DECIDED TO DROP IN!!
BUT IN EXCHANGE FOR MY FREEDOM, I HAD TO PROMISE NOT TO HARM THE FREEDOM FIGHTERS OR YOU, SNIVELY! AND THIS TIME I'M GOING TO KEEP MY WORD...*
*WE'LL SEE HOW LONG THAT LASTS! -Editor
... SO THAT WE CAN SPEND MANY, MANY HAPPY YEARS TOGETHER... WHILE I MAKE YOUR LIFE MISERABLE!!
GULP!!
16

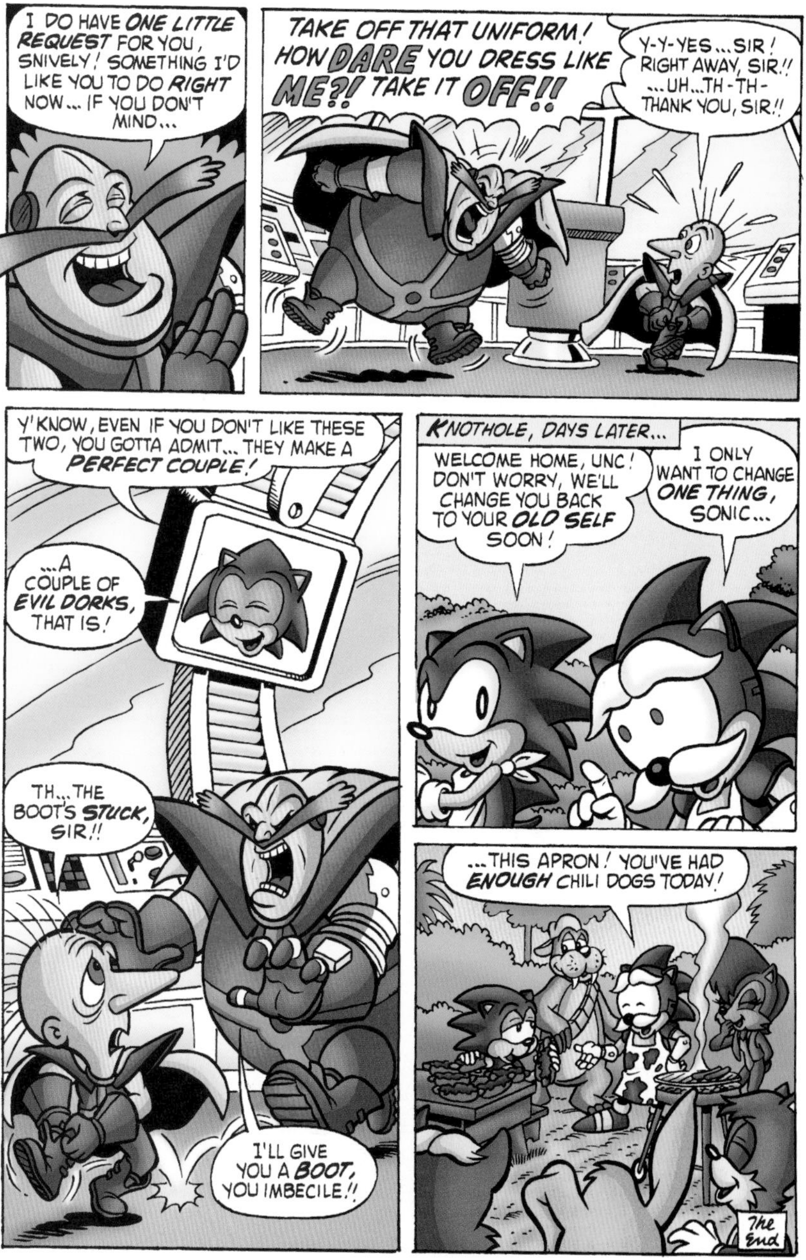
I DO HAVE ONE LITTLE REQUEST FOR YOU, SNIVELY! SOMETHING I'D LIKE YOU TO DO RIGHT NOW... IF YOU DON'T MIND...
TAKE OFF THAT UNIFORM! HOW DARE YOU DRESS LIKE ME?! TAKE IT OFF!!
Y-Y-YES...SIR! RIGHT AWAY, SIR!! ...UH...TH-TH-THANK YOU, SIR!!
Y'KNOW, EVEN IF YOU DON'T LIKE THESE TWO, YOU GOTTA ADMIT... THEY MAKE A PERFECT COUPLE!
...A COUPLE OF EVIL DORKS, THAT IS!
TH...THE BOOT'S STUCK, SIR!!
I'LL GIVE YOU A BOOT, YOU IMBECILE!!
KNOTHOLE, DAYS LATER...
WELCOME HOME, UNC! DON'T WORRY, WE'LL CHANGE YOU BACK TO YOUR OLD SELF SOON!
I ONLY WANT TO CHANGE ONE THING, SONIC...
...THIS APRON! YOU'VE HAD ENOUGH CHILI DOGS TODAY!
The End

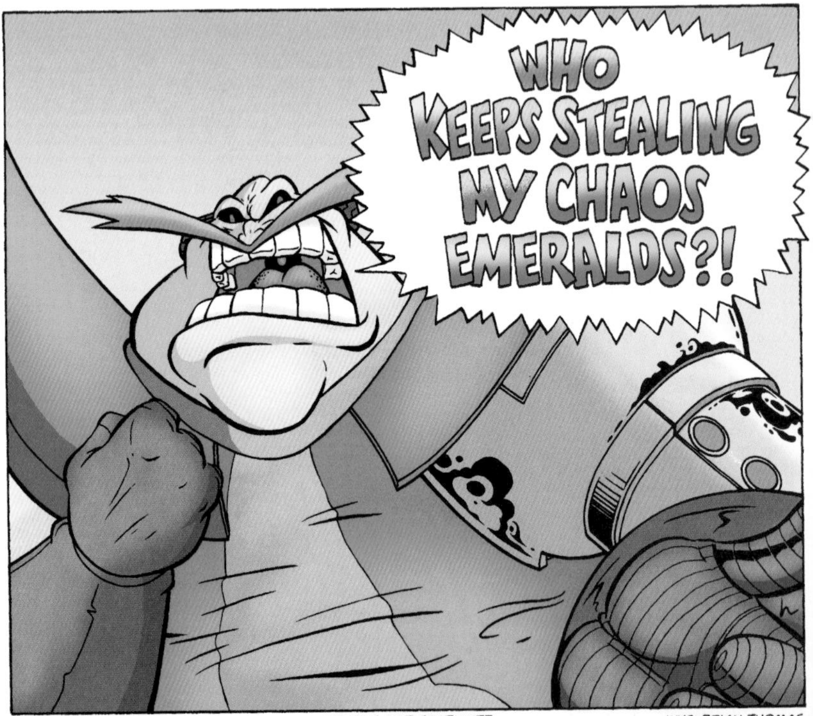
WHO KEEPS STEALING MY CHAOS EMERALDS?!

SCRIPT: PAUL CASTIGLIA PENCILS: PAT SPAZIANTE INKS: BRIAN THOMAS

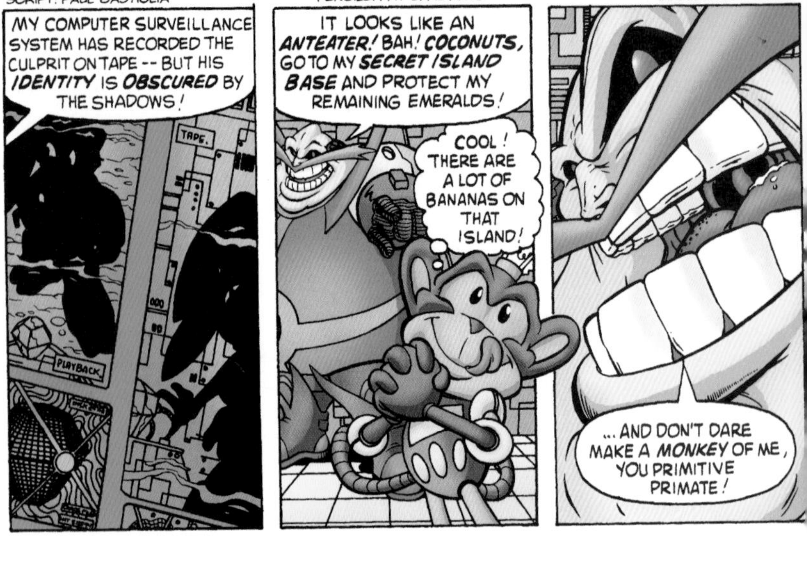
MY COMPUTER SURVEILLANCE SYSTEM HAS RECORDED THE CULPRIT ON TAPE -- BUT HIS *IDENTITY* IS *OBSCURED* BY THE SHADOWS!
TAPE
PLAYBACK
IT LOOKS LIKE AN *ANTEATER!* BAH! *COCONUTS,* GO TO MY *SECRET ISLAND BASE* AND PROTECT MY REMAINING EMERALDS!
COOL! THERE ARE A LOT OF BANANAS ON THAT ISLAND!
...AND DON'T DARE MAKE A *MONKEY* OF ME, YOU PRIMITIVE PRIMATE!

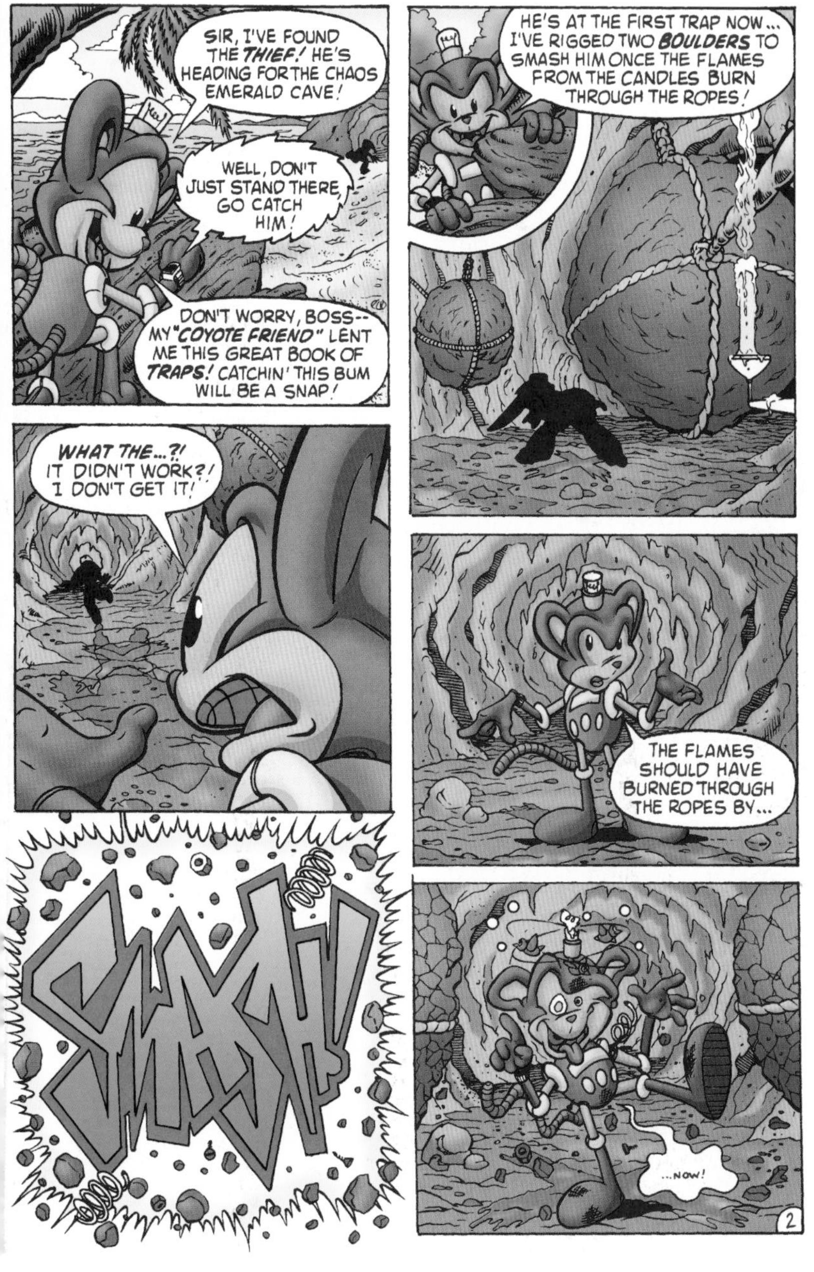
SIR, I'VE FOUND THE THIEF! HE'S HEADING FOR THE CHAOS EMERALD CAVE!
WELL, DON'T JUST STAND THERE, GO CATCH HIM!
DON'T WORRY, BOSS-- MY "COYOTE FRIEND" LENT ME THIS GREAT BOOK OF TRAPS! CATCHIN' THIS BUM WILL BE A SNAP!
HE'S AT THE FIRST TRAP NOW... I'VE RIGGED TWO BOULDERS TO SMASH HIM ONCE THE FLAMES FROM THE CANDLES BURN THROUGH THE ROPES!
WHAT THE...?! IT DIDN'T WORK?! I DON'T GET IT!
THE FLAMES SHOULD HAVE BURNED THROUGH THE ROPES BY...
SMASH!
...NOW!

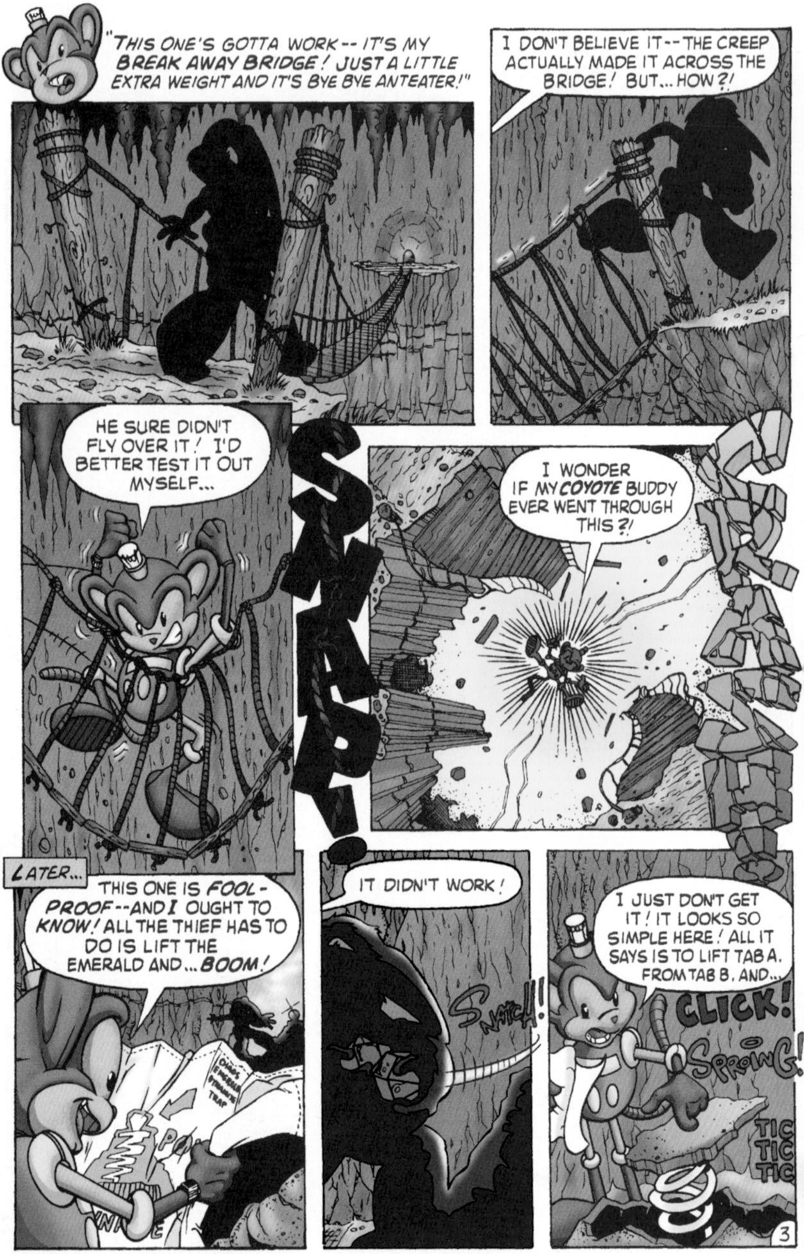
"THIS ONE'S GOTTA WORK -- IT'S MY BREAK AWAY BRIDGE! JUST A LITTLE EXTRA WEIGHT AND IT'S BYE BYE ANTEATER!"
I DON'T BELIEVE IT -- THE CREEP ACTUALLY MADE IT ACROSS THE BRIDGE! BUT... HOW?!
HE SURE DIDN'T FLY OVER IT! I'D BETTER TEST IT OUT MYSELF...
SNAP!
I WONDER IF MY COYOTE BUDDY EVER WENT THROUGH THIS?!
LATER...
THIS ONE IS FOOL-PROOF -- AND I OUGHT TO KNOW! ALL THE THIEF HAS TO DO IS LIFT THE EMERALD AND... BOOM!
CHAOS EMERALD DYNAMITE TRAP
IT DIDN'T WORK!
SNATCH!
I JUST DON'T GET IT! IT LOOKS SO SIMPLE HERE! ALL IT SAYS IS TO LIFT TAB A. FROM TAB B. AND...
CLICK!
SPROING!
TIC TIC TIC
3

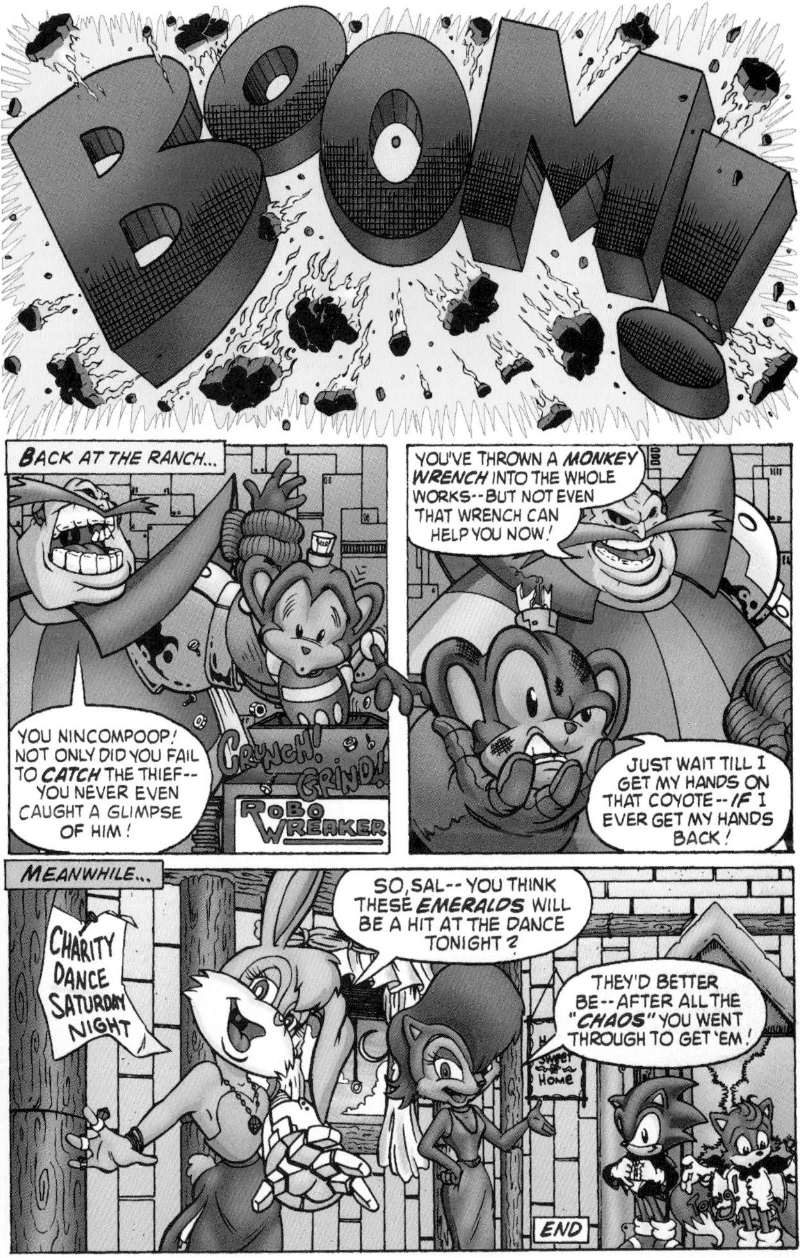
BOOM!!
BACK AT THE RANCH...
YOU NINCOMPOOP! NOT ONLY DID YOU FAIL TO CATCH THE THIEF-- YOU NEVER EVEN CAUGHT A GLIMPSE OF HIM!
CRUNCH! GRIND!
ROBO WREAKER
YOU'VE THROWN A MONKEY WRENCH INTO THE WHOLE WORKS--BUT NOT EVEN THAT WRENCH CAN HELP YOU NOW!
JUST WAIT TILL I GET MY HANDS ON THAT COYOTE--IF I EVER GET MY HANDS BACK!
MEANWHILE...
CHARITY DANCE SATURDAY NIGHT
SO, SAL-- YOU THINK THESE EMERALDS WILL BE A HIT AT THE DANCE TONIGHT?
THEY'D BETTER BE--AFTER ALL THE "CHAOS" YOU WENT THROUGH TO GET 'EM!
HOME
END

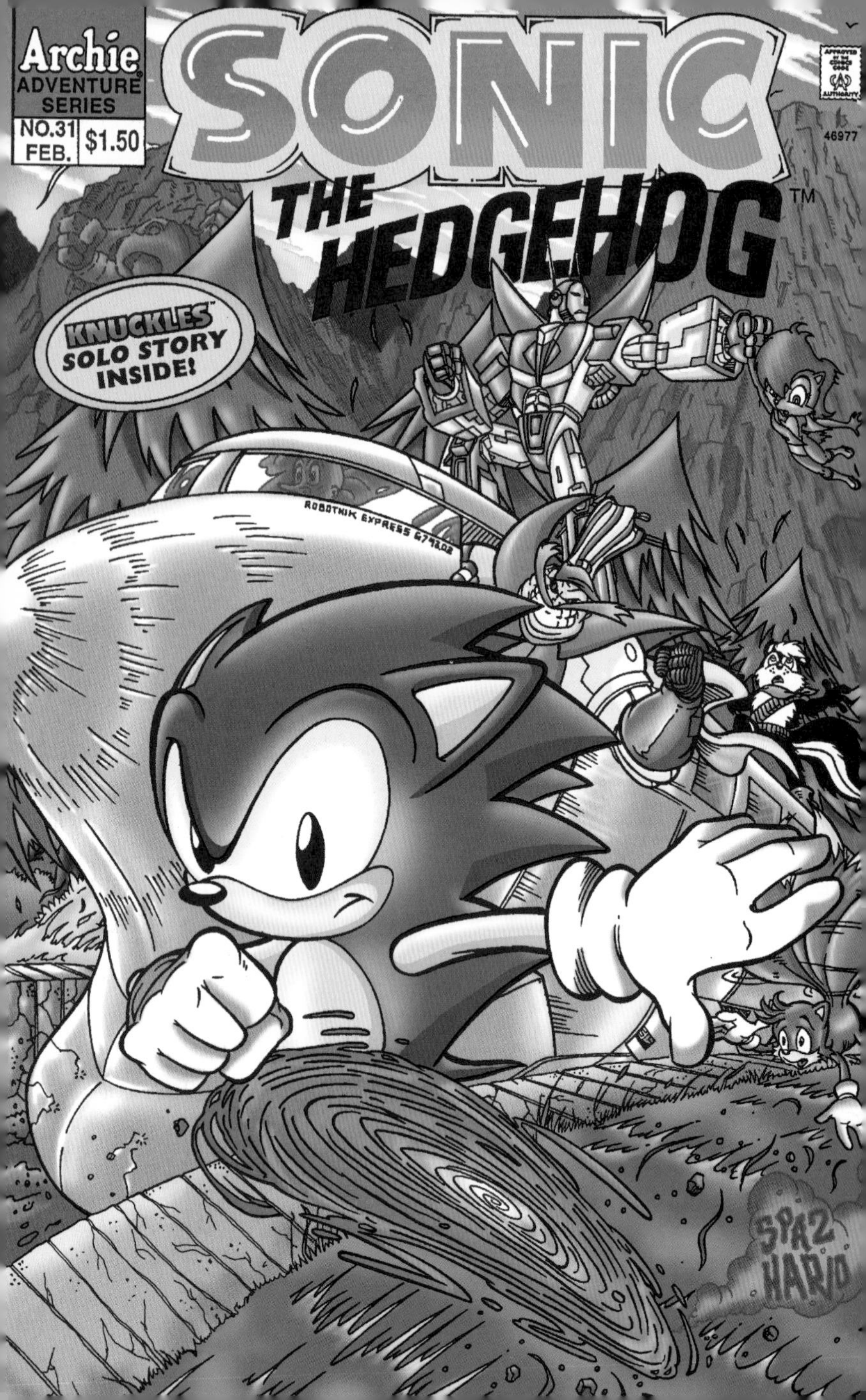

Archie
ADVENTURE SERIES
NO.31
FEB.
$1.50
SONIC THE HEDGEHOG™
46977
KNUCKLES™ SOLO STORY INSIDE!
ROBOTNIK EXPRESS 674202
SPAZ HARVO

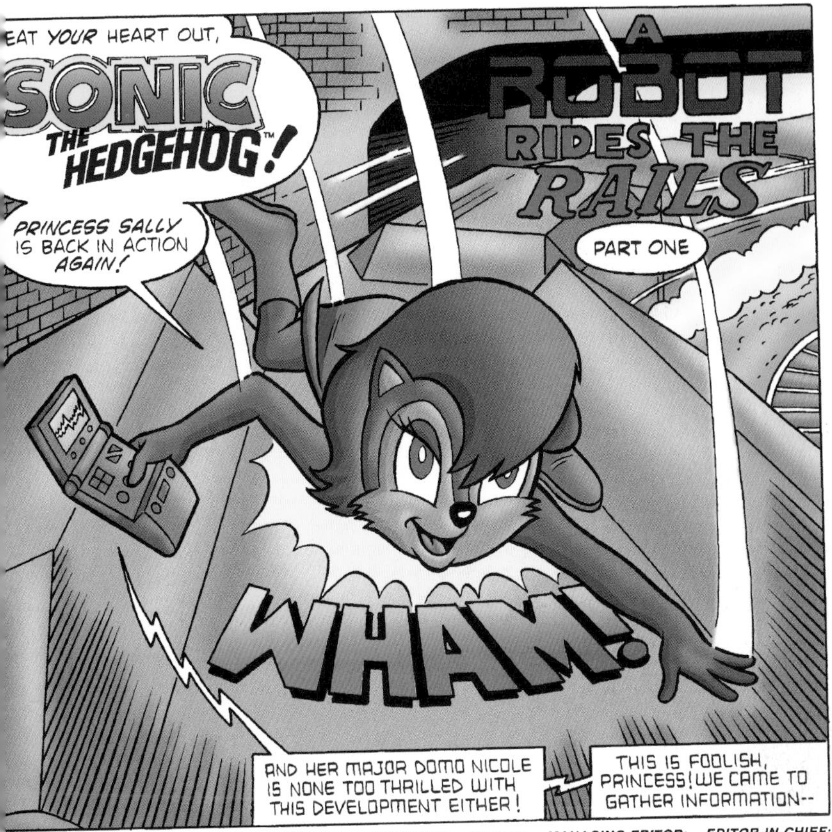
EAT YOUR HEART OUT,
SONIC THE HEDGEHOG™!
A ROBOT RIDES THE RAILS
PART ONE
PRINCESS SALLY IS BACK IN ACTION AGAIN!
WHAM!
AND HER MAJOR DOMO NICOLE IS NONE TOO THRILLED WITH THIS DEVELOPMENT EITHER!
THIS IS FOOLISH, PRINCESS! WE CAME TO GATHER INFORMATION--

SCRIPT & PENCILS: KEN PENDERS INKS: JON D'AGOSTINO LETTERING: MINDY EISMAN COLORING: BARRY GROSSMAN EDITOR: SCOTT FULOP MANAGING EDITOR: VICTOR GORELICK EDITOR-IN-CHIEF: RICHARD GOLDWATER

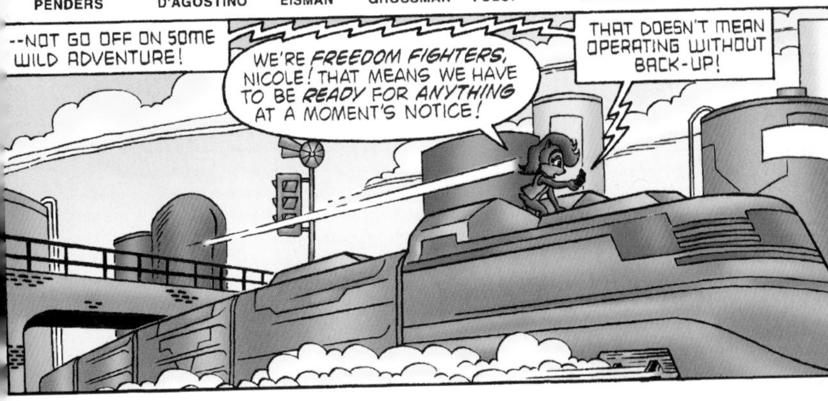
--NOT GO OFF ON SOME WILD ADVENTURE!
WE'RE FREEDOM FIGHTERS, NICOLE! THAT MEANS WE HAVE TO BE READY FOR ANYTHING AT A MOMENT'S NOTICE!
THAT DOESN'T MEAN OPERATING WITHOUT BACK-UP!

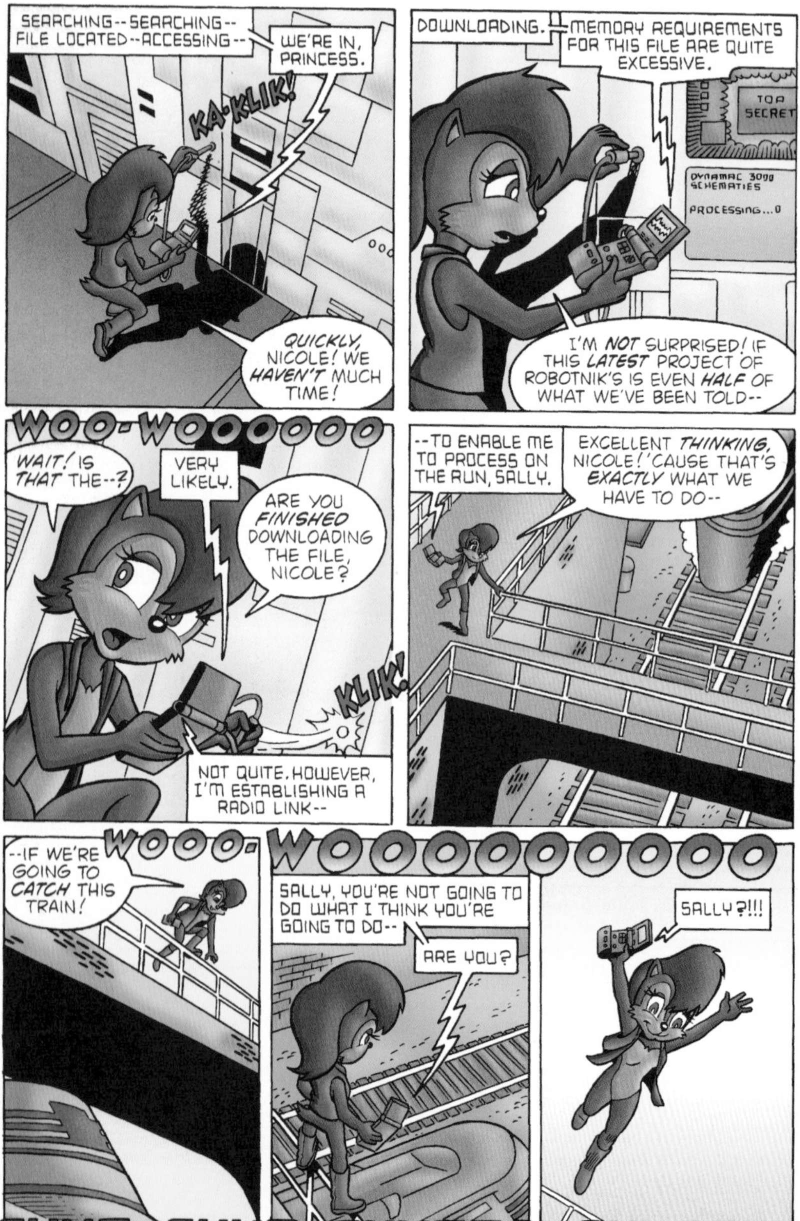
SEARCHING--SEARCHING--
FILE LOCATED--ACCESSING--
WE'RE IN, PRINCESS.
KA-KLIK!
QUICKLY, NICOLE! WE HAVEN'T MUCH TIME!
DOWNLOADING.
MEMORY REQUIREMENTS FOR THIS FILE ARE QUITE EXCESSIVE.
TOP SECRET
DYNAMAC 3000 SCHEMATICS
PROCESSING...0
I'M NOT SURPRISED! IF THIS LATEST PROJECT OF ROBOTNIK'S IS EVEN HALF OF WHAT WE'VE BEEN TOLD--
WOO-WOOOOOO
WAIT! IS THAT THE--?
VERY LIKELY.
ARE YOU FINISHED DOWNLOADING THE FILE, NICOLE?
KLIK!
NOT QUITE. HOWEVER, I'M ESTABLISHING A RADIO LINK--
--TO ENABLE ME TO PROCESS ON THE RUN, SALLY.
EXCELLENT THINKING, NICOLE! 'CAUSE THAT'S EXACTLY WHAT WE HAVE TO DO--
WOOO-WOOOOOOOOOO
--IF WE'RE GOING TO CATCH THIS TRAIN!
SALLY, YOU'RE NOT GOING TO DO WHAT I THINK YOU'RE GOING TO DO--
ARE YOU?
SALLY?!!!
CHUG-CHUG-CHUGGA-CHUGGA-

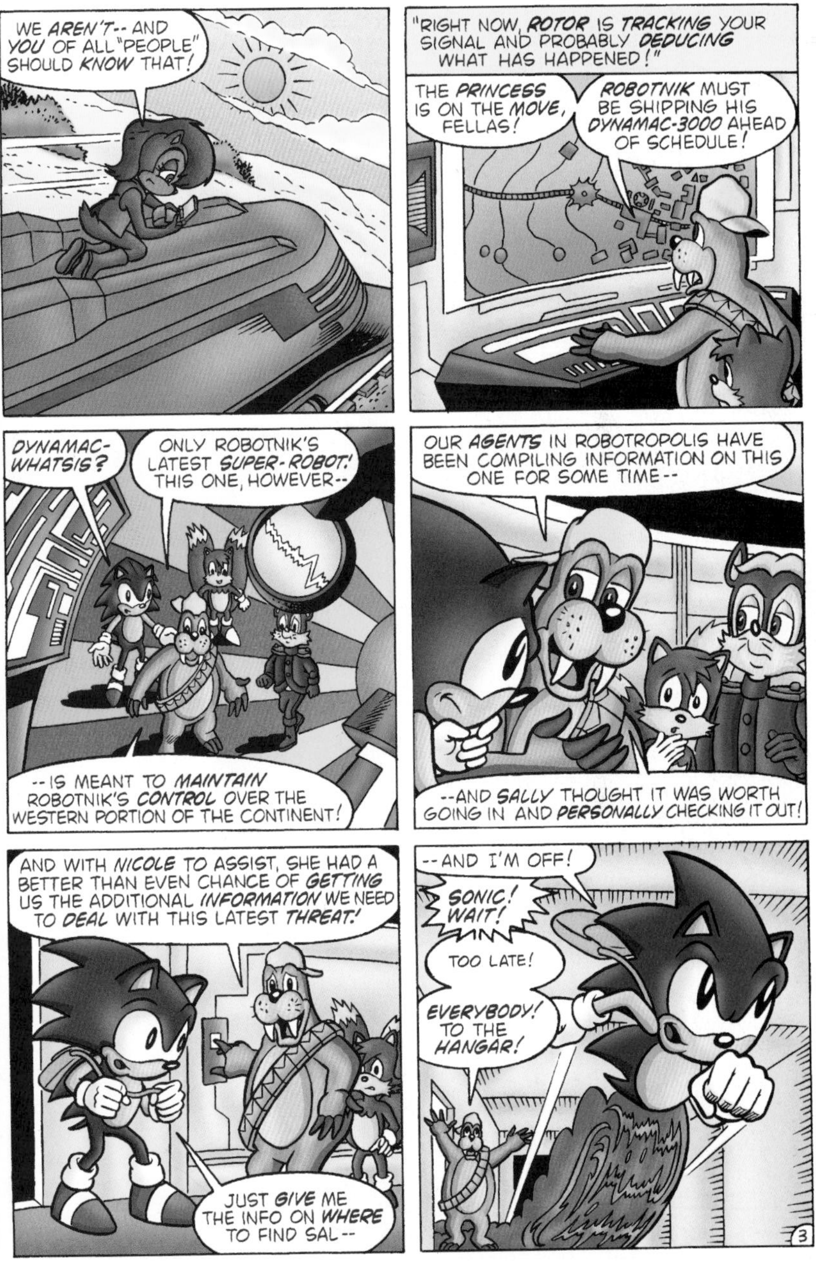
WE AREN'T-- AND YOU OF ALL "PEOPLE" SHOULD KNOW THAT!
"RIGHT NOW, ROTOR IS TRACKING YOUR SIGNAL AND PROBABLY DEDUCING WHAT HAS HAPPENED!"
THE PRINCESS IS ON THE MOVE, FELLAS!
ROBOTNIK MUST BE SHIPPING HIS DYNAMAC-3000 AHEAD OF SCHEDULE!
DYNAMAC-WHATSIS?
ONLY ROBOTNIK'S LATEST SUPER-ROBOT! THIS ONE, HOWEVER--
--IS MEANT TO MAINTAIN ROBOTNIK'S CONTROL OVER THE WESTERN PORTION OF THE CONTINENT!
OUR AGENTS IN ROBOTROPOLIS HAVE BEEN COMPILING INFORMATION ON THIS ONE FOR SOME TIME--
--AND SALLY THOUGHT IT WAS WORTH GOING IN AND PERSONALLY CHECKING IT OUT!
AND WITH NICOLE TO ASSIST, SHE HAD A BETTER THAN EVEN CHANCE OF GETTING US THE ADDITIONAL INFORMATION WE NEED TO DEAL WITH THIS LATEST THREAT!
JUST GIVE ME THE INFO ON WHERE TO FIND SAL--
--AND I'M OFF!
SONIC! WAIT!
TOO LATE!
EVERYBODY! TO THE HANGAR!
3

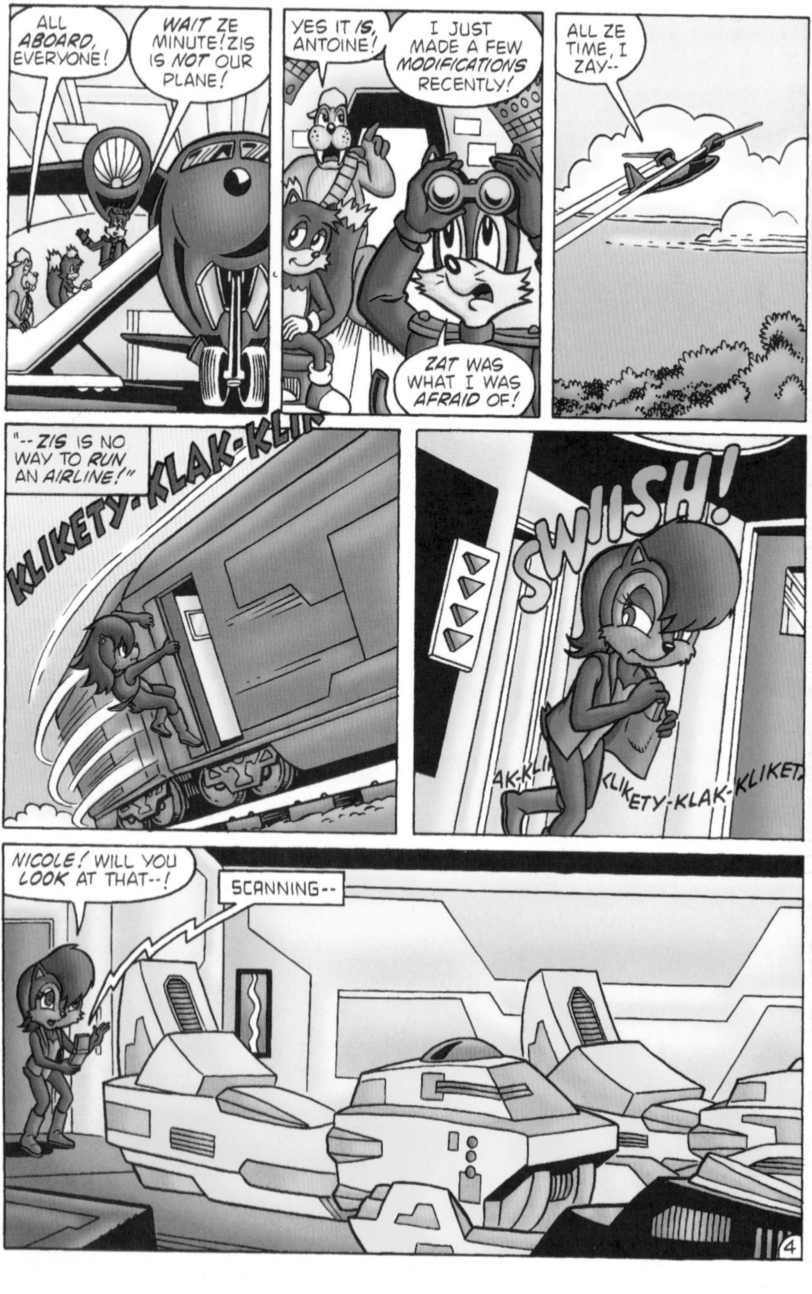
ALL ABOARD, EVERYONE!
WAIT ZE MINUTE! ZIS IS NOT OUR PLANE!
YES IT IS, ANTOINE!
I JUST MADE A FEW MODIFICATIONS RECENTLY!
ZAT WAS WHAT I WAS AFRAID OF!
ALL ZE TIME, I ZAY--
"--ZIS IS NO WAY TO RUN AN AIRLINE!"
KLIKETY-KLAK-KLIK
SWIISH!
AK-KLIK
KLIKETY-KLAK-KLIKETY
NICOLE! WILL YOU LOOK AT THAT--!
SCANNING--
4

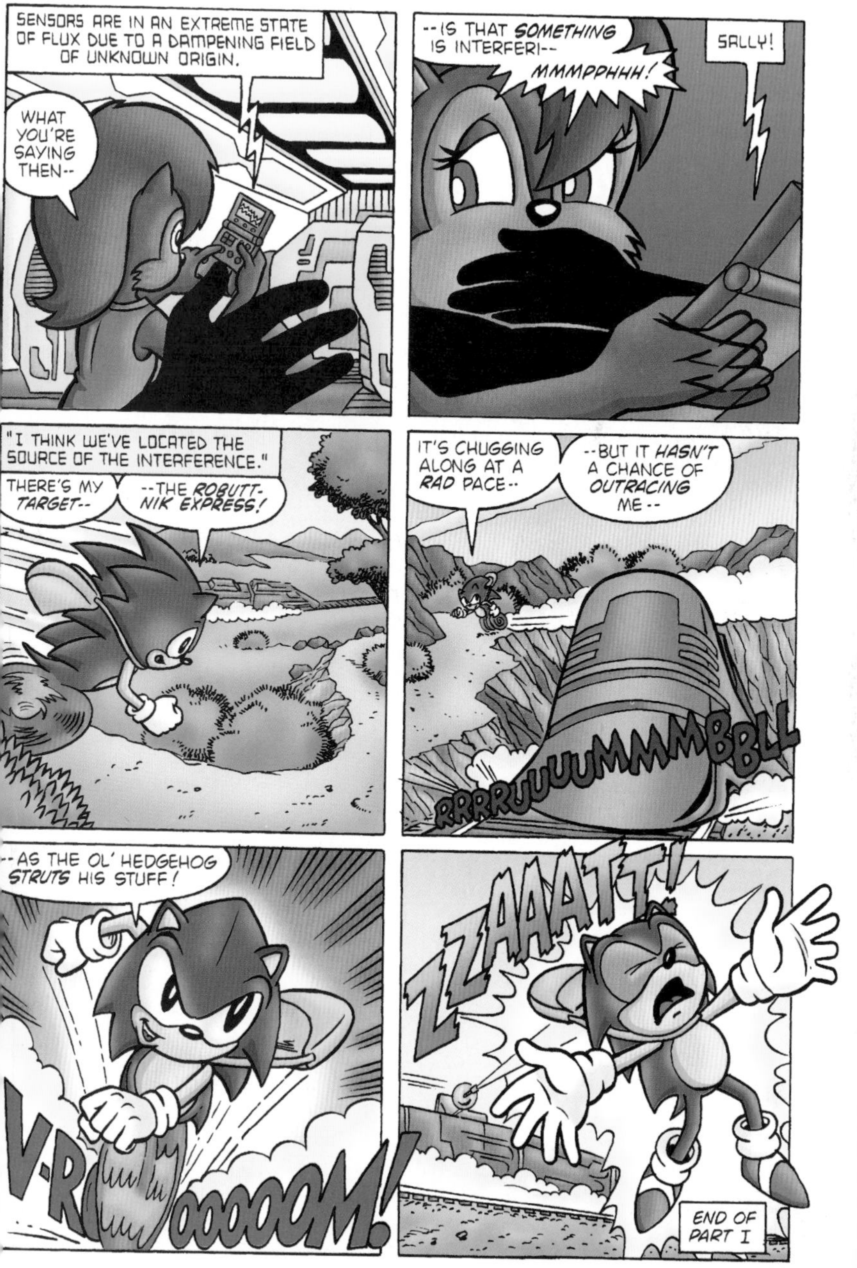
SENSORS ARE IN AN EXTREME STATE OF FLUX DUE TO A DAMPENING FIELD OF UNKNOWN ORIGIN.
WHAT YOU'RE SAYING THEN--
--IS THAT SOMETHING IS INTERFERI--
MMMPPHHH!
SALLY!
"I THINK WE'VE LOCATED THE SOURCE OF THE INTERFERENCE."
THERE'S MY TARGET--
--THE ROBUTT-NIK EXPRESS!
IT'S CHUGGING ALONG AT A RAD PACE--
--BUT IT HASN'T A CHANCE OF OUTRACING ME--
RRRRUUUUMMMMBBLL
--AS THE OL' HEDGEHOG STRUTS HIS STUFF!
V-ROOOOOOM!
ZZAAATT!
END OF PART I

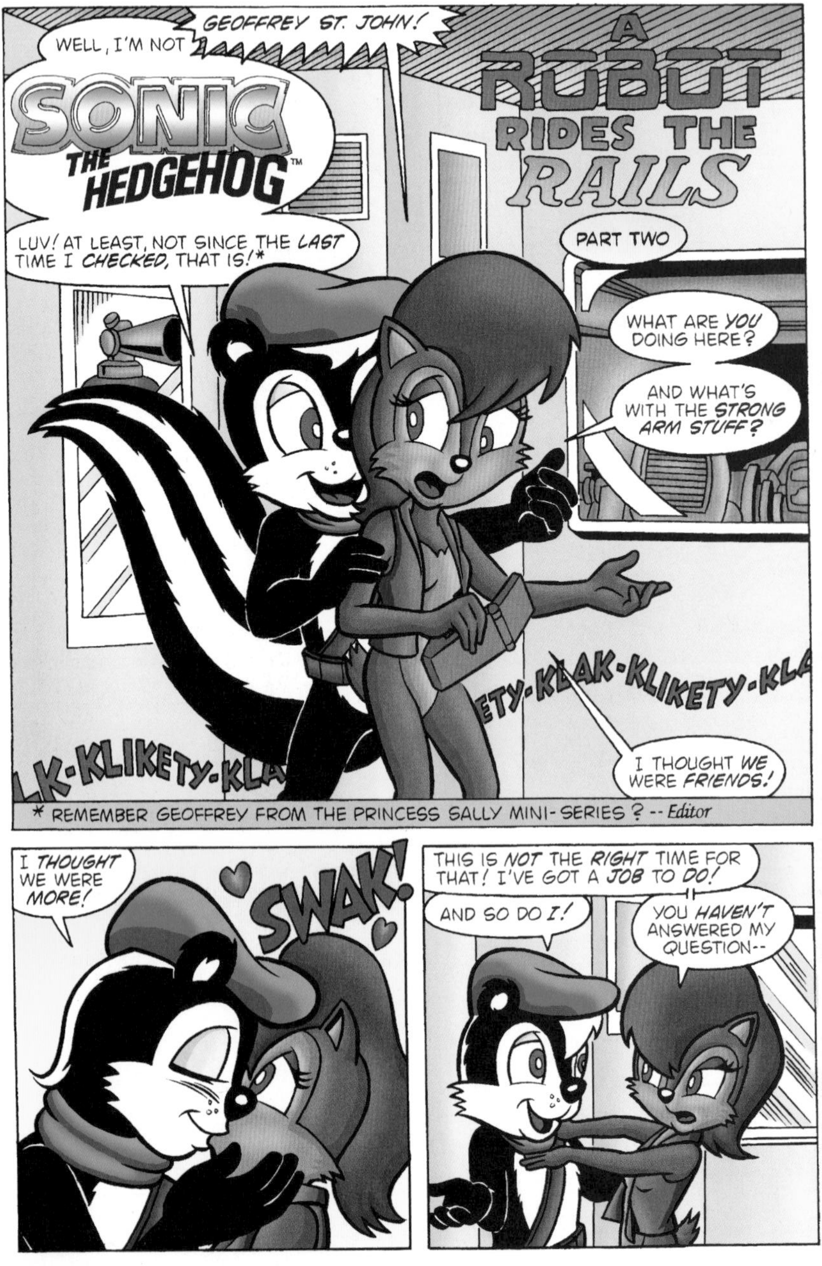
WELL, I'M NOT
GEOFFREY ST. JOHN!
SONIC THE HEDGEHOG™
A ROBOT RIDES THE RAILS
LUV! AT LEAST, NOT SINCE THE LAST TIME I CHECKED, THAT IS!*
PART TWO
WHAT ARE YOU DOING HERE?
AND WHAT'S WITH THE STRONG ARM STUFF?
ETY-KLAK-KLIKETY-KLA
LK-KLIKETY-KLA
I THOUGHT WE WERE FRIENDS!
* REMEMBER GEOFFREY FROM THE PRINCESS SALLY MINI-SERIES? -- Editor
I THOUGHT WE WERE MORE!
SWAK!
THIS IS NOT THE RIGHT TIME FOR THAT! I'VE GOT A JOB TO DO!
AND SO DO I!
YOU HAVEN'T ANSWERED MY QUESTION--

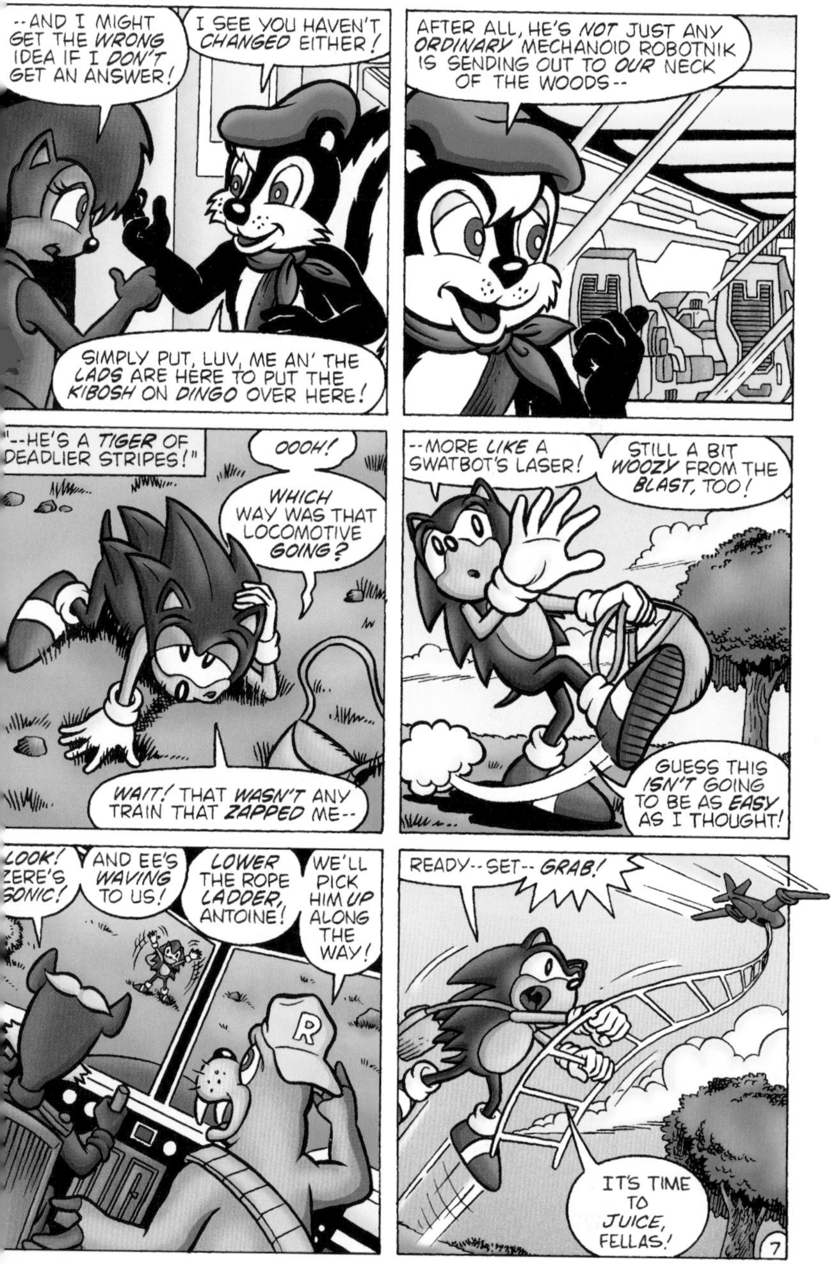
--AND I MIGHT GET THE WRONG IDEA IF I DON'T GET AN ANSWER!
I SEE YOU HAVEN'T CHANGED EITHER!
SIMPLY PUT, LUV, ME AN' THE LADS ARE HERE TO PUT THE KIBOSH ON DINGO OVER HERE!
AFTER ALL, HE'S NOT JUST ANY ORDINARY MECHANOID ROBOTNIK IS SENDING OUT TO OUR NECK OF THE WOODS--
"--HE'S A TIGER OF DEADLIER STRIPES!"
OOOH!
WHICH WAY WAS THAT LOCOMOTIVE GOING?
WAIT! THAT WASN'T ANY TRAIN THAT ZAPPED ME--
--MORE LIKE A SWATBOT'S LASER!
STILL A BIT WOOZY FROM THE BLAST, TOO!
GUESS THIS ISN'T GOING TO BE AS EASY AS I THOUGHT!
LOOK! ZERE'S SONIC!
AND EE'S WAVING TO US!
LOWER THE ROPE LADDER, ANTOINE!
WE'LL PICK HIM UP ALONG THE WAY!
R
READY--SET--GRAB!
IT'S TIME TO JUICE, FELLAS!

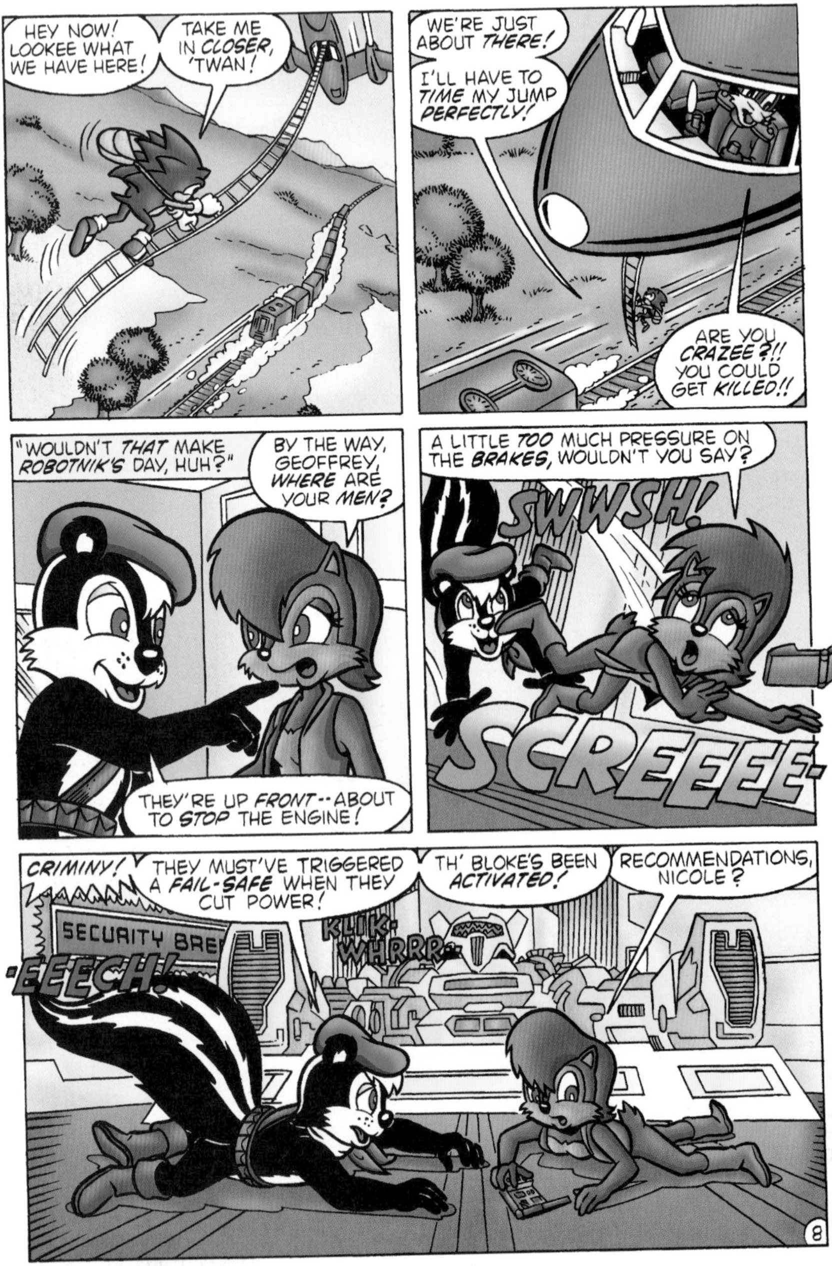

HEY NOW! LOOKEE WHAT WE HAVE HERE!
TAKE ME IN CLOSER, 'TWAN!
WE'RE JUST ABOUT THERE!
I'LL HAVE TO TIME MY JUMP PERFECTLY!
ARE YOU CRAZEE?!! YOU COULD GET KILLED!!
"WOULDN'T THAT MAKE ROBOTNIK'S DAY, HUH?"
BY THE WAY, GEOFFREY, WHERE ARE YOUR MEN?
THEY'RE UP FRONT--ABOUT TO STOP THE ENGINE!
A LITTLE TOO MUCH PRESSURE ON THE BRAKES, WOULDN'T YOU SAY?
SWWSH!
SCREEEE-
-EEECH!
CRIMINY!
THEY MUST'VE TRIGGERED A FAIL-SAFE WHEN THEY CUT POWER!
SECURITY BRE
KLIK-WHRRR-
TH' BLOKE'S BEEN ACTIVATED!
RECOMMENDATIONS, NICOLE?

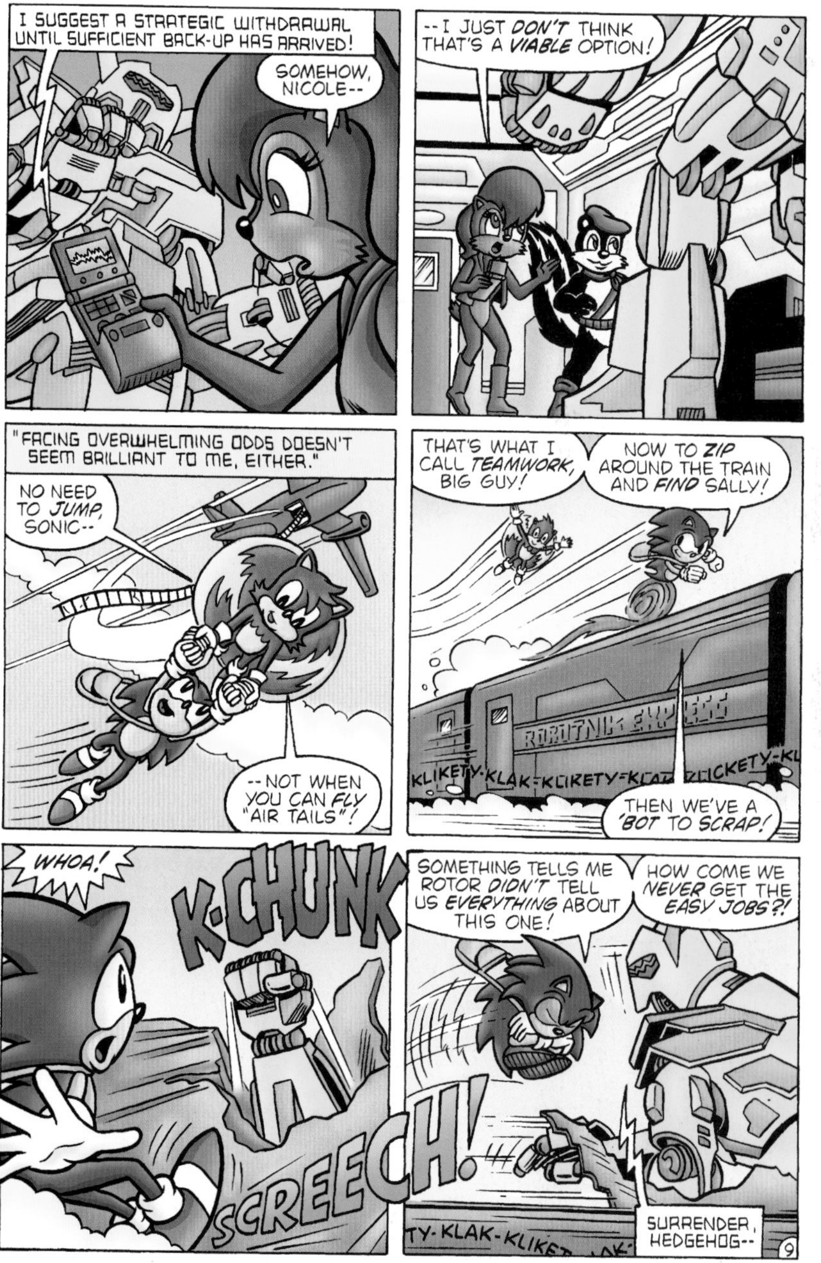
I SUGGEST A STRATEGIC WITHDRAWAL UNTIL SUFFICIENT BACK-UP HAS ARRIVED!
SOMEHOW, NICOLE--
--I JUST DON'T THINK THAT'S A VIABLE OPTION!
"FACING OVERWHELMING ODDS DOESN'T SEEM BRILLIANT TO ME, EITHER."
NO NEED TO JUMP, SONIC--
--NOT WHEN YOU CAN FLY "AIR TAILS"!
THAT'S WHAT I CALL TEAMWORK, BIG GUY!
NOW TO ZIP AROUND THE TRAIN AND FIND SALLY!
KLIKETY-KLAK=KLIKETY=
THEN WE'VE A 'BOT TO SCRAP!
WHOA!
K-CHUNK
SCREEECH!
SOMETHING TELLS ME ROTOR DIDN'T TELL US EVERYTHING ABOUT THIS ONE!
HOW COME WE NEVER GET THE EASY JOBS?!
TY-KLAK-
SURRENDER, HEDGEHOG--

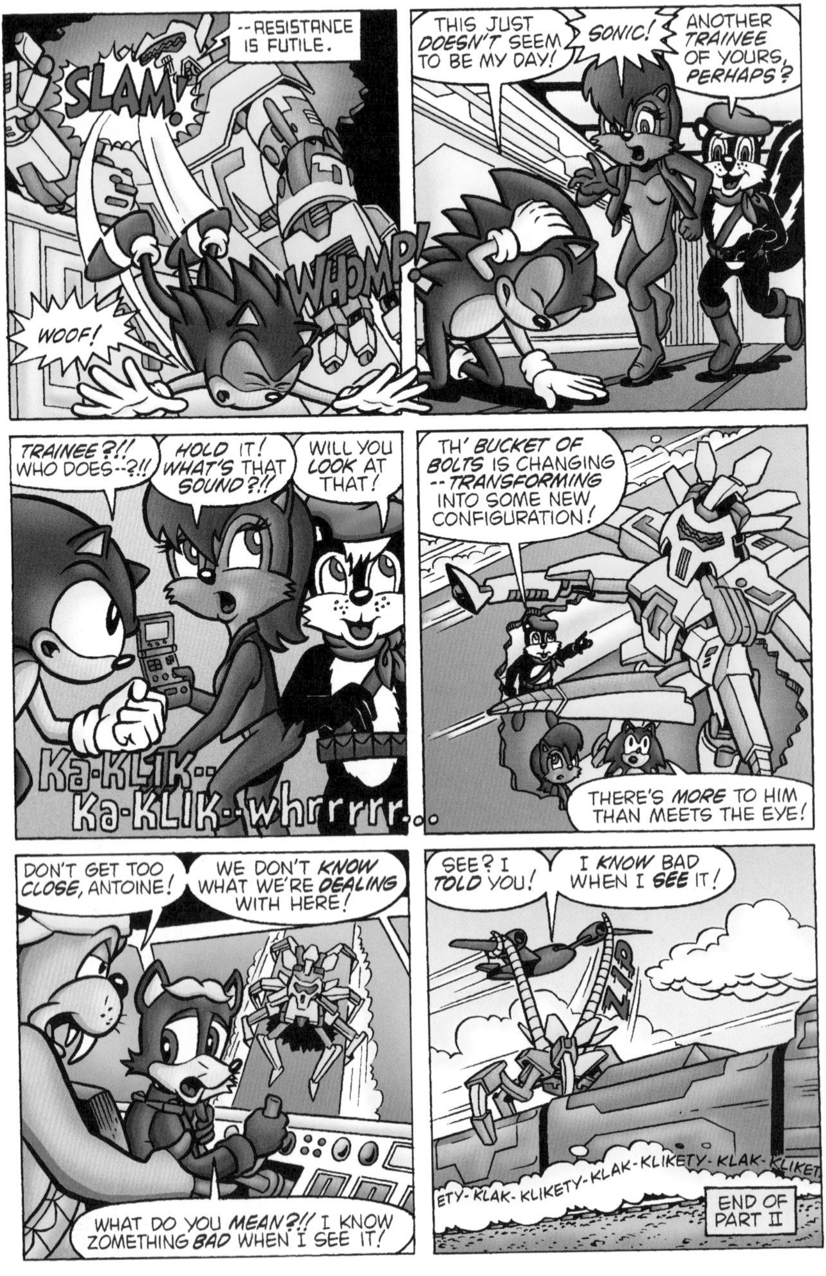
--RESISTANCE IS FUTILE.
SLAM!
WOOF!
WHOMP!
THIS JUST DOESN'T SEEM TO BE MY DAY!
SONIC!
ANOTHER TRAINEE OF YOURS, PERHAPS?
TRAINEE?!! WHO DOES--?!!
HOLD IT! WHAT'S THAT SOUND?!!
WILL YOU LOOK AT THAT!
Ka-KLIK--
Ka-KLIK--whrrrrr...
TH' BUCKET OF BOLTS IS CHANGING --TRANSFORMING INTO SOME NEW CONFIGURATION!
THERE'S MORE TO HIM THAN MEETS THE EYE!
DON'T GET TOO CLOSE, ANTOINE!
WE DON'T KNOW WHAT WE'RE DEALING WITH HERE!
WHAT DO YOU MEAN?!! I KNOW ZOMETHING BAD WHEN I SEE IT!
SEE? I TOLD YOU!
I KNOW BAD WHEN I SEE IT!
ZIP
ETY-KLAK-KLIKETY-KLAK-KLIKETY-KLAK-KLIKET
END OF PART II

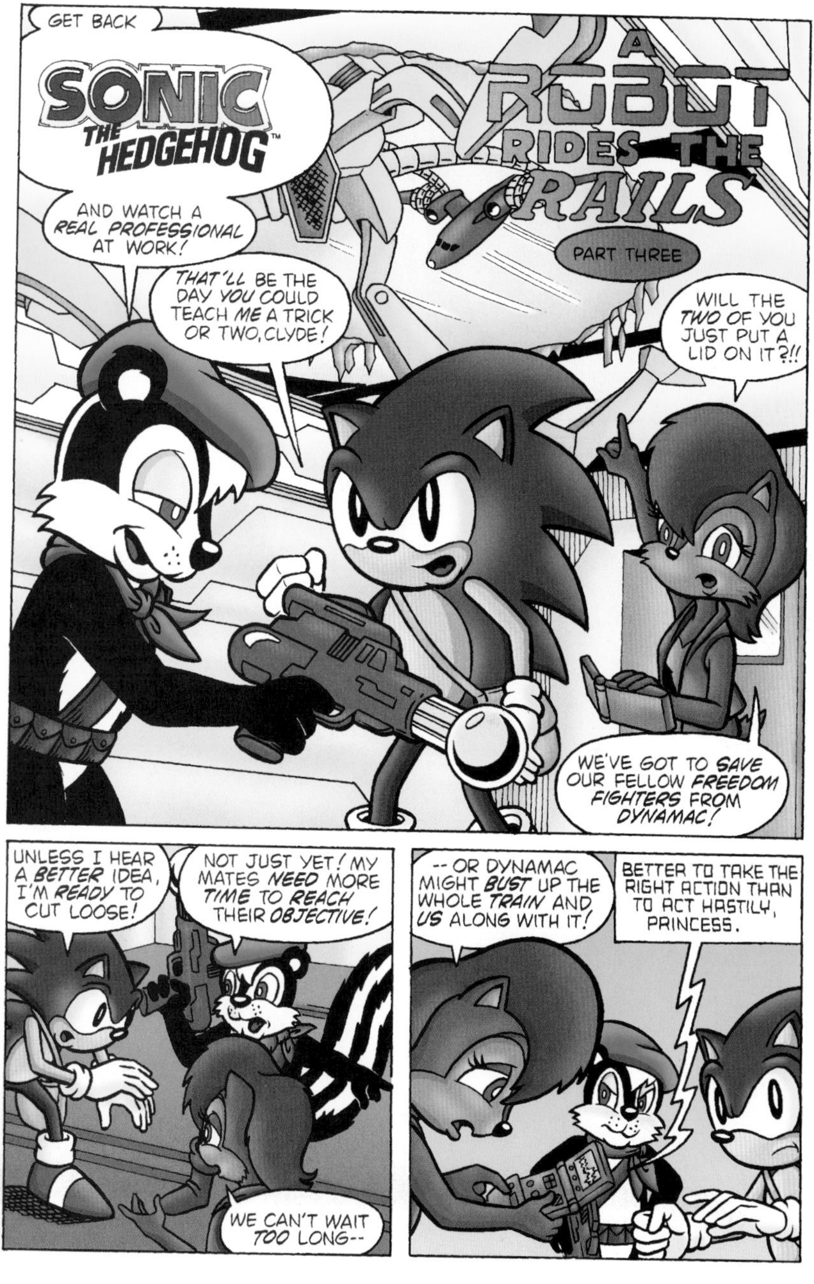
GET BACK
SONIC THE HEDGEHOG™
A ROBOT RIDES THE RAILS
PART THREE
AND WATCH A REAL PROFESSIONAL AT WORK!
THAT'LL BE THE DAY YOU COULD TEACH ME A TRICK OR TWO, CLYDE!
WILL THE TWO OF YOU JUST PUT A LID ON IT?!!
WE'VE GOT TO SAVE OUR FELLOW FREEDOM FIGHTERS FROM DYNAMAC!
UNLESS I HEAR A BETTER IDEA, I'M READY TO CUT LOOSE!
NOT JUST YET! MY MATES NEED MORE TIME TO REACH THEIR OBJECTIVE!
WE CAN'T WAIT TOO LONG--
-- OR DYNAMAC MIGHT BUST UP THE WHOLE TRAIN AND US ALONG WITH IT!
BETTER TO TAKE THE RIGHT ACTION THAN TO ACT HASTILY, PRINCESS.

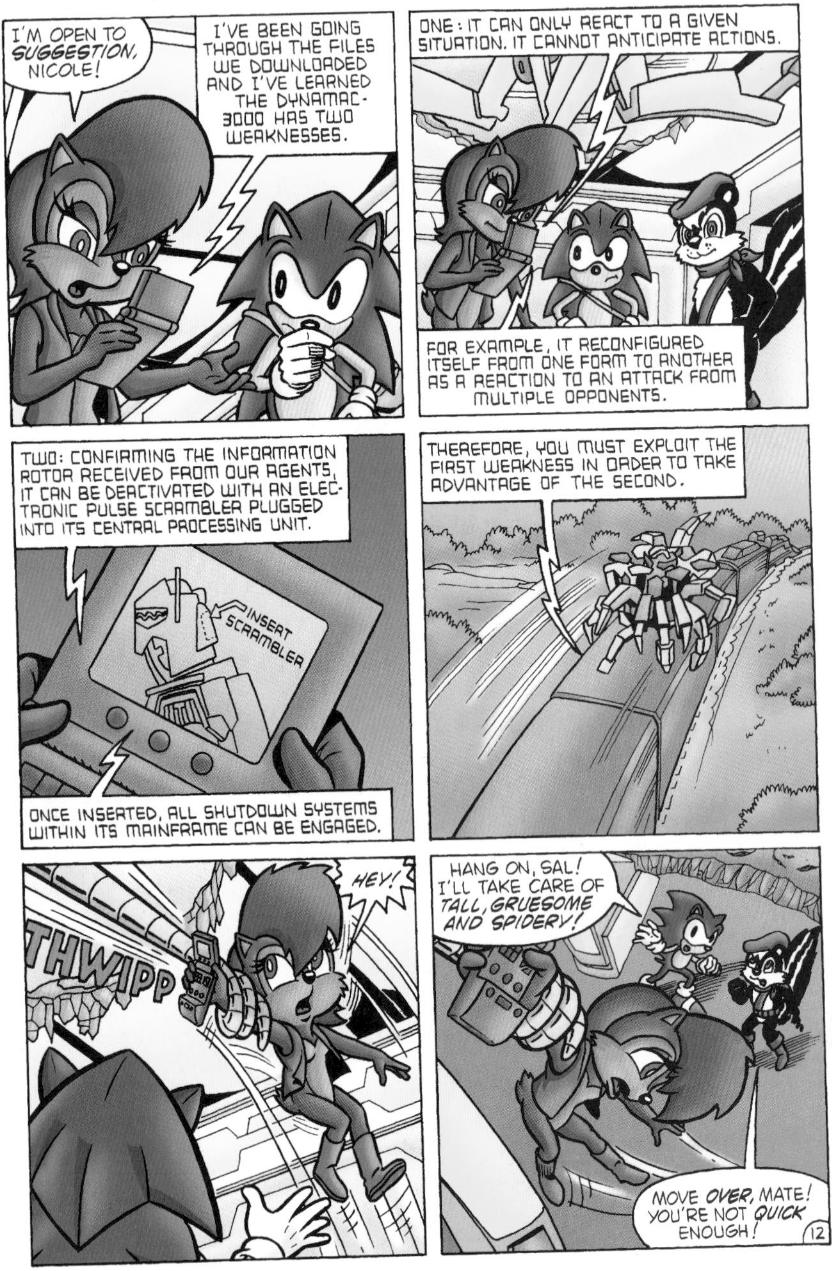
I'M OPEN TO SUGGESTION, NICOLE!
I'VE BEEN GOING THROUGH THE FILES WE DOWNLOADED AND I'VE LEARNED THE DYNAMAC-3000 HAS TWO WEAKNESSES.
ONE: IT CAN ONLY REACT TO A GIVEN SITUATION. IT CANNOT ANTICIPATE ACTIONS.
FOR EXAMPLE, IT RECONFIGURED ITSELF FROM ONE FORM TO ANOTHER AS A REACTION TO AN ATTACK FROM MULTIPLE OPPONENTS.
TWO: CONFIRMING THE INFORMATION ROTOR RECEIVED FROM OUR AGENTS, IT CAN BE DEACTIVATED WITH AN ELECTRONIC PULSE SCRAMBLER PLUGGED INTO ITS CENTRAL PROCESSING UNIT.
INSERT SCRAMBLER
ONCE INSERTED, ALL SHUTDOWN SYSTEMS WITHIN ITS MAINFRAME CAN BE ENGAGED.
THEREFORE, YOU MUST EXPLOIT THE FIRST WEAKNESS IN ORDER TO TAKE ADVANTAGE OF THE SECOND.
THWIPP
HEY!
HANG ON, SAL! I'LL TAKE CARE OF TALL, GRUESOME AND SPIDERY!
MOVE OVER, MATE! YOU'RE NOT QUICK ENOUGH!
12

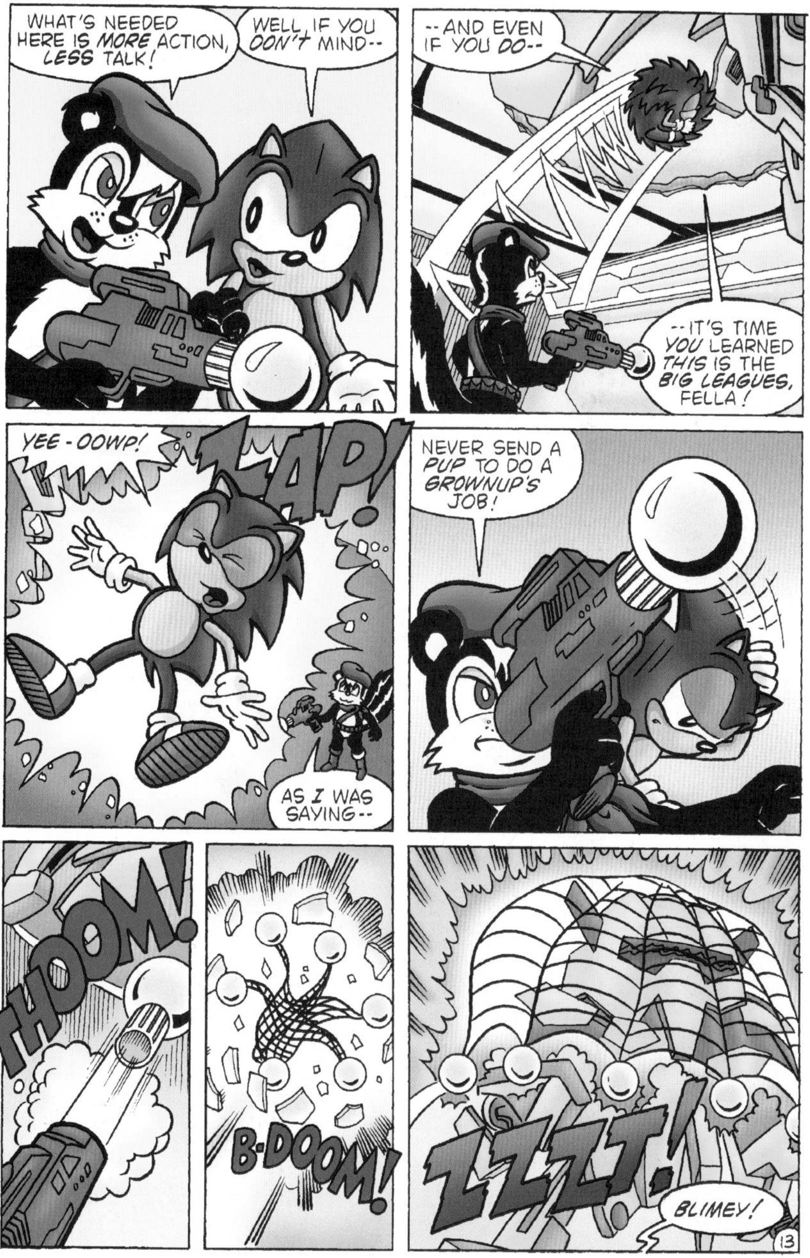
WHAT'S NEEDED HERE IS MORE ACTION, LESS TALK!
WELL, IF YOU DON'T MIND--
--AND EVEN IF YOU DO--
--IT'S TIME YOU LEARNED THIS IS THE BIG LEAGUES, FELLA!
YEE-OOWP!
ZAP!
AS I WAS SAYING--
NEVER SEND A PUP TO DO A GROWNUP'S JOB!
THOOM!
B-DOOM!
ZZZT!
BLIMEY!

THE *BOLAS* DIDN'T PACK ENOUGH *JUICE!*

WE NEED SOMETHING WITH A *STRONGER* CHARGE!

DON'T HAVE THE SAME *GET-UP-'N'-GO* THAT SOME OF *US* HAVE, EH?

UH-OH!

I *DON'T* THINK IT'S TOO *HAPPY* WITH US!

K-CHUNKT!

WE NEED TO GET TO THE *ROOF!*

FRIENDLY SORT, ISN'T IT?

I HATE T' BE A *KILLJOY*, MATE, BUT WE'RE *REALLY* LEAVING OURSELVES *OUT* IN TH' OPEN HERE!

KLIKETY- KLAK- KLIKETY- KLAK— KLIKETY

IN MY *KNAPSACK* IS SOMETHING ROTOR ANTICIPATED WE'D NEED!

ETY-KLAK-KLIK Y-KLAK-KLIKETY-KLAK

THIS LITTLE DOOHICKEY *SHOULD* SCRAMBLE THAT 'BOTS ELECTRONICS, AND RATTLE HIM *BIG TIME!*

YOU STAND *READY* TO FOLLOW THROUGH WHILE I *DISTRACT HEAVY METAL!*

KETY- KLAK-KLIKETY-K

BOINK!

LET'S SEE IF THE *DYNAMAC* CAN PLAY *SPINBALL* MY WAY!

14

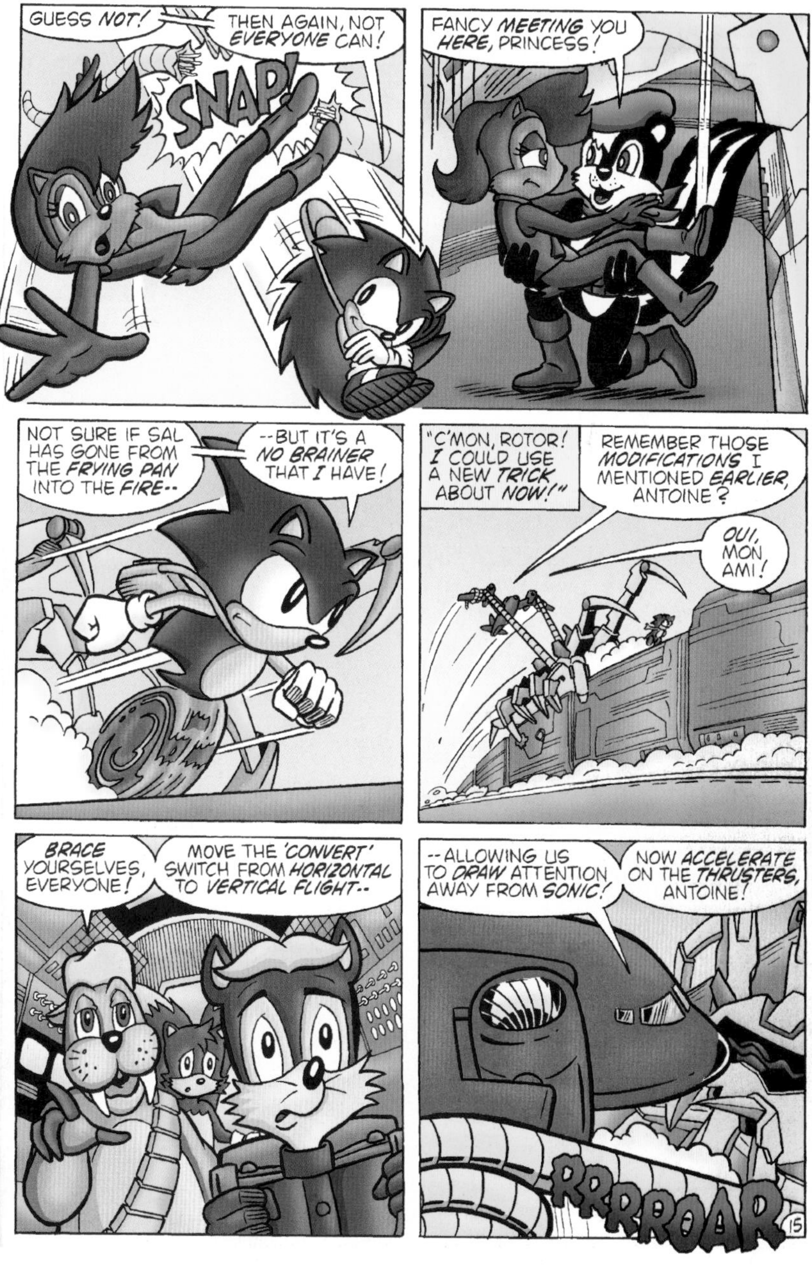
GUESS NOT!
THEN AGAIN, NOT EVERYONE CAN!
SNAP!
FANCY MEETING YOU HERE, PRINCESS!
NOT SURE IF SAL HAS GONE FROM THE FRYING PAN INTO THE FIRE--
--BUT IT'S A NO BRAINER THAT I HAVE!
"C'MON, ROTOR! I COULD USE A NEW TRICK ABOUT NOW!"
REMEMBER THOSE MODIFICATIONS I MENTIONED EARLIER, ANTOINE?
OUI, MON AMI!
BRACE YOURSELVES, EVERYONE!
MOVE THE 'CONVERT' SWITCH FROM HORIZONTAL TO VERTICAL FLIGHT--
--ALLOWING US TO DRAW ATTENTION AWAY FROM SONIC!
NOW ACCELERATE ON THE THRUSTERS, ANTOINE!
RRRROAR

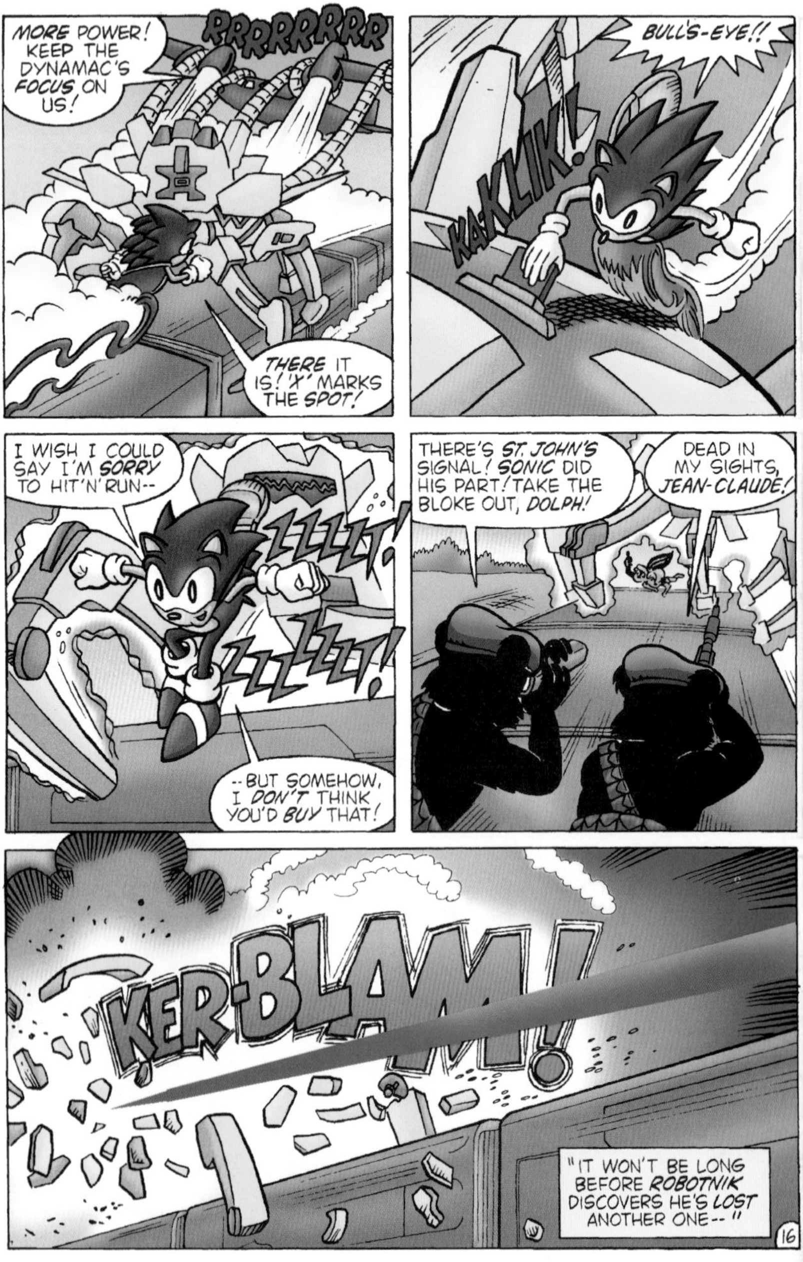
MORE POWER! KEEP THE DYNAMAC'S FOCUS ON US!
RRRRRRRR
THERE IT IS! 'X' MARKS THE SPOT!
BULL'S-EYE!!
KA-KLIK!
I WISH I COULD SAY I'M SORRY TO HIT'N'RUN--
ZZZZT!
ZZZZZZZT!
--BUT SOMEHOW, I DON'T THINK YOU'D BUY THAT!
THERE'S ST. JOHN'S SIGNAL! SONIC DID HIS PART! TAKE THE BLOKE OUT, DOLPH!
DEAD IN MY SIGHTS, JEAN-CLAUDE!
KER-BLAM!
"IT WON'T BE LONG BEFORE ROBOTNIK DISCOVERS HE'S LOST ANOTHER ONE--"

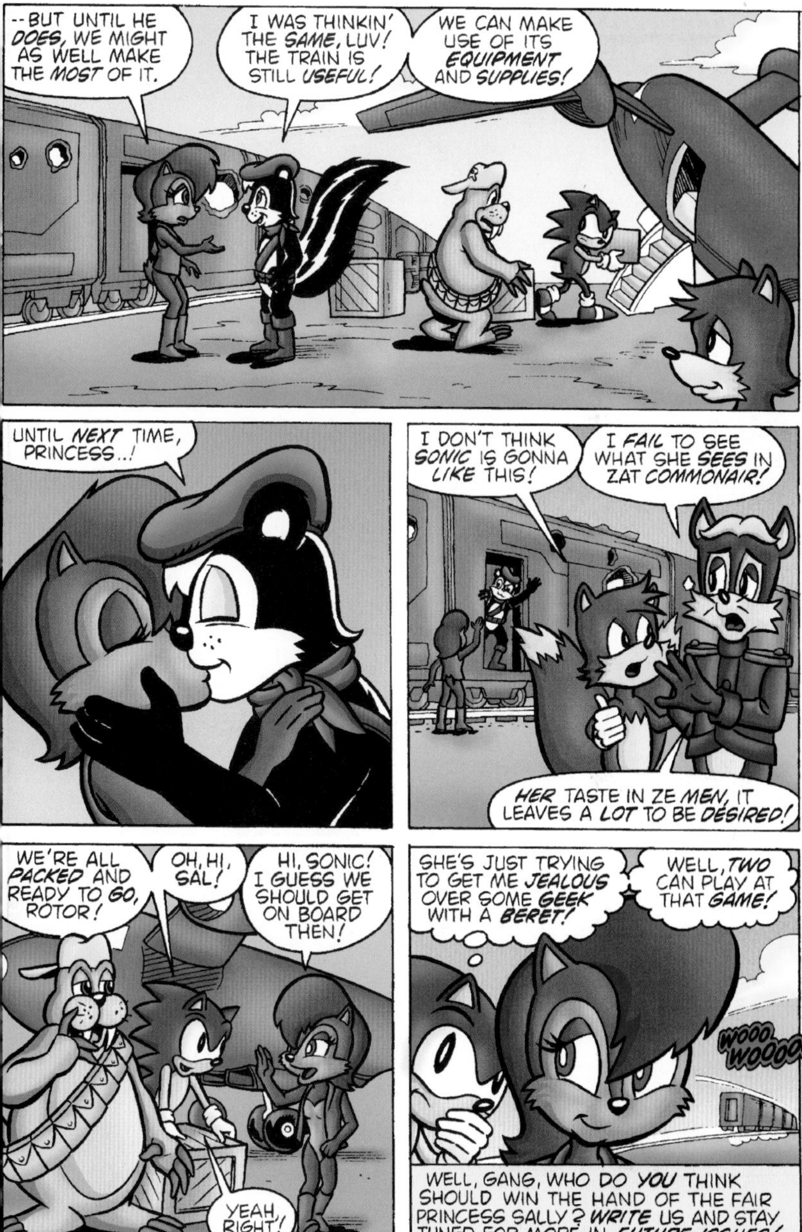
--BUT UNTIL HE DOES, WE MIGHT AS WELL MAKE THE MOST OF IT.
I WAS THINKIN' THE SAME, LUV! THE TRAIN IS STILL USEFUL!
WE CAN MAKE USE OF ITS EQUIPMENT AND SUPPLIES!
UNTIL NEXT TIME, PRINCESS...!
I DON'T THINK SONIC IS GONNA LIKE THIS!
I FAIL TO SEE WHAT SHE SEES IN ZAT COMMONAIR!
HER TASTE IN ZE MEN, IT LEAVES A LOT TO BE DÉSIRED!
WE'RE ALL PACKED AND READY TO GO, ROTOR!
OH, HI, SAL!
HI, SONIC! I GUESS WE SHOULD GET ON BOARD THEN!
YEAH, RIGHT!
SHE'S JUST TRYING TO GET ME JEALOUS OVER SOME GEEK WITH A BERET!
WELL, TWO CAN PLAY AT THAT GAME!
WOOO WOOOOO
WELL, GANG, WHO DO YOU THINK SHOULD WIN THE HAND OF THE FAIR PRINCESS SALLY? WRITE US AND STAY TUNED FOR MORE IN FUTURE ISSUES!

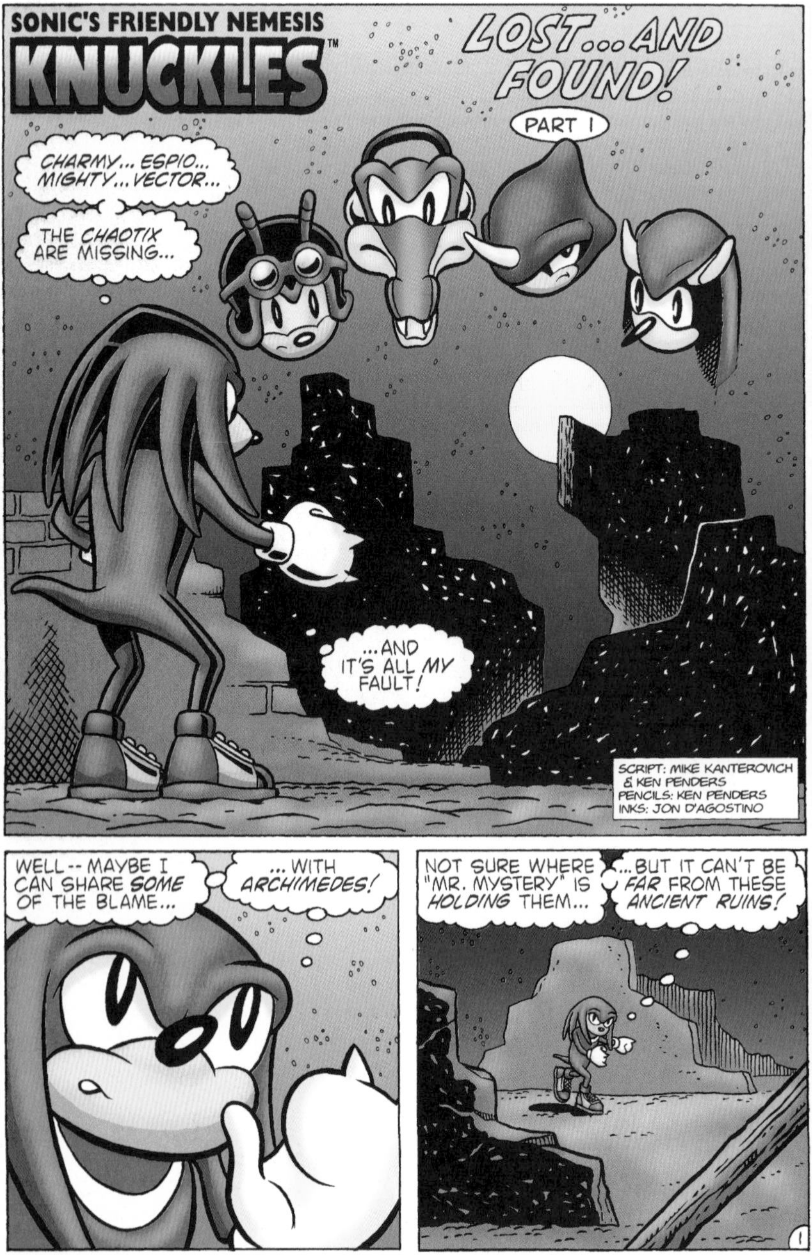

SONIC'S FRIENDLY NEMESIS
KNUCKLES™
LOST... AND FOUND!
PART 1
CHARMY... ESPIO... MIGHTY... VECTOR...
THE CHAOTIX ARE MISSING...
...AND IT'S ALL MY FAULT!
SCRIPT: MIKE KANTEROVICH & KEN PENDERS
PENCILS: KEN PENDERS
INKS: JON D'AGOSTINO
WELL -- MAYBE I CAN SHARE SOME OF THE BLAME...
... WITH ARCHIMEDES!
NOT SURE WHERE "MR. MYSTERY" IS HOLDING THEM...
...BUT IT CAN'T BE FAR FROM THESE ANCIENT RUINS!
1

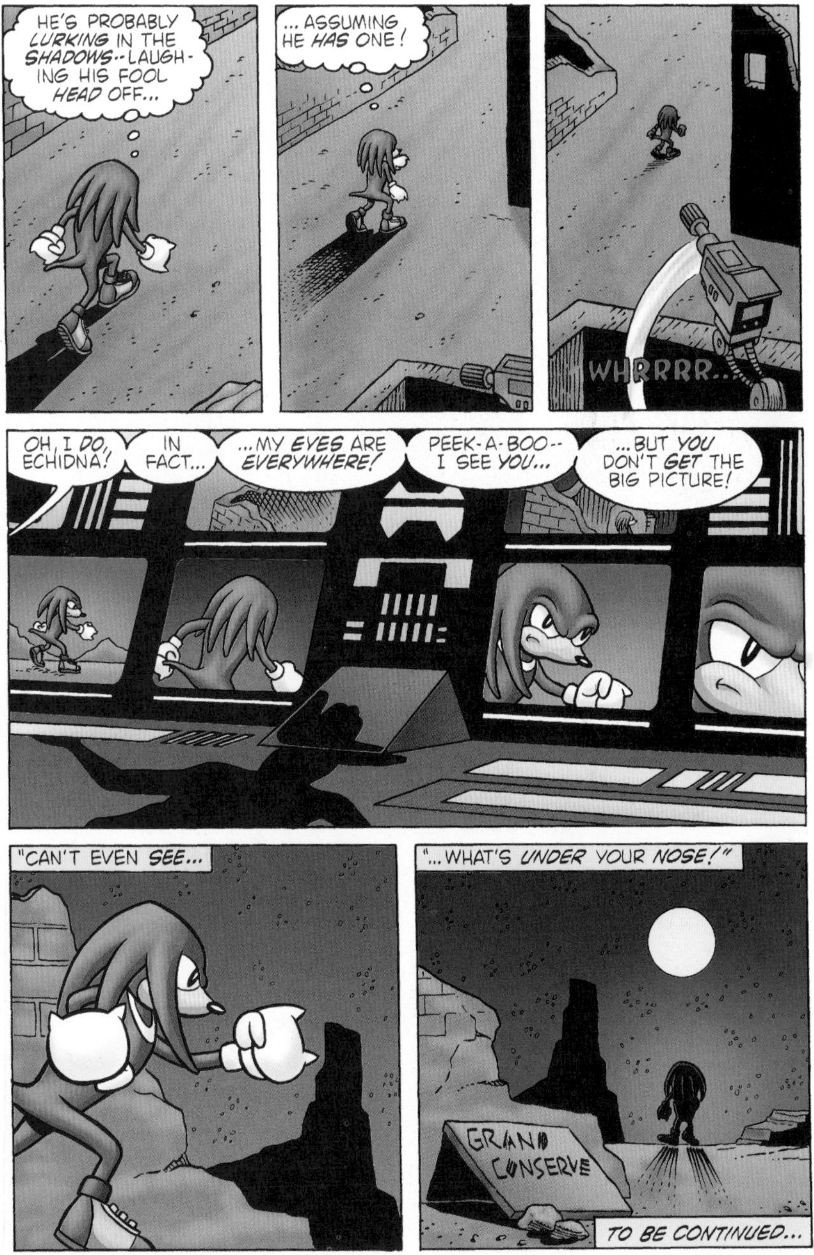
HE'S PROBABLY LURKING IN THE SHADOWS--LAUGHING HIS FOOL HEAD OFF...
...ASSUMING HE HAS ONE!
WHRRRR...
OH, I DO, ECHIDNA!
IN FACT...
...MY EYES ARE EVERYWHERE!
PEEK-A-BOO-- I SEE YOU...
...BUT YOU DON'T GET THE BIG PICTURE!
"CAN'T EVEN SEE...
"...WHAT'S UNDER YOUR NOSE!"
GRAND CONSERVE
TO BE CONTINUED...

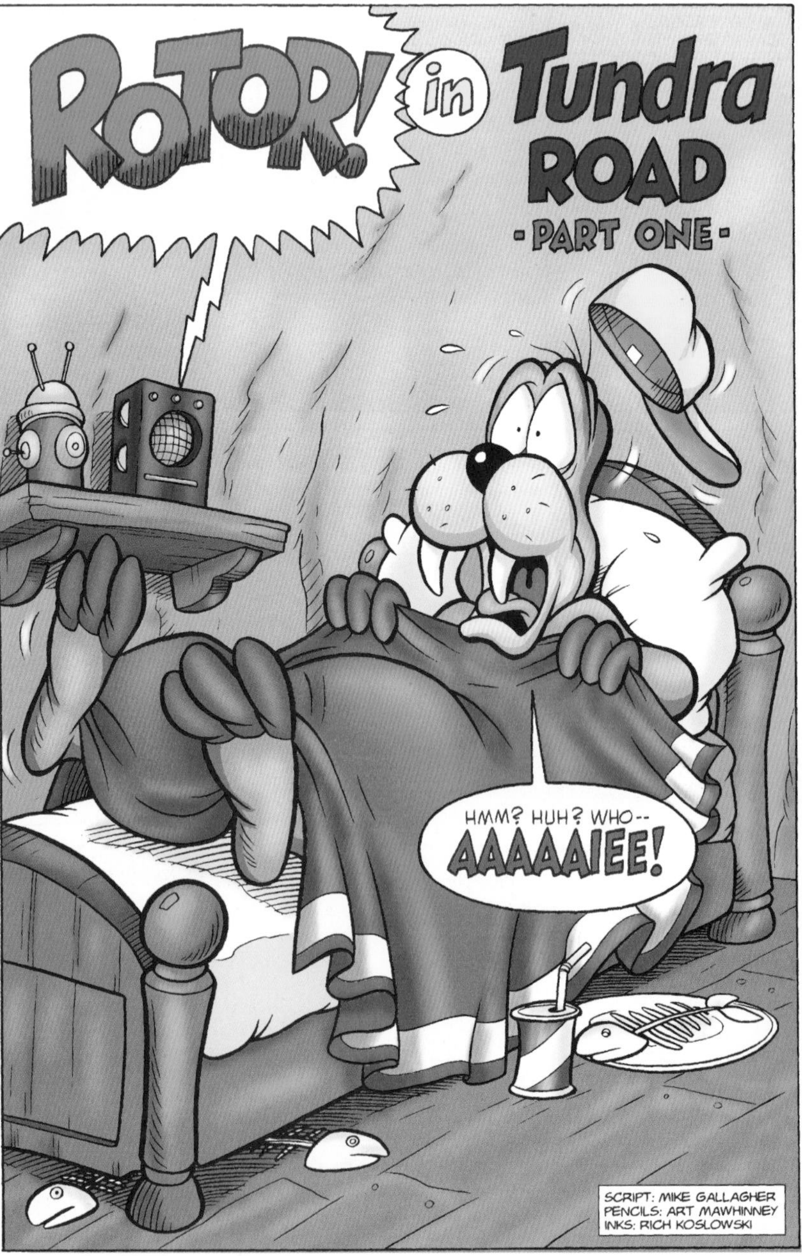
ROTOR! in Tundra ROAD
-PART ONE-
HMM? HUH? WHO--
AAAAAIEE!
SCRIPT: MIKE GALLAGHER
PENCILS: ART MAWHINNEY
INKS: RICH KOSLOWSKI

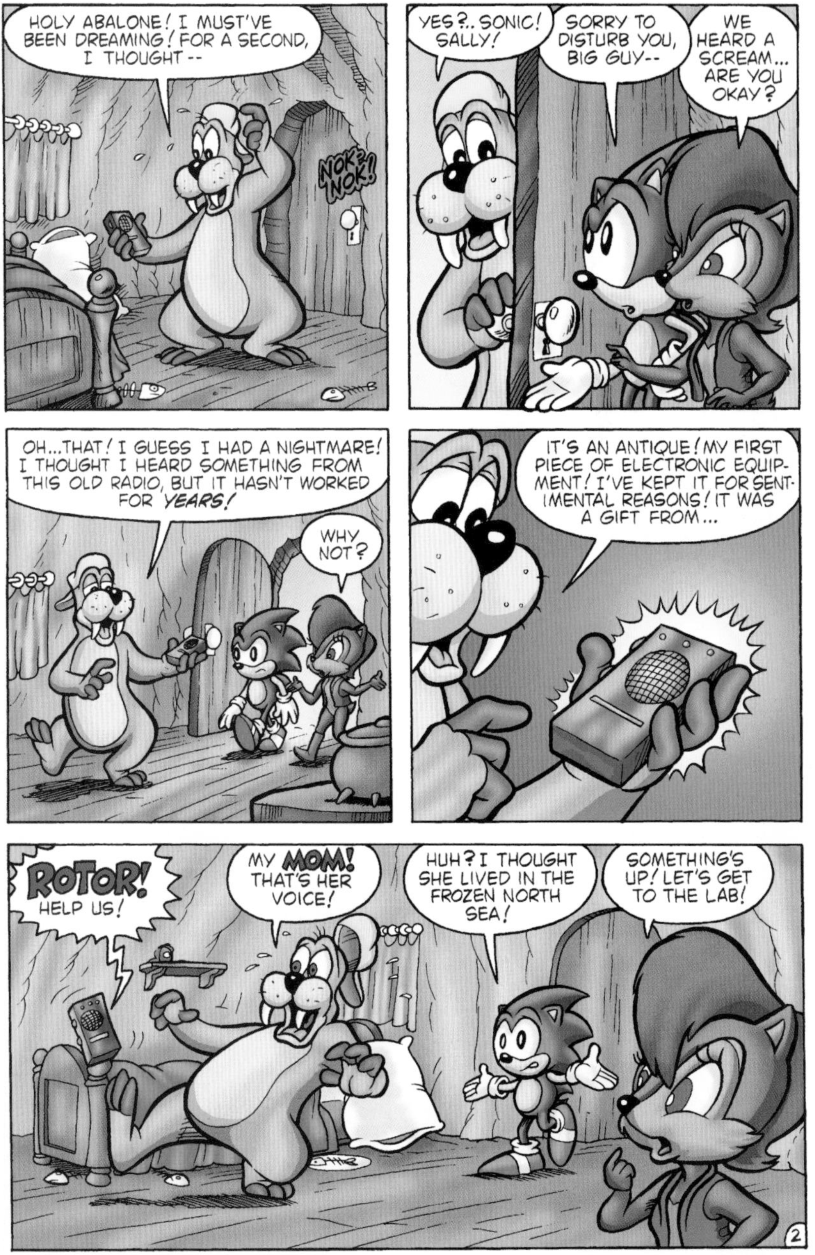
HOLY ABALONE! I MUST'VE BEEN DREAMING! FOR A SECOND, I THOUGHT --
NOK? NOK!
YES?.. SONIC! SALLY!
SORRY TO DISTURB YOU, BIG GUY--
WE HEARD A SCREAM... ARE YOU OKAY?
OH...THAT! I GUESS I HAD A NIGHTMARE! I THOUGHT I HEARD SOMETHING FROM THIS OLD RADIO, BUT IT HASN'T WORKED FOR YEARS!
WHY NOT?
IT'S AN ANTIQUE! MY FIRST PIECE OF ELECTRONIC EQUIPMENT! I'VE KEPT IT FOR SENTIMENTAL REASONS! IT WAS A GIFT FROM...
ROTOR! HELP US!
MY MOM! THAT'S HER VOICE!
HUH? I THOUGHT SHE LIVED IN THE FROZEN NORTH SEA!
SOMETHING'S UP! LET'S GET TO THE LAB!
2

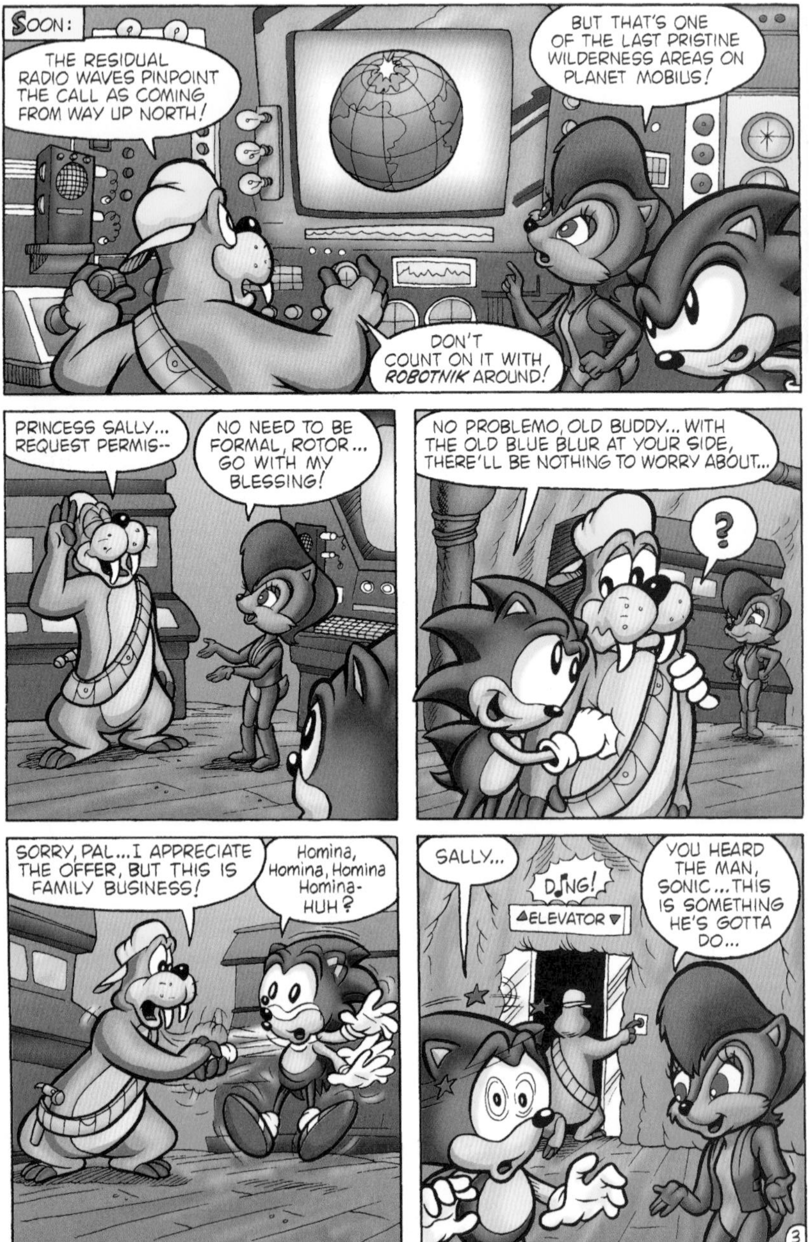
SOON:
THE RESIDUAL RADIO WAVES PINPOINT THE CALL AS COMING FROM WAY UP NORTH!
BUT THAT'S ONE OF THE LAST PRISTINE WILDERNESS AREAS ON PLANET MOBIUS!
DON'T COUNT ON IT WITH ROBOTNIK AROUND!
PRINCESS SALLY... REQUEST PERMIS--
NO NEED TO BE FORMAL, ROTOR... GO WITH MY BLESSING!
NO PROBLEMO, OLD BUDDY... WITH THE OLD BLUE BLUR AT YOUR SIDE, THERE'LL BE NOTHING TO WORRY ABOUT...
?
SORRY, PAL... I APPRECIATE THE OFFER, BUT THIS IS FAMILY BUSINESS!
Homina, Homina, Homina Homina- HUH?
SALLY...
DING!
ELEVATOR
YOU HEARD THE MAN, SONIC... THIS IS SOMETHING HE'S GOTTA DO...
3

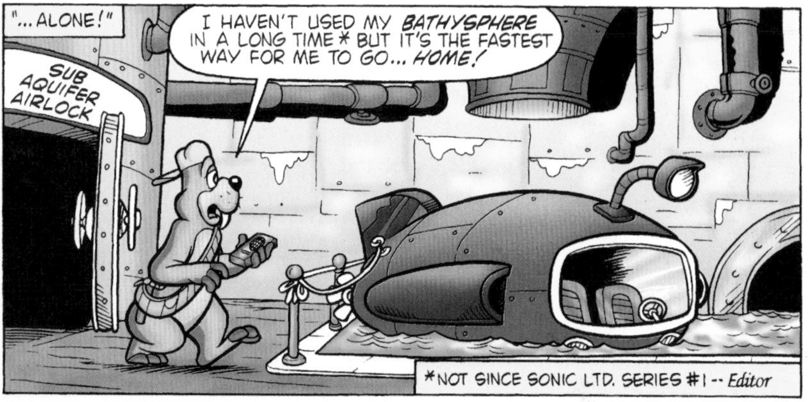
"... ALONE!"
I HAVEN'T USED MY BATHYSPHERE IN A LONG TIME * BUT IT'S THE FASTEST WAY FOR ME TO GO... HOME!
SUB AQUIFER AIRLOCK
*NOT SINCE SONIC LTD. SERIES #1 -- Editor

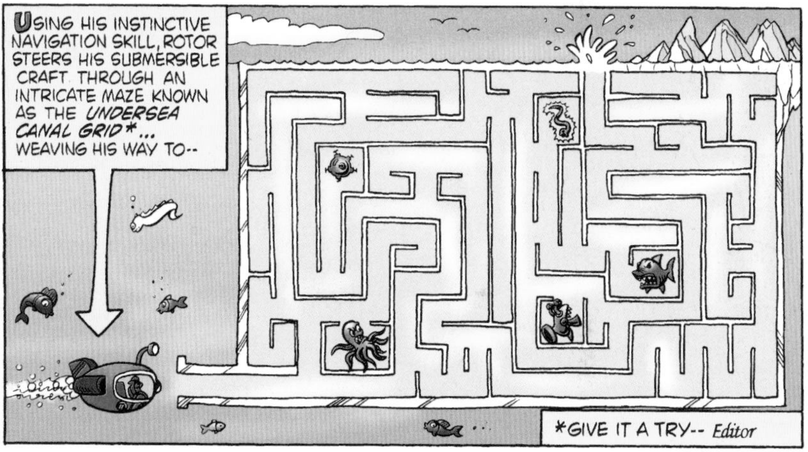
USING HIS INSTINCTIVE NAVIGATION SKILL, ROTOR STEERS HIS SUBMERSIBLE CRAFT THROUGH AN INTRICATE MAZE KNOWN AS THE UNDERSEA CANAL GRID*... WEAVING HIS WAY TO--
*GIVE IT A TRY-- Editor

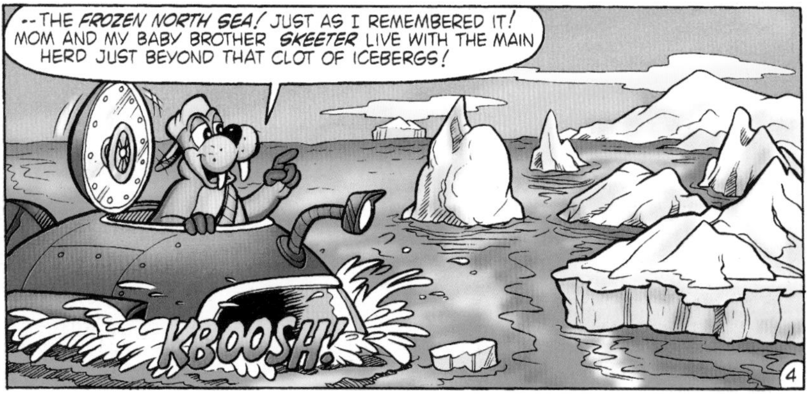
--THE FROZEN NORTH SEA! JUST AS I REMEMBERED IT! MOM AND MY BABY BROTHER SKEETER LIVE WITH THE MAIN HERD JUST BEYOND THAT CLOT OF ICEBERGS!
KBOOSH!

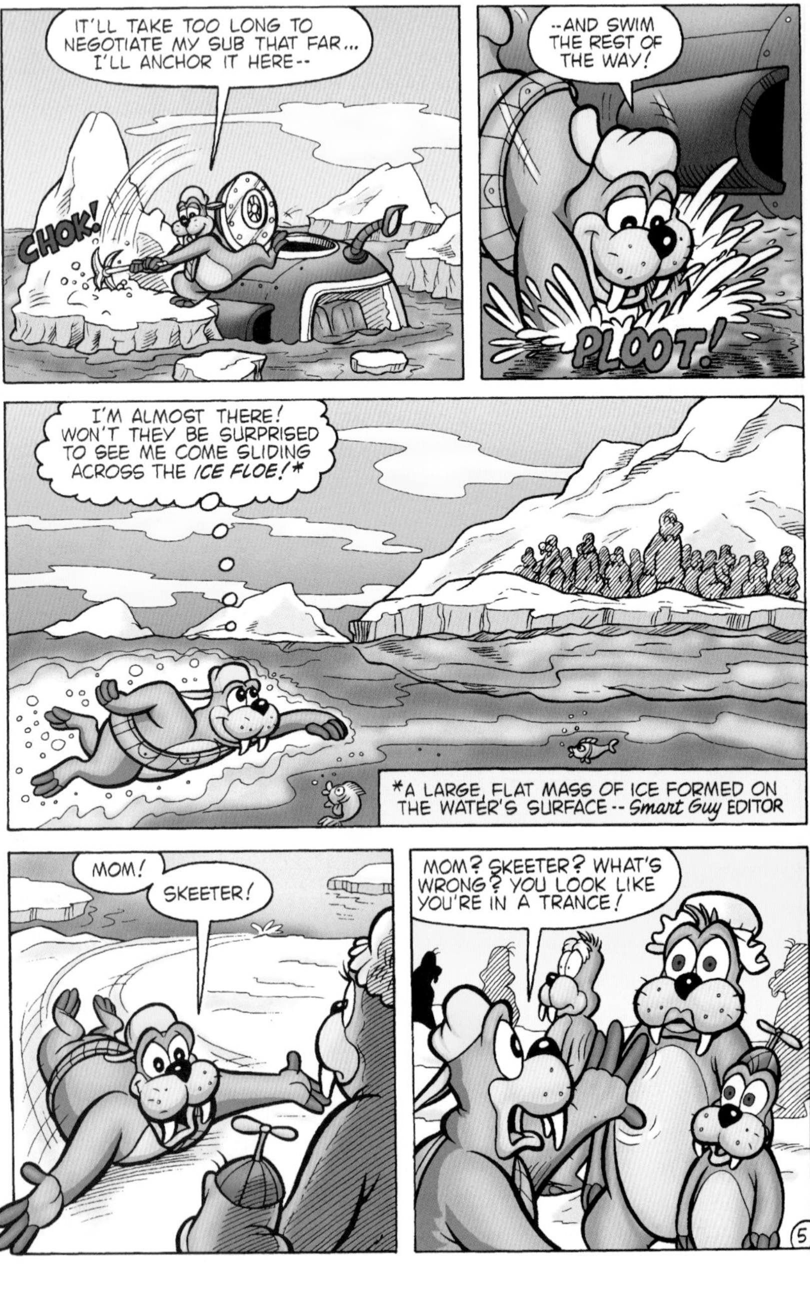
IT'LL TAKE TOO LONG TO NEGOTIATE MY SUB THAT FAR... I'LL ANCHOR IT HERE--
CHOK!
--AND SWIM THE REST OF THE WAY!
PLOOT!
I'M ALMOST THERE! WON'T THEY BE SURPRISED TO SEE ME COME SLIDING ACROSS THE ICE FLOE!*
*A LARGE, FLAT MASS OF ICE FORMED ON THE WATER'S SURFACE -- Smart Guy EDITOR
MOM!
SKEETER!
MOM? SKEETER? WHAT'S WRONG? YOU LOOK LIKE YOU'RE IN A TRANCE!

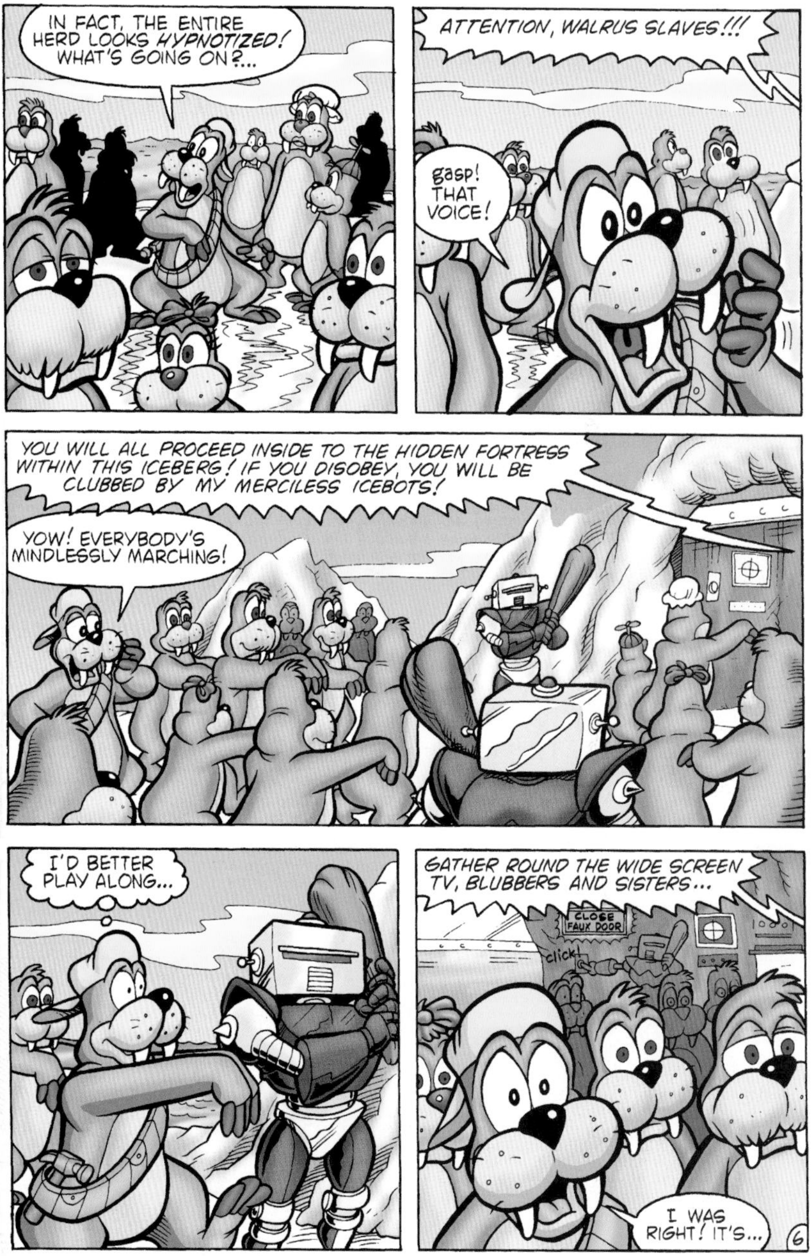

IN FACT, THE ENTIRE HERD LOOKS *HYPNOTIZED*! WHAT'S GOING ON?...
ATTENTION, WALRUS SLAVES!!!
gasp! THAT VOICE!
YOU WILL ALL PROCEED INSIDE TO THE HIDDEN FORTRESS WITHIN THIS ICEBERG! IF YOU DISOBEY, YOU WILL BE CLUBBED BY MY MERCILESS ICEBOTS!
YOW! EVERYBODY'S MINDLESSLY MARCHING!
I'D BETTER PLAY ALONG...
GATHER ROUND THE WIDE SCREEN TV, BLUBBERS AND SISTERS...
CLOSE FAUX DOOR
click!
I WAS RIGHT! IT'S...
6

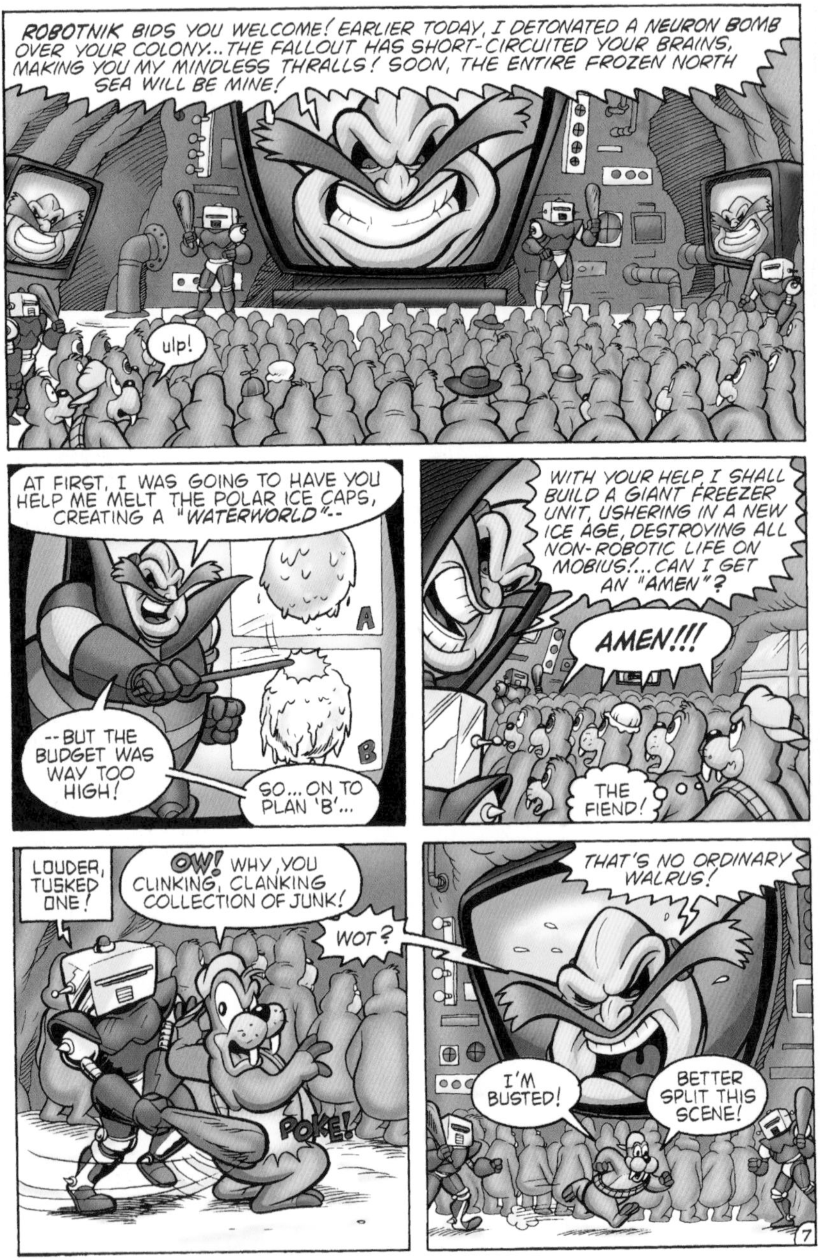

ROBOTNIK BIDS YOU WELCOME! EARLIER TODAY, I DETONATED A NEURON BOMB OVER YOUR COLONY...THE FALLOUT HAS SHORT-CIRCUITED YOUR BRAINS, MAKING YOU MY MINDLESS THRALLS! SOON, THE ENTIRE FROZEN NORTH SEA WILL BE MINE!
ulp!
AT FIRST, I WAS GOING TO HAVE YOU HELP ME MELT THE POLAR ICE CAPS, CREATING A "WATERWORLD"--
A
B
--BUT THE BUDGET WAS WAY TOO HIGH!
SO... ON TO PLAN 'B'...
WITH YOUR HELP I SHALL BUILD A GIANT FREEZER UNIT, USHERING IN A NEW ICE AGE, DESTROYING ALL NON-ROBOTIC LIFE ON MOBIUS!...CAN I GET AN "AMEN"?
AMEN!!!
THE FIEND!
LOUDER, TUSKED ONE!
OW! WHY, YOU CLINKING, CLANKING COLLECTION OF JUNK!
POKE!
WOT?
THAT'S NO ORDINARY WALRUS!
I'M BUSTED!
BETTER SPLIT THIS SCENE!

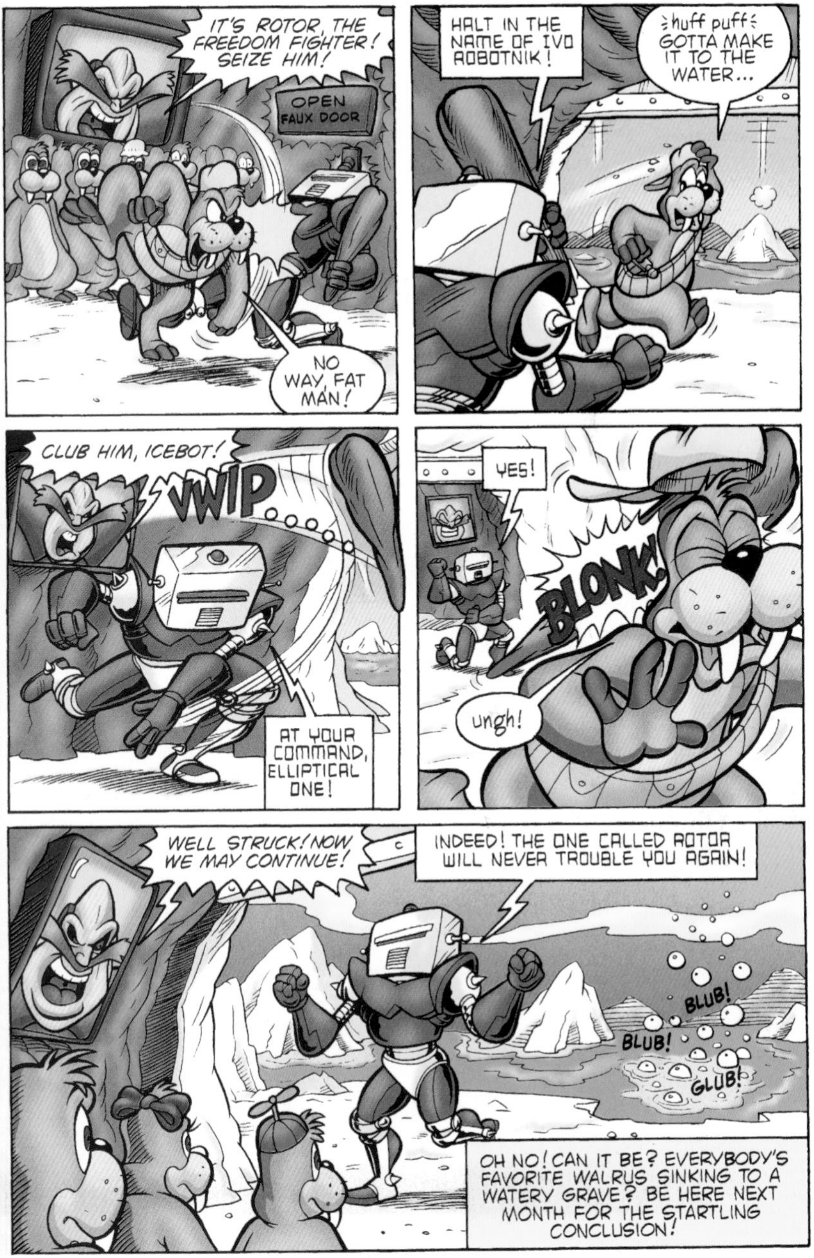
IT'S ROTOR, THE FREEDOM FIGHTER! SEIZE HIM!
OPEN FAUX DOOR
NO WAY, FAT MAN!
HALT IN THE NAME OF IVO ROBOTNIK!
huff puff GOTTA MAKE IT TO THE WATER...
CLUB HIM, ICEBOT!
VWIP
AT YOUR COMMAND, ELLIPTICAL ONE!
YES!
BLONK!
ungh!
WELL STRUCK! NOW WE MAY CONTINUE!
INDEED! THE ONE CALLED ROTOR WILL NEVER TROUBLE YOU AGAIN!
BLUB!
BLUB!
GLUB!
OH NO! CAN IT BE? EVERYBODY'S FAVORITE WALRUS SINKING TO A WATERY GRAVE? BE HERE NEXT MONTH FOR THE STARTLING CONCLUSION!

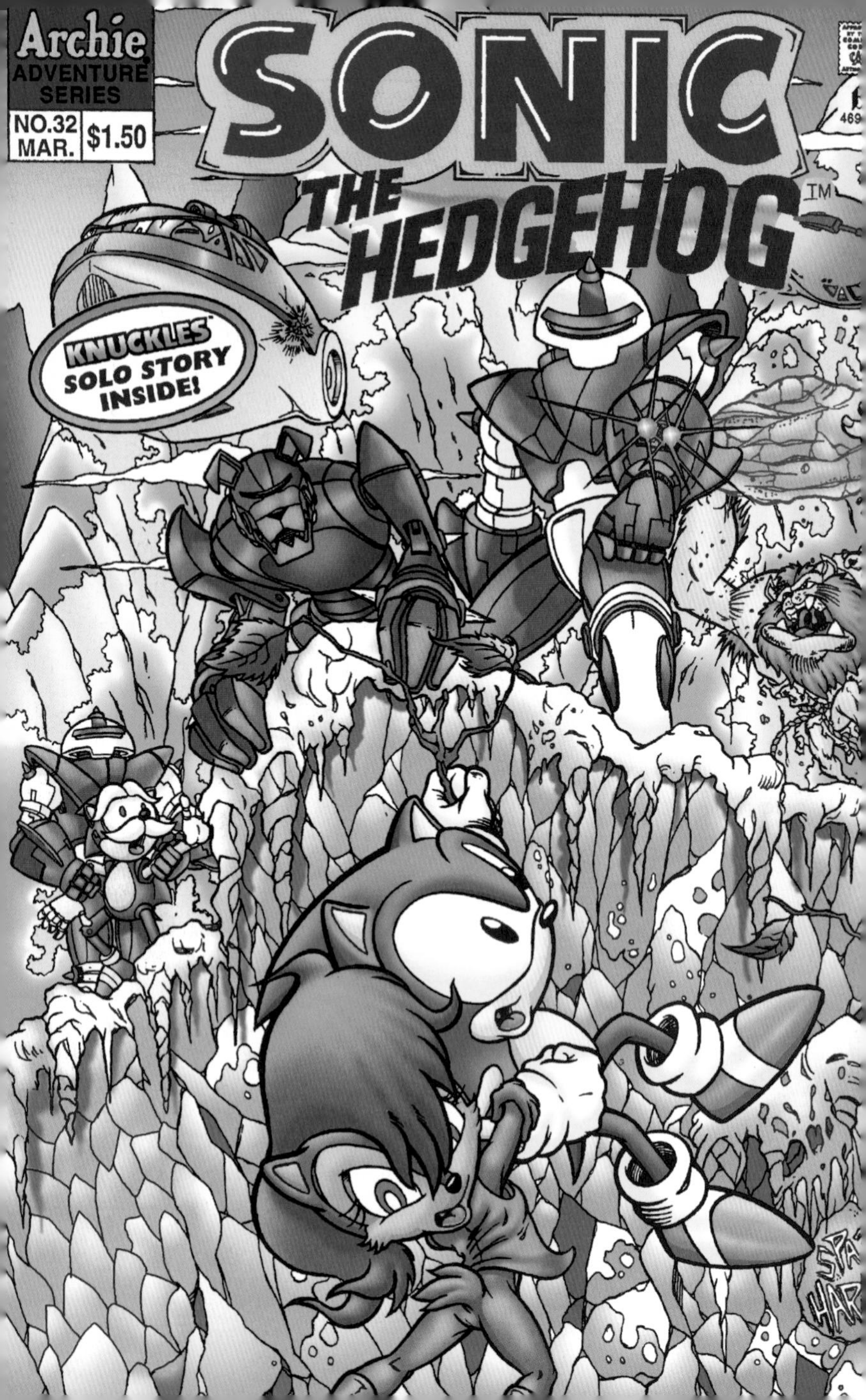
Archie
ADVENTURE
SERIES
NO.32
MAR.
$1.50
SONIC
THE HEDGEHOG™
KNUCKLES™
SOLO STORY
INSIDE!

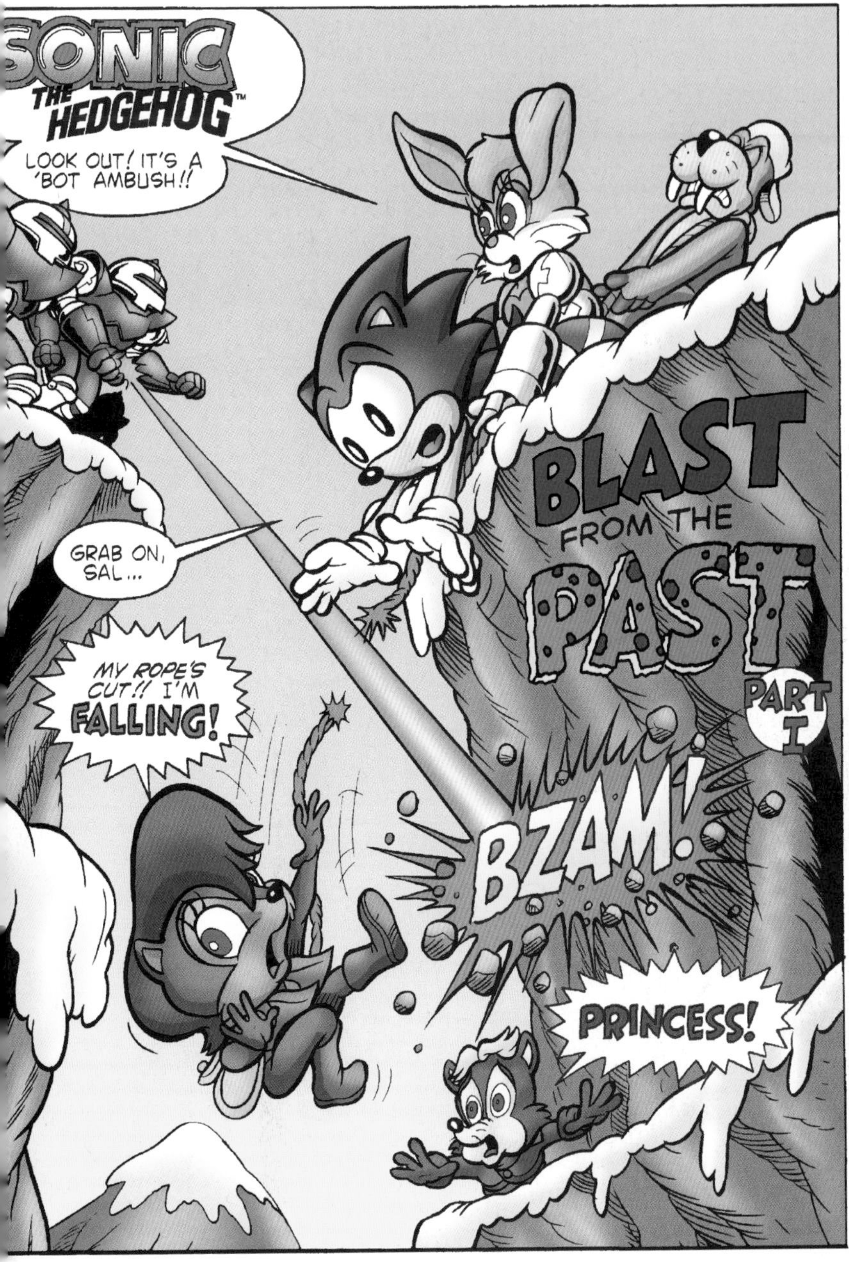
SONIC THE HEDGEHOG™
LOOK OUT! IT'S A 'BOT AMBUSH!!
BLAST FROM THE PAST PART I
GRAB ON, SAL...
MY ROPE'S CUT!! I'M FALLING!
BZAM!
PRINCESS!

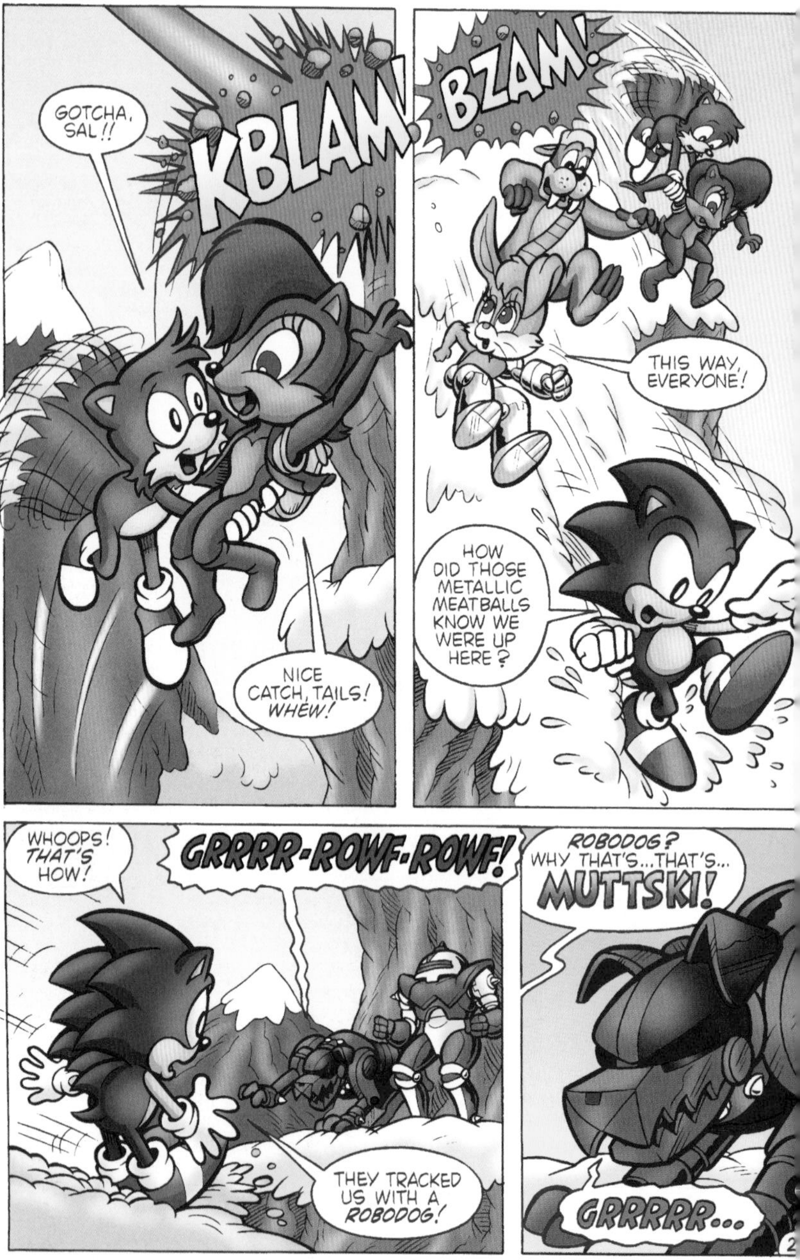

GOTCHA, SAL!!
KBLAM!
BZAM!
NICE CATCH, TAILS! WHEW!
THIS WAY, EVERYONE!
HOW DID THOSE METALLIC MEATBALLS KNOW WE WERE UP HERE?
WHOOPS! THAT'S HOW!
GRRRR-ROWF-ROWF!
THEY TRACKED US WITH A ROBODOG!
ROBODOG? WHY THAT'S...THAT'S... MUTTSKI!
GRRRRR...

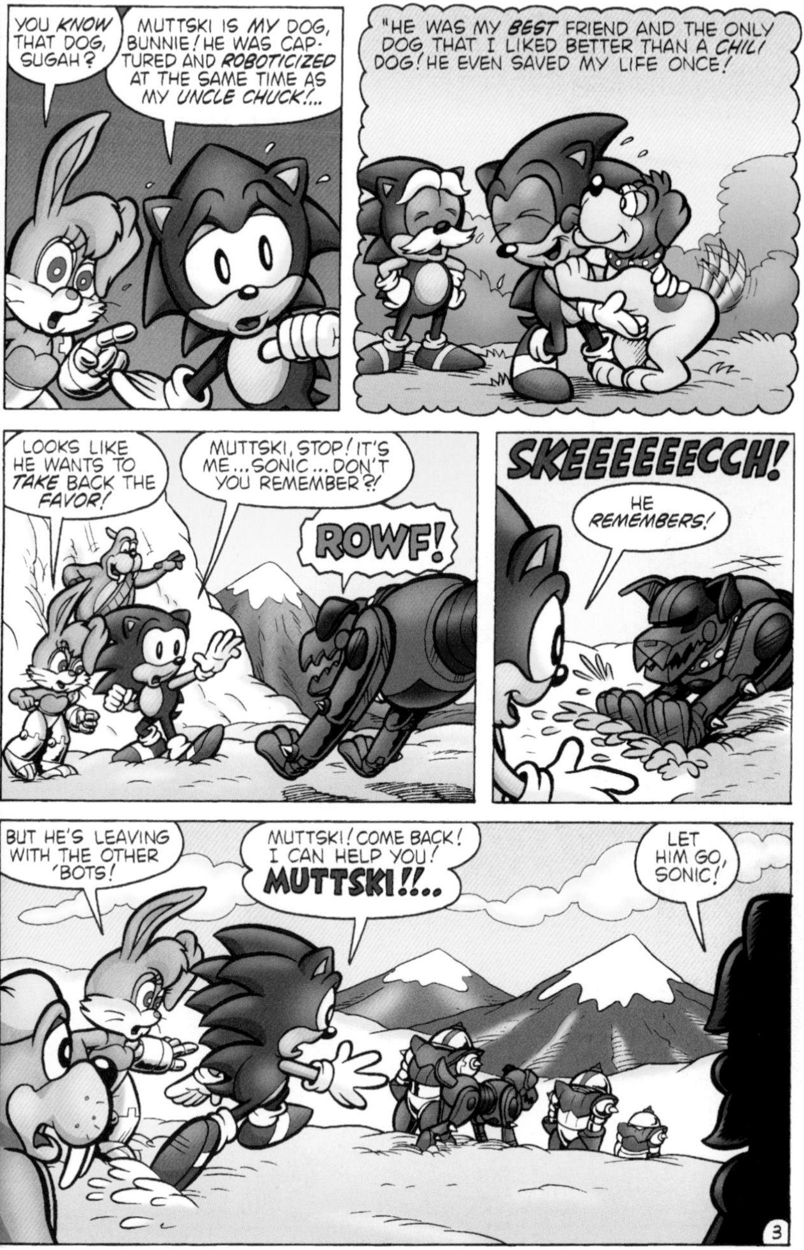
YOU KNOW THAT DOG, SUGAH?
MUTTSKI IS MY DOG, BUNNIE! HE WAS CAPTURED AND ROBOTICIZED AT THE SAME TIME AS MY UNCLE CHUCK!...
"HE WAS MY BEST FRIEND AND THE ONLY DOG THAT I LIKED BETTER THAN A CHILI DOG! HE EVEN SAVED MY LIFE ONCE!
LOOKS LIKE HE WANTS TO TAKE BACK THE FAVOR!
MUTTSKI, STOP! IT'S ME...SONIC...DON'T YOU REMEMBER?!
ROWF!
SKEEEEEEECCH!
HE REMEMBERS!
BUT HE'S LEAVING WITH THE OTHER 'BOTS!
MUTTSKI! COME BACK! I CAN HELP YOU! MUTTSKI!!..
LET HIM GO, SONIC!

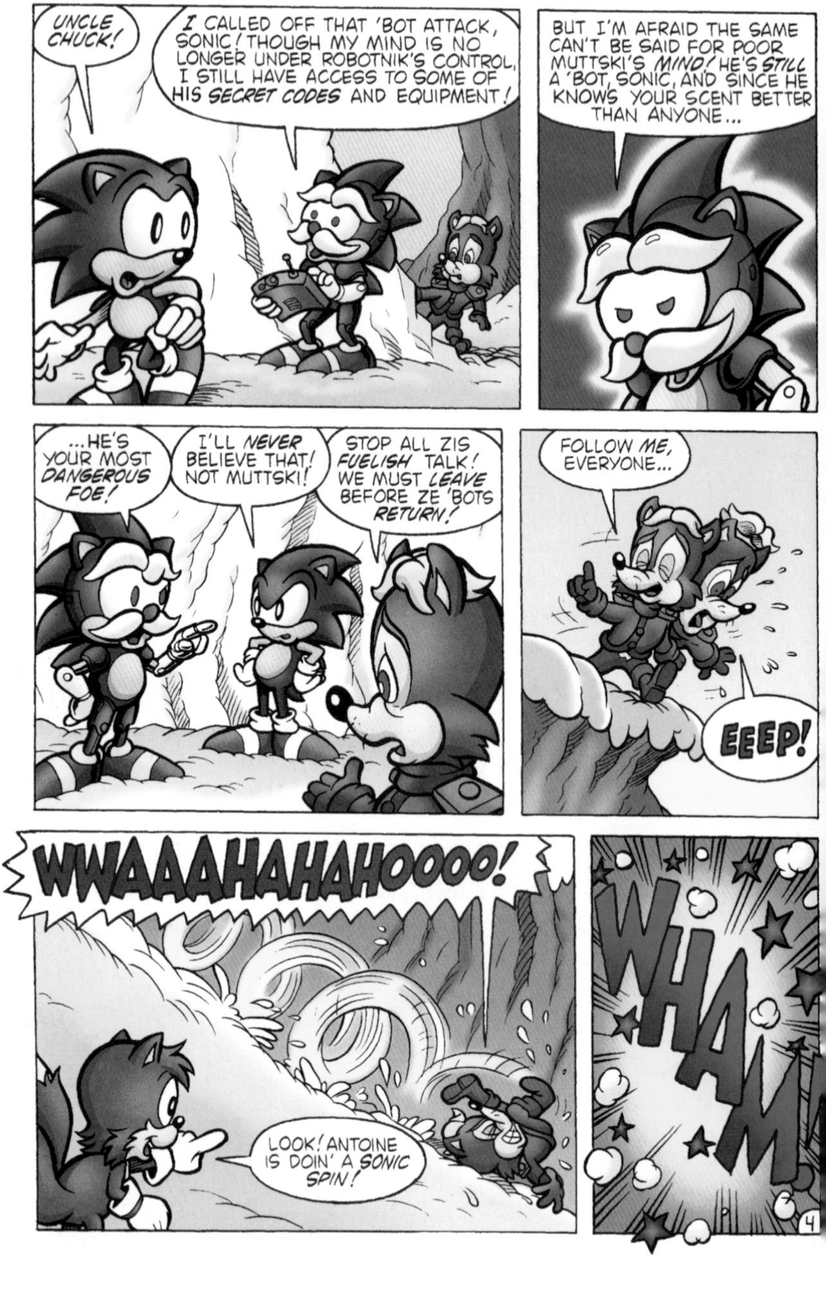
UNCLE CHUCK!
I CALLED OFF THAT 'BOT ATTACK, SONIC! THOUGH MY MIND IS NO LONGER UNDER ROBOTNIK'S CONTROL, I STILL HAVE ACCESS TO SOME OF HIS SECRET CODES AND EQUIPMENT!
BUT I'M AFRAID THE SAME CAN'T BE SAID FOR POOR MUTTSKI'S MIND! HE'S STILL A 'BOT, SONIC, AND SINCE HE KNOWS YOUR SCENT BETTER THAN ANYONE...
...HE'S YOUR MOST DANGEROUS FOE!
I'LL NEVER BELIEVE THAT! NOT MUTTSKI!
STOP ALL ZIS FUELISH TALK! WE MUST LEAVE BEFORE ZE 'BOTS RETURN!
FOLLOW ME, EVERYONE...
EEEP!
WWAAAHAHAHOOOO!
LOOK! ANTOINE IS DOIN' A SONIC SPIN!
WHAM
4

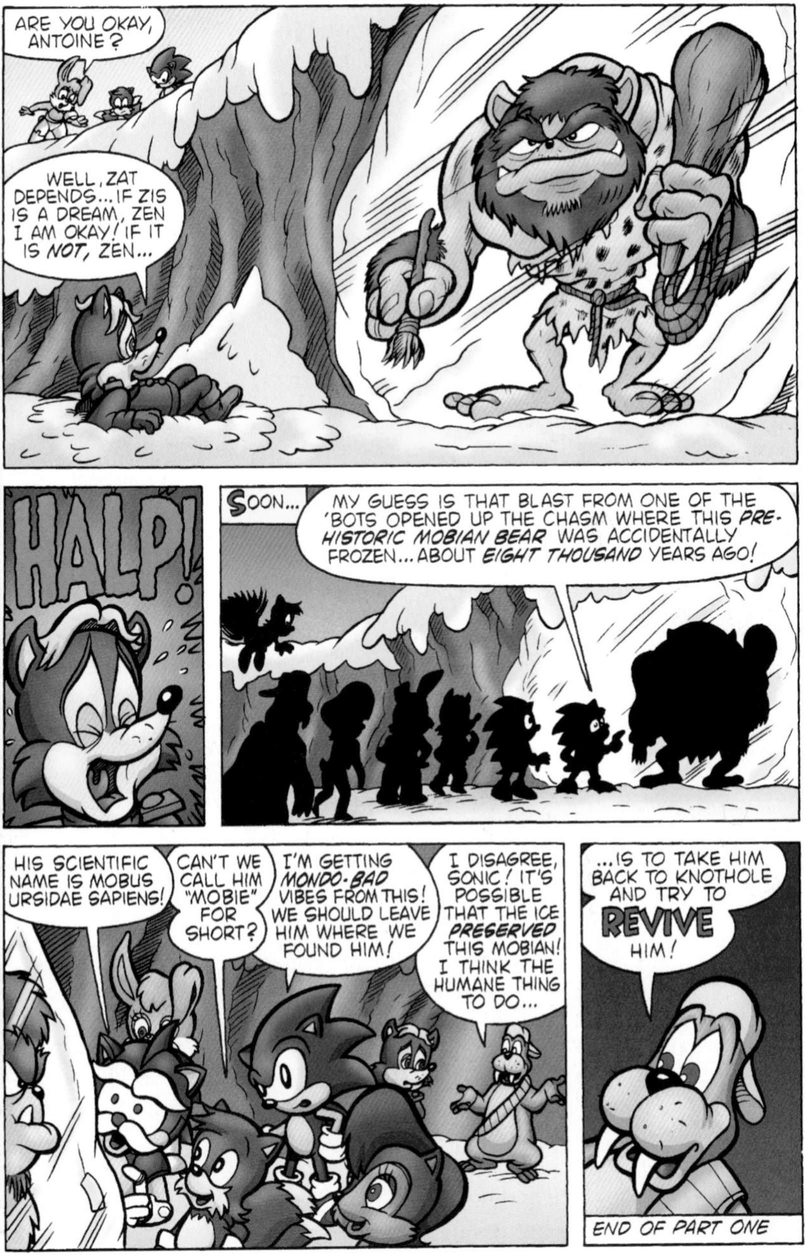
ARE YOU OKAY, ANTOINE?
WELL, ZAT DEPENDS... IF ZIS IS A DREAM, ZEN I AM OKAY! IF IT IS *NOT*, ZEN...
HALP!
SOON...
MY GUESS IS THAT BLAST FROM ONE OF THE 'BOTS OPENED UP THE CHASM WHERE THIS *PRE-HISTORIC MOBIAN BEAR* WAS ACCIDENTALLY FROZEN... ABOUT *EIGHT THOUSAND* YEARS AGO!
HIS SCIENTIFIC NAME IS MOBUS URSIDAE SAPIENS!
CAN'T WE CALL HIM "MOBIE" FOR SHORT?
I'M GETTING *MONDO-BAD* VIBES FROM THIS! WE SHOULD LEAVE HIM WHERE WE FOUND HIM!
I DISAGREE, SONIC! IT'S POSSIBLE THAT THE ICE *PRESERVED* THIS MOBIAN! I THINK THE HUMANE THING TO DO...
...IS TO TAKE HIM BACK TO KNOTHOLE AND TRY TO REVIVE HIM!
END OF PART ONE

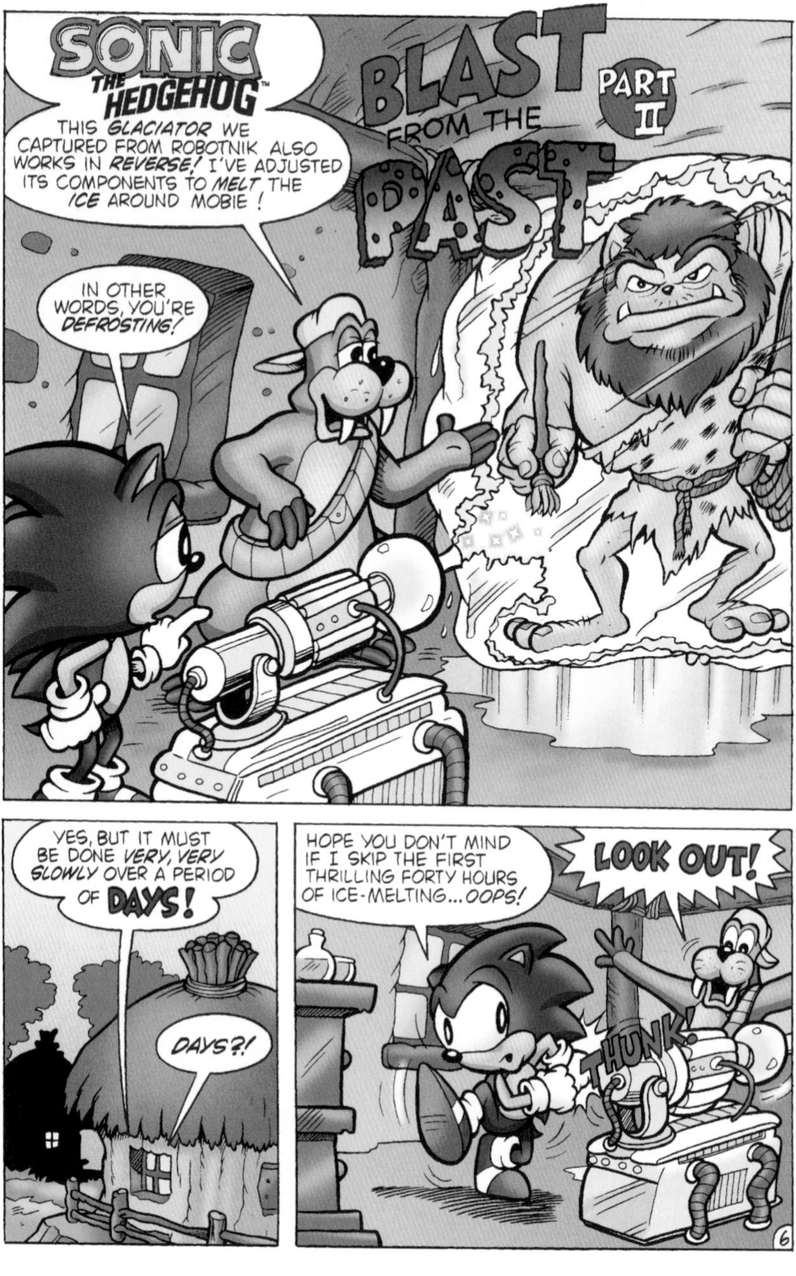
SONIC THE HEDGEHOG™
BLAST FROM THE PAST PART II
THIS GLACIATOR WE CAPTURED FROM ROBOTNIK ALSO WORKS IN REVERSE! I'VE ADJUSTED ITS COMPONENTS TO MELT THE ICE AROUND MOBIE!
IN OTHER WORDS, YOU'RE DEFROSTING!
YES, BUT IT MUST BE DONE VERY, VERY SLOWLY OVER A PERIOD OF DAYS!
DAYS?!
HOPE YOU DON'T MIND IF I SKIP THE FIRST THRILLING FORTY HOURS OF ICE-MELTING... OOPS!
LOOK OUT!
THUNK!
6

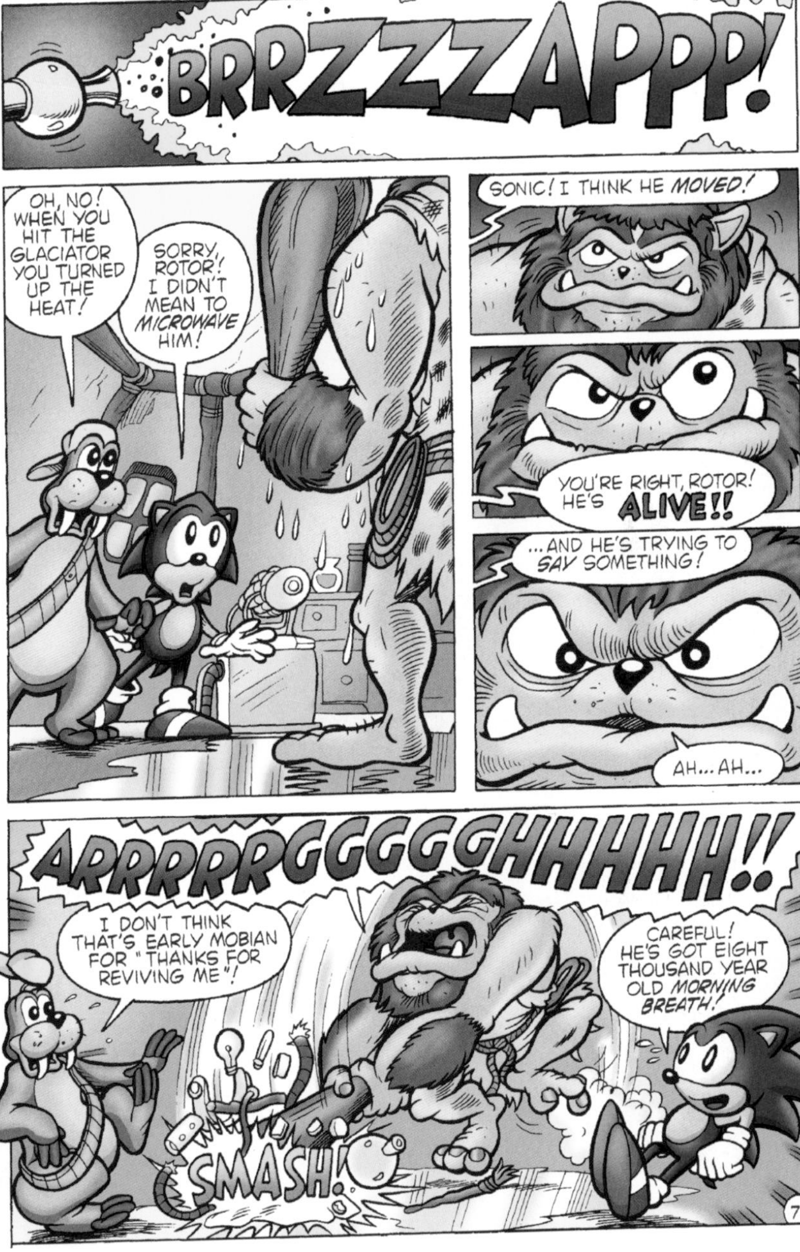
BRRZZZZAPPP!
OH, NO! WHEN YOU HIT THE GLACIATOR YOU TURNED UP THE HEAT!
SORRY, ROTOR! I DIDN'T MEAN TO MICROWAVE HIM!
SONIC! I THINK HE MOVED!
YOU'RE RIGHT, ROTOR! HE'S ALIVE!!
...AND HE'S TRYING TO SAY SOMETHING!
AH... AH...
ARRRRRGGGGGHHHHH!!
I DON'T THINK THAT'S EARLY MOBIAN FOR "THANKS FOR REVIVING ME"!
CAREFUL! HE'S GOT EIGHT THOUSAND YEAR OLD MORNING BREATH!
SMASH!

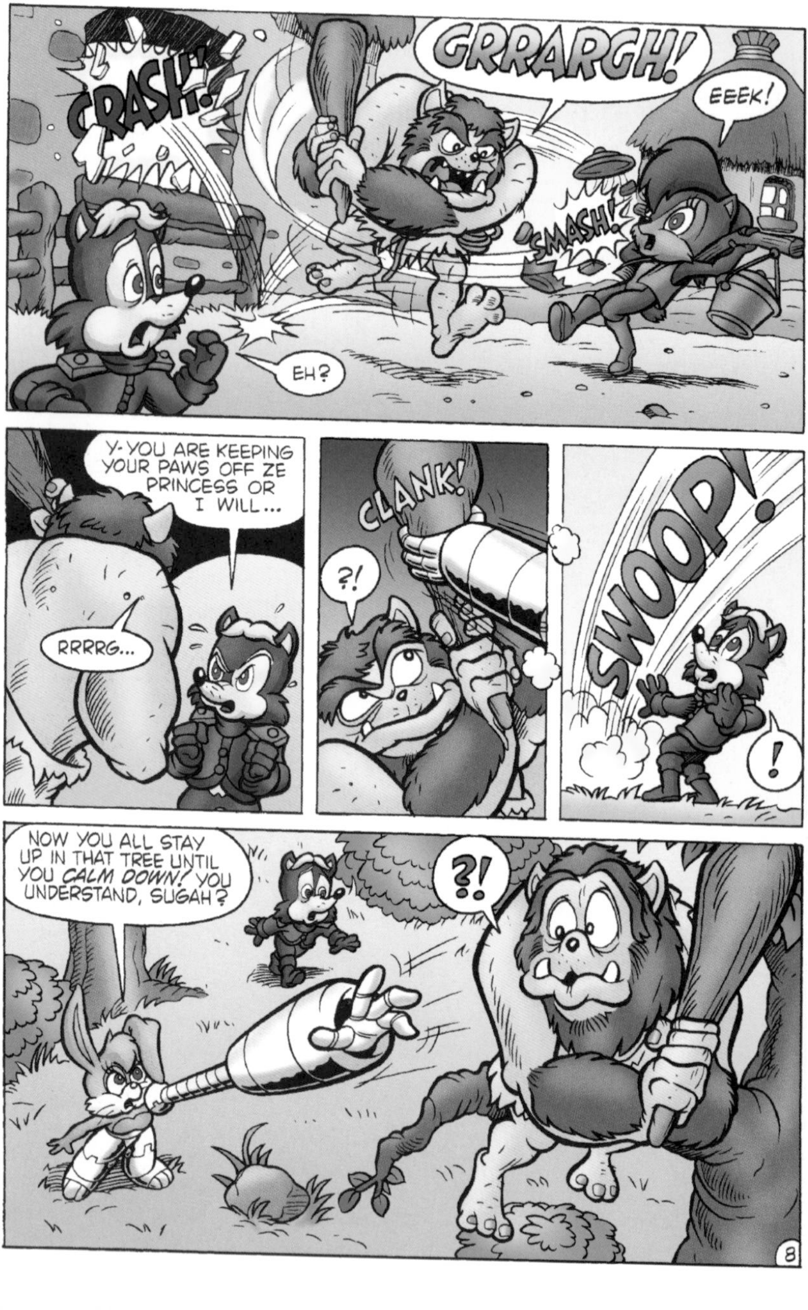
CRASH!
GRRARGH!
EEEK!
SMASH!
EH?
Y-YOU ARE KEEPING YOUR PAWS OFF ZE PRINCESS OR I WILL...
RRRRG...
CLANK!
?!
SWOOP!
!
NOW YOU ALL STAY UP IN THAT TREE UNTIL YOU *CALM DOWN!* YOU UNDERSTAND, SUGAH?
?!

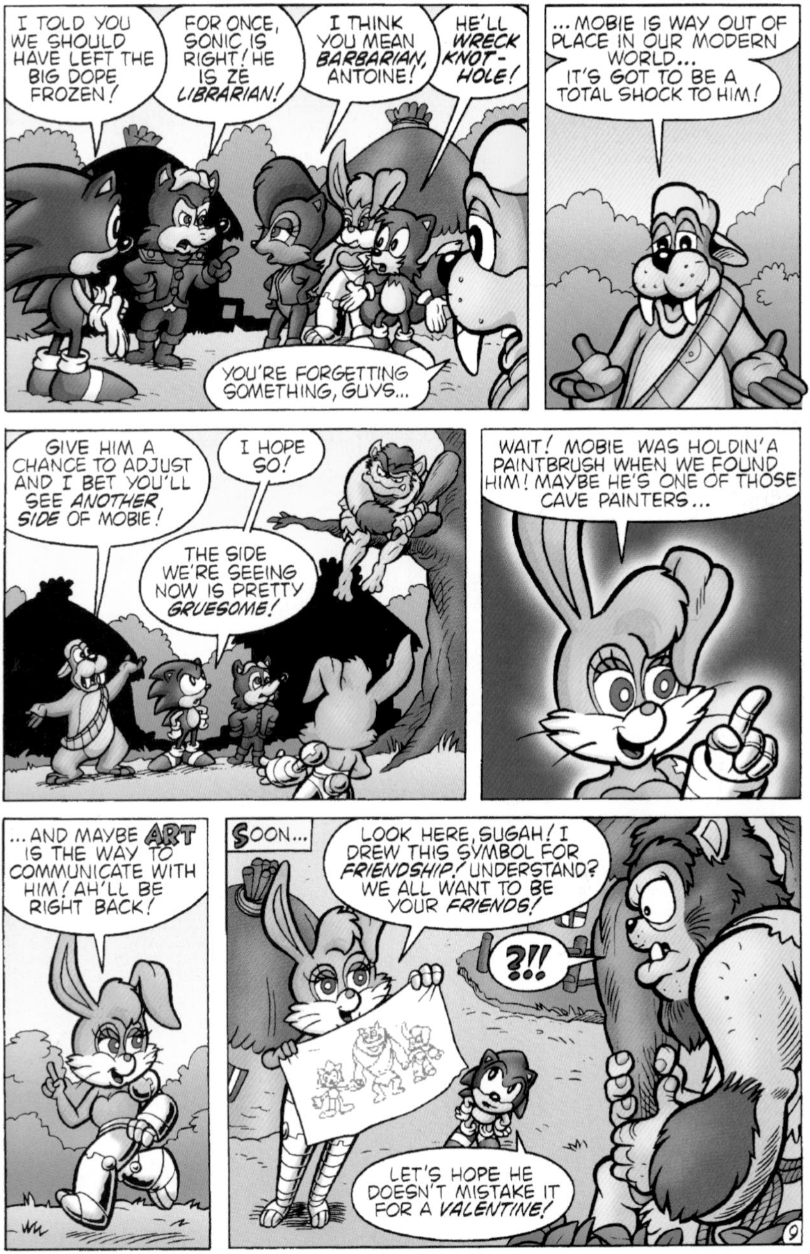
I TOLD YOU WE SHOULD HAVE LEFT THE BIG DOPE FROZEN!
FOR ONCE, SONIC IS RIGHT! HE IS ZE *LIBRARIAN!*
I THINK YOU MEAN *BARBARIAN*, ANTOINE!
HE'LL *WRECK KNOT-HOLE!*
YOU'RE FORGETTING SOMETHING, GUYS...
...MOBIE IS WAY OUT OF PLACE IN OUR MODERN WORLD... IT'S GOT TO BE A TOTAL SHOCK TO HIM!
GIVE HIM A CHANCE TO ADJUST AND I BET YOU'LL SEE *ANOTHER SIDE* OF MOBIE!
I HOPE SO!
THE SIDE WE'RE SEEING NOW IS PRETTY *GRUESOME!*
WAIT! MOBIE WAS HOLDIN' A PAINTBRUSH WHEN WE FOUND HIM! MAYBE HE'S ONE OF THOSE CAVE PAINTERS...
...AND MAYBE **ART** IS THE WAY TO COMMUNICATE WITH HIM! AH'LL BE RIGHT BACK!
SOON...
LOOK HERE, SUGAH! I DREW THIS SYMBOL FOR *FRIENDSHIP!* UNDERSTAND? WE ALL WANT TO BE YOUR *FRIENDS!*
?!!
LET'S HOPE HE DOESN'T MISTAKE IT FOR A *VALENTINE!*
9

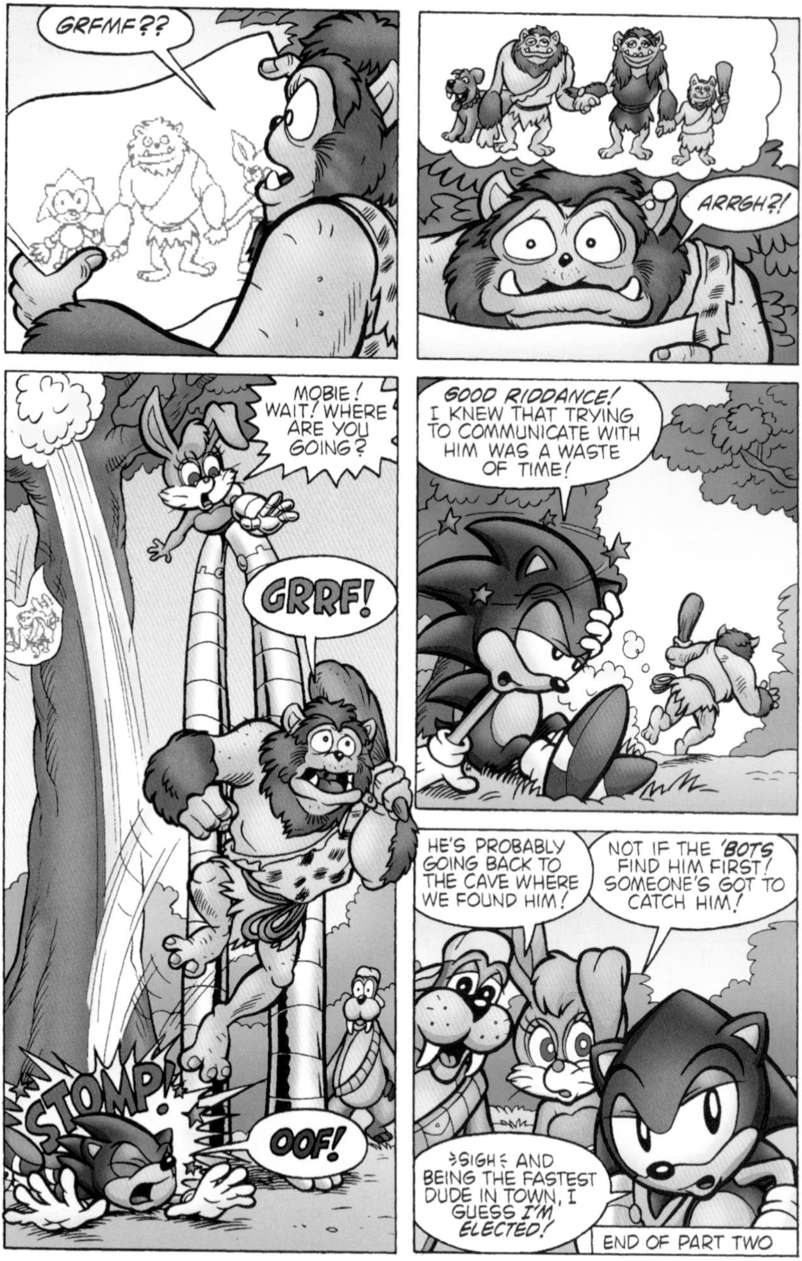
GRFMF??
ARRGH?!
MOBIE! WAIT! WHERE ARE YOU GOING?
GRRF!
STOMP!
OOF!
GOOD RIDDANCE! I KNEW THAT TRYING TO COMMUNICATE WITH HIM WAS A WASTE OF TIME!
HE'S PROBABLY GOING BACK TO THE CAVE WHERE WE FOUND HIM!
NOT IF THE 'BOTS FIND HIM FIRST! SOMEONE'S GOT TO CATCH HIM!
≶SIGH≷ AND BEING THE FASTEST DUDE IN TOWN, I GUESS I'M ELECTED!
END OF PART TWO

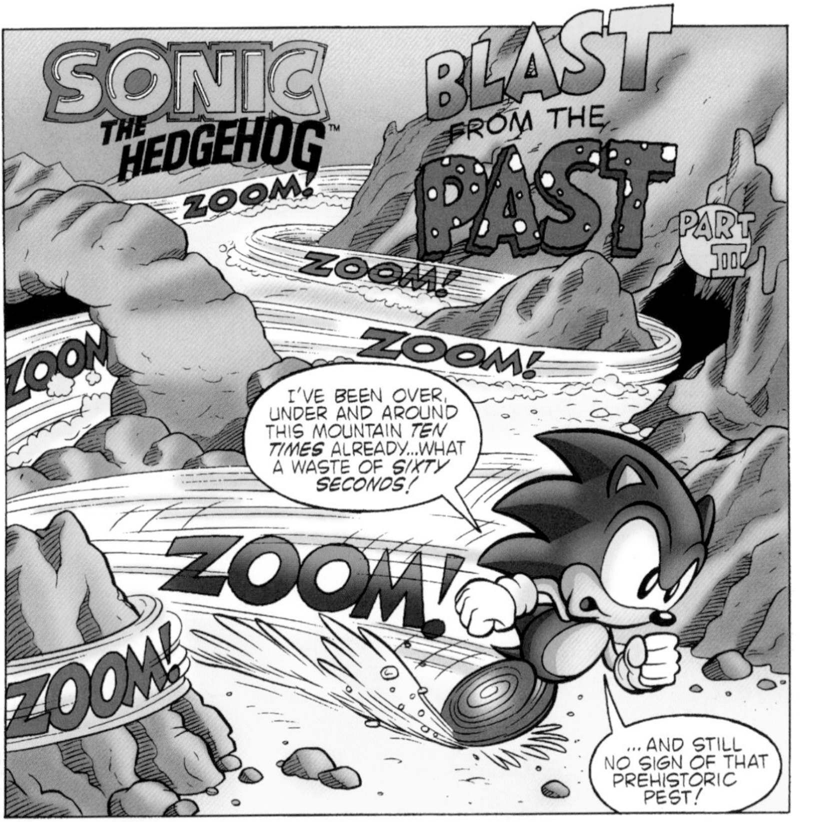
SONIC THE HEDGEHOG™
BLAST FROM THE PAST
PART III
ZOOM!
ZOOM!
ZOOM!
ZOOM!
I'VE BEEN OVER, UNDER AND AROUND THIS MOUNTAIN *TEN TIMES* ALREADY...WHAT A WASTE OF *SIXTY SECONDS!*
ZOOM!
ZOOM!
...AND STILL NO SIGN OF THAT PREHISTORIC PEST!

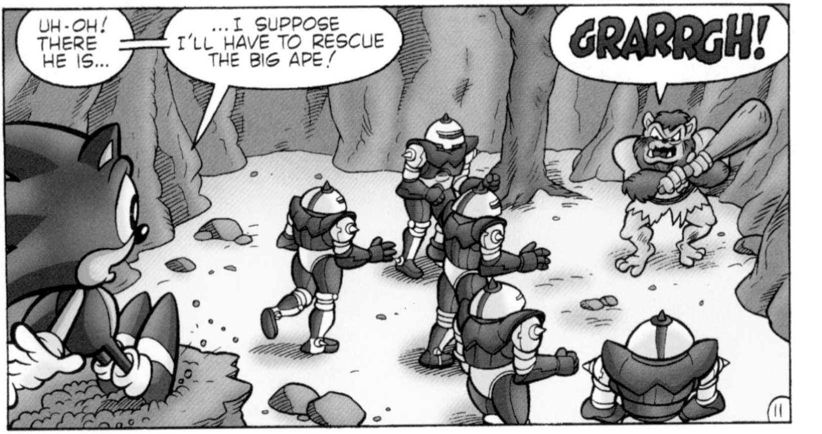
UH-OH! THERE HE IS...
...I SUPPOSE I'LL HAVE TO RESCUE THE BIG APE!
GRARRGH!

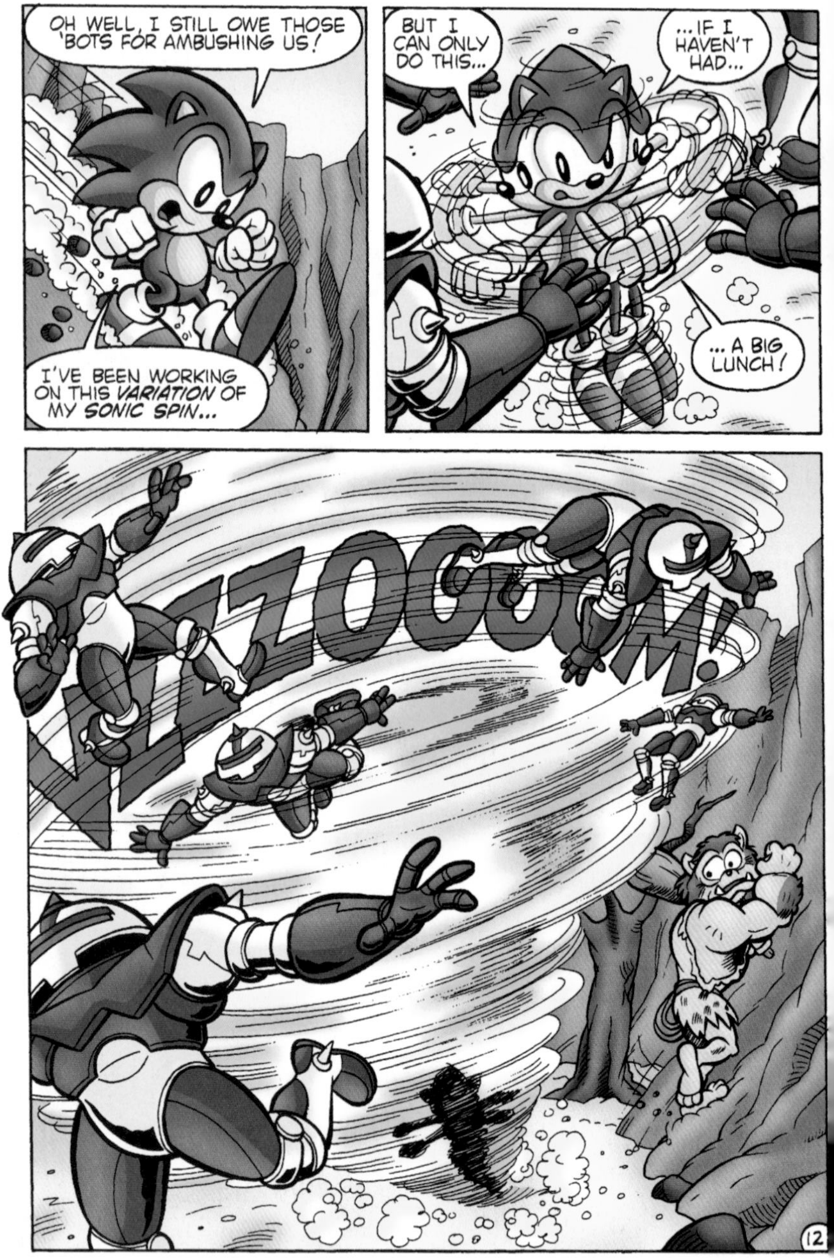

OH WELL, I STILL OWE THOSE 'BOTS FOR AMBUSHING US!
I'VE BEEN WORKING ON THIS *VARIATION* OF MY *SONIC SPIN*...
BUT I CAN ONLY DO THIS...
...IF I HAVEN'T HAD...
...A BIG LUNCH!
ZZZOGGOOM!

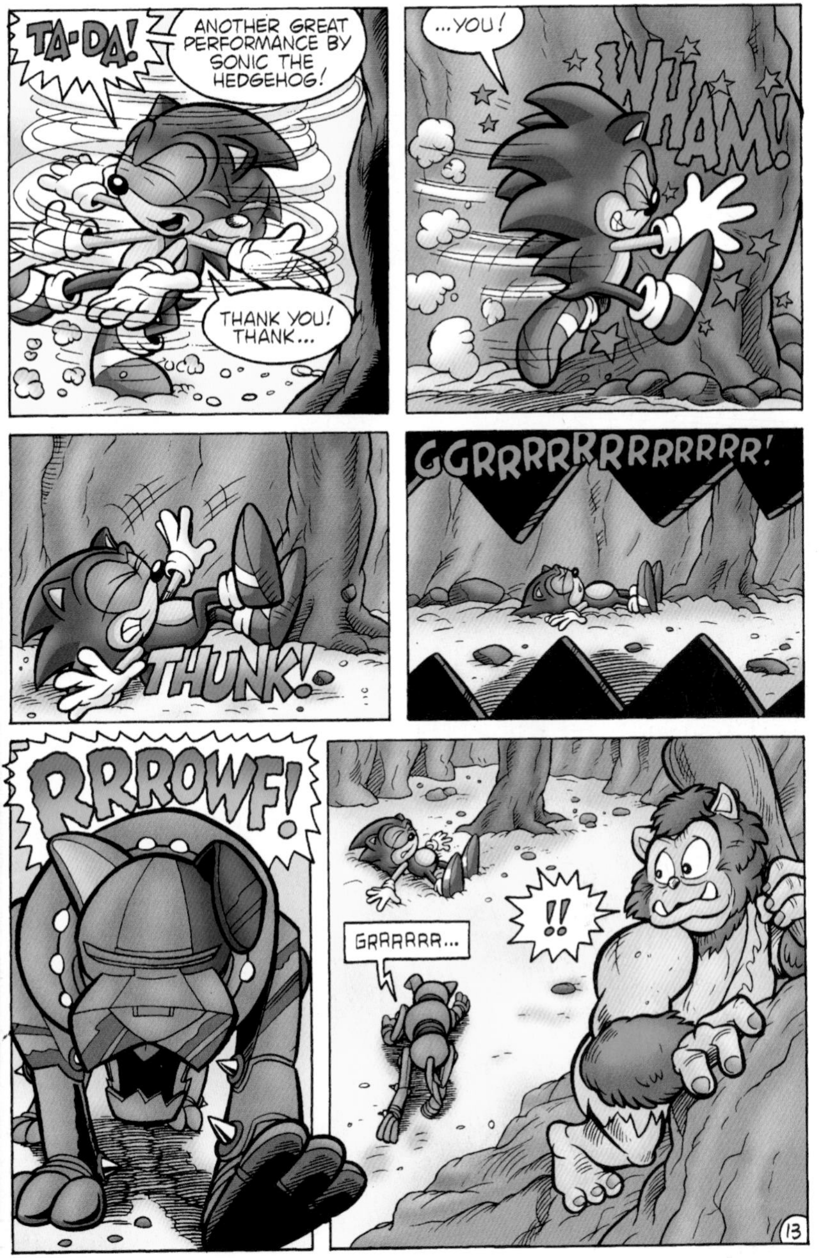
TA-DA!
ANOTHER GREAT PERFORMANCE BY SONIC THE HEDGEHOG!
THANK YOU! THANK...
...YOU!
WHAM!
THUNK!
GGRRRRRRRRRRRR!
RRROWF!
GRRRRRR...
!!

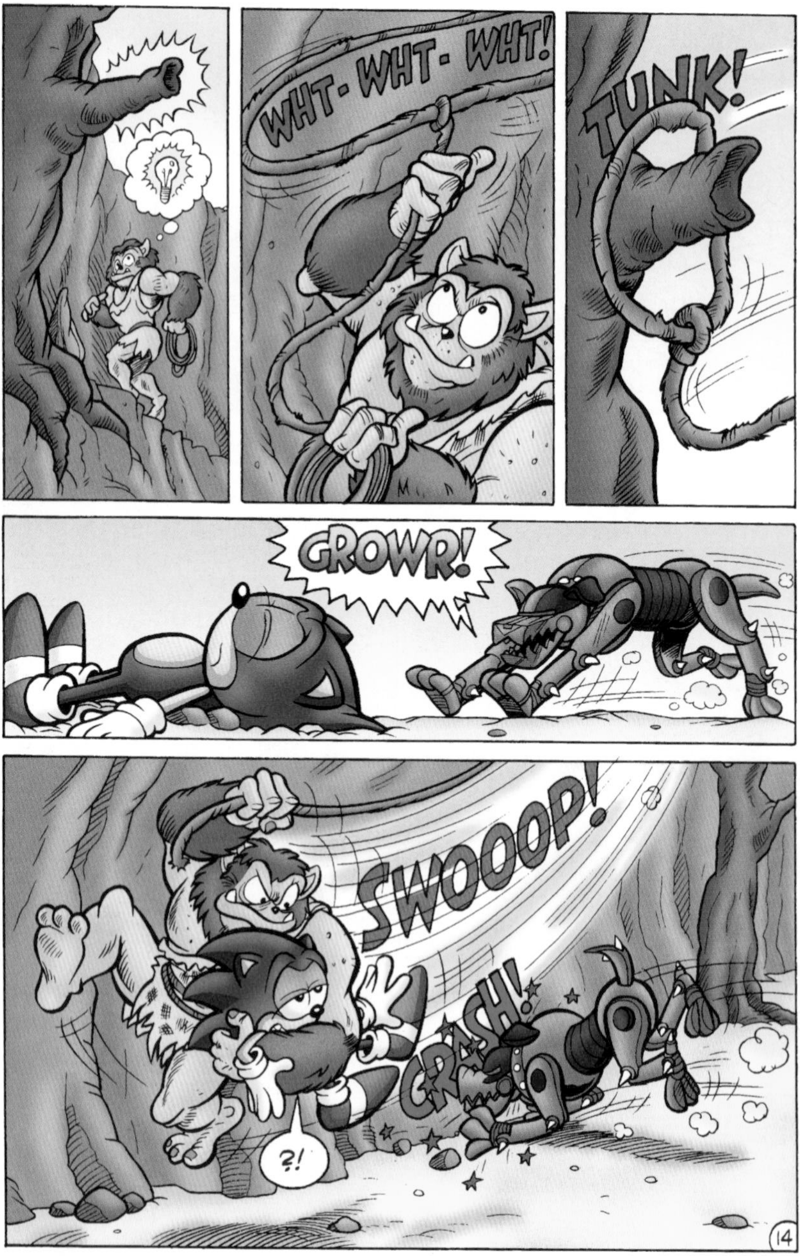
WHT-WHT-WHT!
TUNK!
GROWR!
SWOOOP!
CRASH!
?!

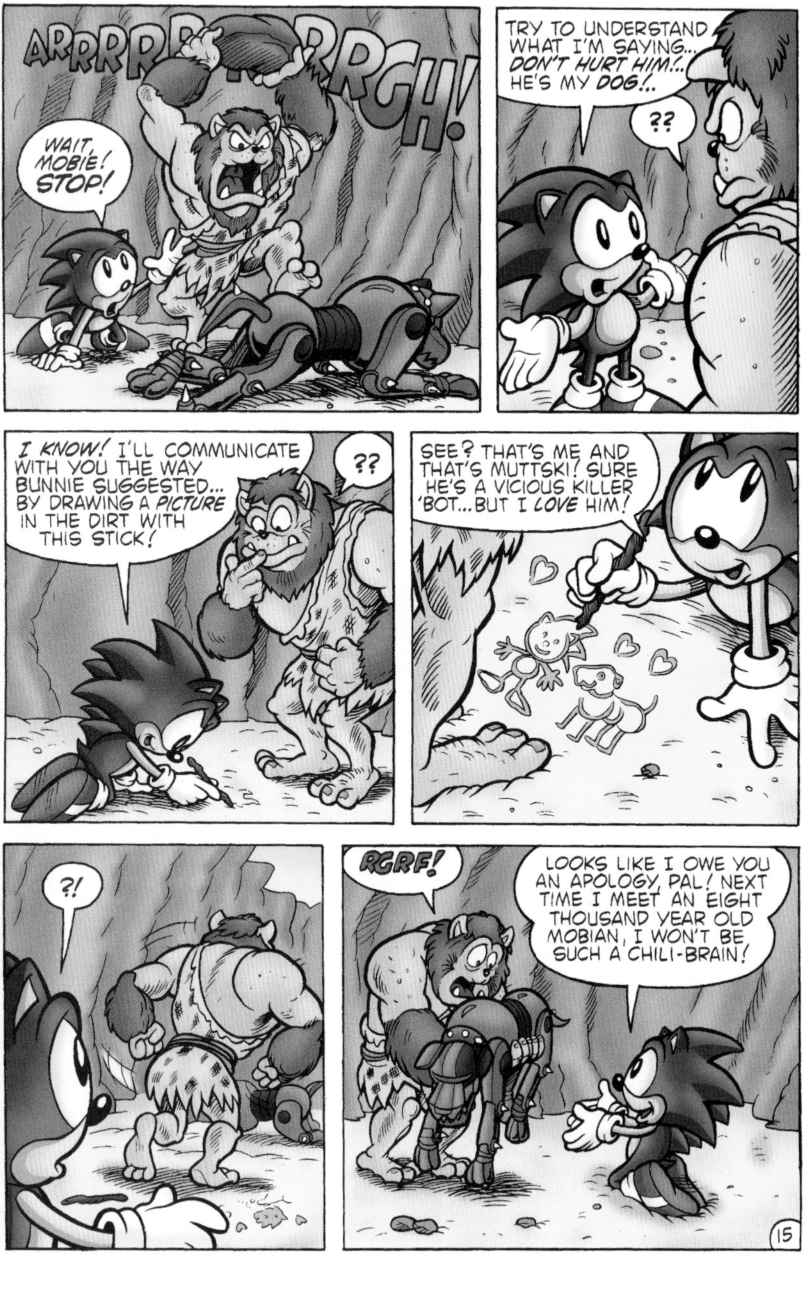

ARRRRRRRRRGH!
WAIT, MOBIE! STOP!
TRY TO UNDERSTAND WHAT I'M SAYING... DON'T HURT HIM!.. HE'S MY DOG!..
??
I KNOW! I'LL COMMUNICATE WITH YOU THE WAY BUNNIE SUGGESTED... BY DRAWING A PICTURE IN THE DIRT WITH THIS STICK!
??
SEE? THAT'S ME AND THAT'S MUTTSKI! SURE HE'S A VICIOUS KILLER 'BOT... BUT I LOVE HIM!
?!
RGRF!
LOOKS LIKE I OWE YOU AN APOLOGY, PAL! NEXT TIME I MEET AN EIGHT THOUSAND YEAR OLD MOBIAN, I WON'T BE SUCH A CHILI-BRAIN!

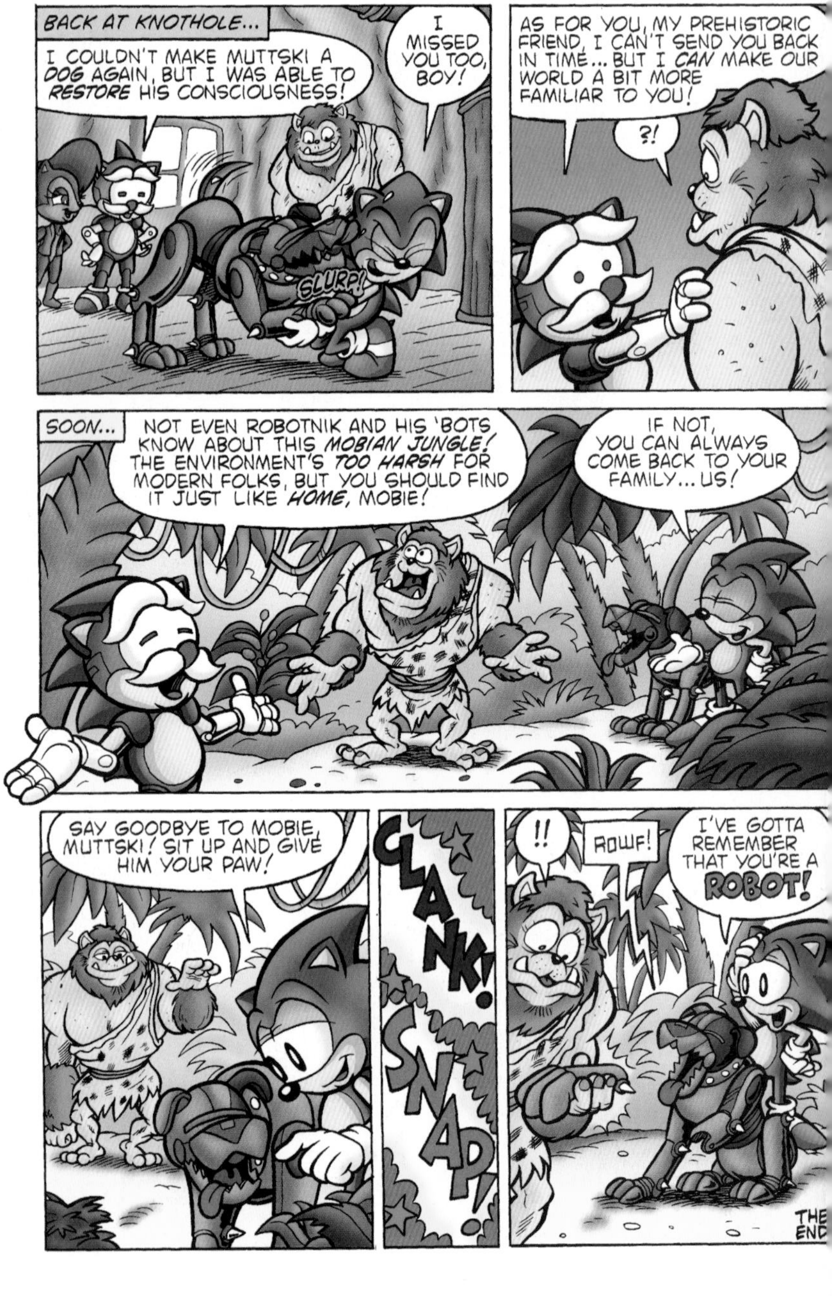
BACK AT KNOTHOLE...
I COULDN'T MAKE MUTTSKI A DOG AGAIN, BUT I WAS ABLE TO RESTORE HIS CONSCIOUSNESS!
I MISSED YOU TOO, BOY!
SLURP!
AS FOR YOU, MY PREHISTORIC FRIEND, I CAN'T SEND YOU BACK IN TIME... BUT I CAN MAKE OUR WORLD A BIT MORE FAMILIAR TO YOU!
?!
SOON...
NOT EVEN ROBOTNIK AND HIS 'BOTS KNOW ABOUT THIS MOBIAN JUNGLE! THE ENVIRONMENT'S TOO HARSH FOR MODERN FOLKS, BUT YOU SHOULD FIND IT JUST LIKE HOME, MOBIE!
IF NOT, YOU CAN ALWAYS COME BACK TO YOUR FAMILY... US!
SAY GOODBYE TO MOBIE, MUTTSKI! SIT UP AND GIVE HIM YOUR PAW!
CLANK!
SNAP!
!!
ROWF!
I'VE GOTTA REMEMBER THAT YOU'RE A ROBOT!
THE END

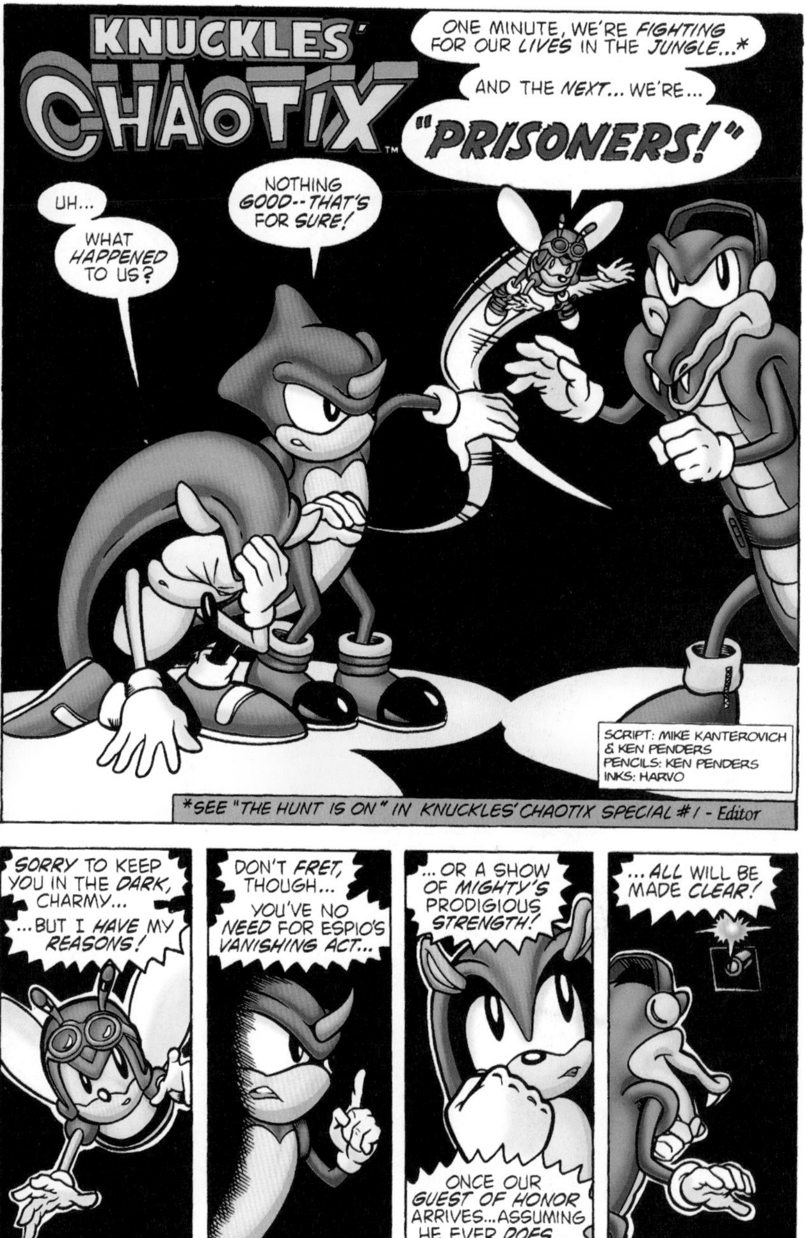
KNUCKLES' CHAOTIX™
ONE MINUTE, WE'RE FIGHTING FOR OUR LIVES IN THE JUNGLE...*
AND THE NEXT... WE'RE...
"PRISONERS!"
UH...
WHAT HAPPENED TO US?
NOTHING GOOD--THAT'S FOR SURE!
SCRIPT: MIKE KANTEROVICH & KEN PENDERS
PENCILS: KEN PENDERS
INKS: HARVO
*SEE "THE HUNT IS ON" IN KNUCKLES' CHAOTIX SPECIAL #1 - Editor
SORRY TO KEEP YOU IN THE DARK, CHARMY...
...BUT I HAVE MY REASONS!
DON'T FRET, THOUGH...
YOU'VE NO NEED FOR ESPIO'S VANISHING ACT...
...OR A SHOW OF MIGHTY'S PRODIGIOUS STRENGTH!
ONCE OUR GUEST OF HONOR ARRIVES...ASSUMING HE EVER DOES...
...ALL WILL BE MADE CLEAR!

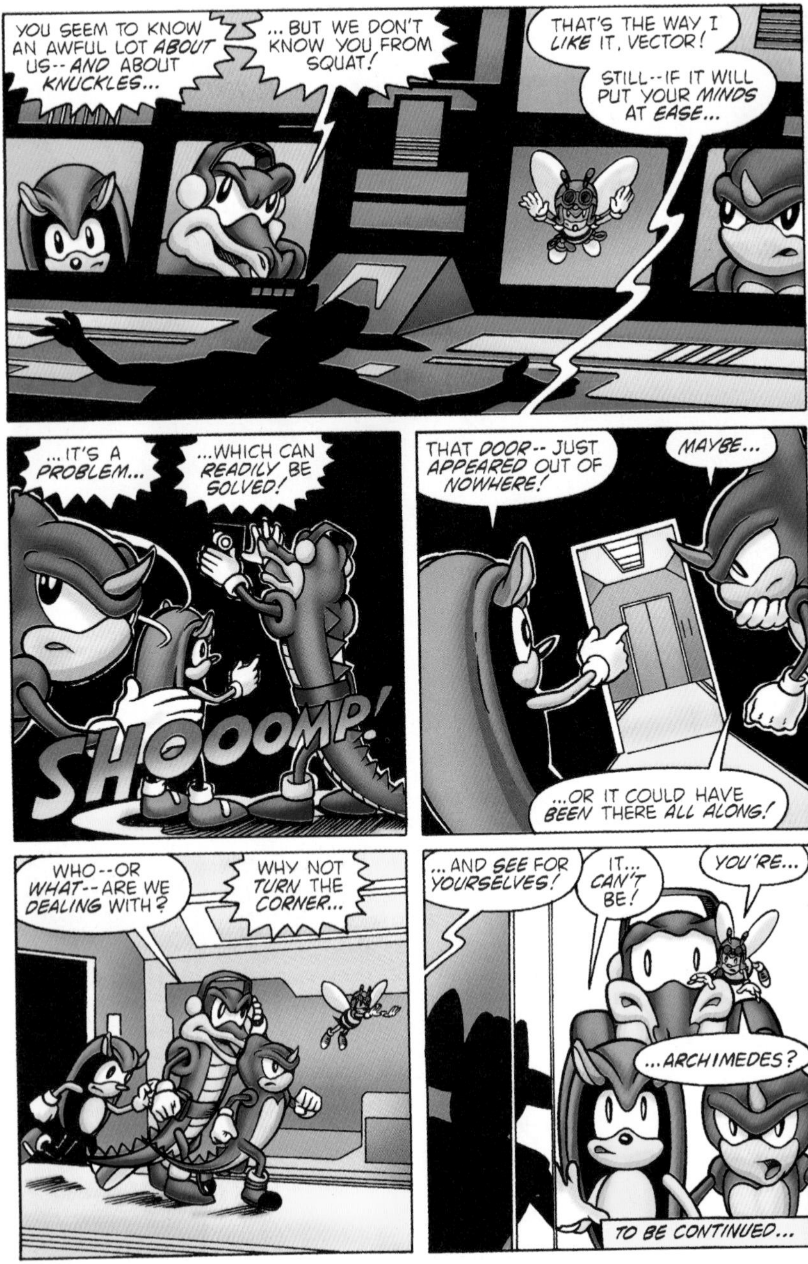
YOU SEEM TO KNOW AN AWFUL LOT ABOUT US--AND ABOUT KNUCKLES...
...BUT WE DON'T KNOW YOU FROM SQUAT!
THAT'S THE WAY I LIKE IT, VECTOR!
STILL--IF IT WILL PUT YOUR MINDS AT EASE...
...IT'S A PROBLEM...
...WHICH CAN READILY BE SOLVED!
SHOOOMP!
THAT DOOR--JUST APPEARED OUT OF NOWHERE!
MAYBE...
...OR IT COULD HAVE BEEN THERE ALL ALONG!
WHO--OR WHAT--ARE WE DEALING WITH?
WHY NOT TURN THE CORNER...
...AND SEE FOR YOURSELVES!
IT... CAN'T BE!
YOU'RE...
...ARCHIMEDES?
TO BE CONTINUED...

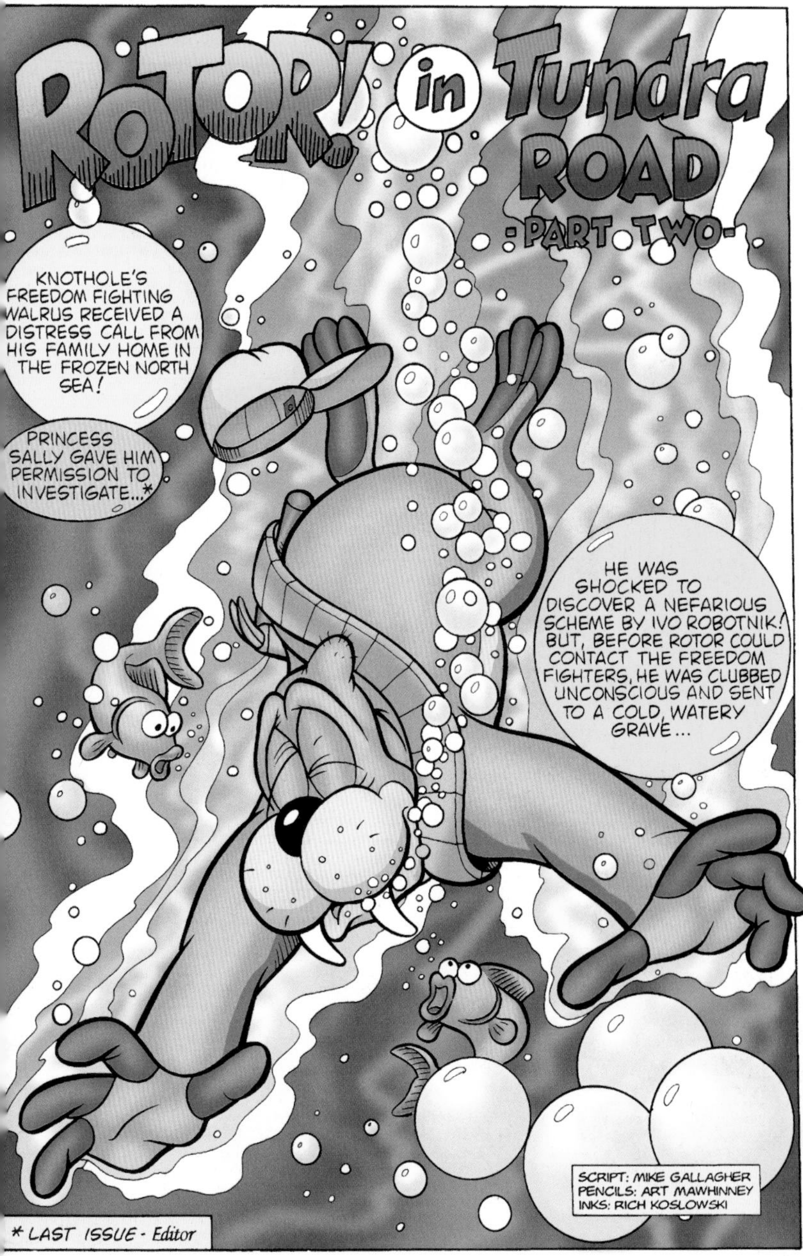
ROTOR! in Tundra ROAD
-PART TWO-
KNOTHOLE'S FREEDOM FIGHTING WALRUS RECEIVED A DISTRESS CALL FROM HIS FAMILY HOME IN THE FROZEN NORTH SEA!
PRINCESS SALLY GAVE HIM PERMISSION TO INVESTIGATE...*
HE WAS SHOCKED TO DISCOVER A NEFARIOUS SCHEME BY IVO ROBOTNIK! BUT, BEFORE ROTOR COULD CONTACT THE FREEDOM FIGHTERS, HE WAS CLUBBED UNCONSCIOUS AND SENT TO A COLD, WATERY GRAVE...
SCRIPT: MIKE GALLAGHER
PENCILS: ART MAWHINNEY
INKS: RICH KOSLOWSKI
* LAST ISSUE - Editor

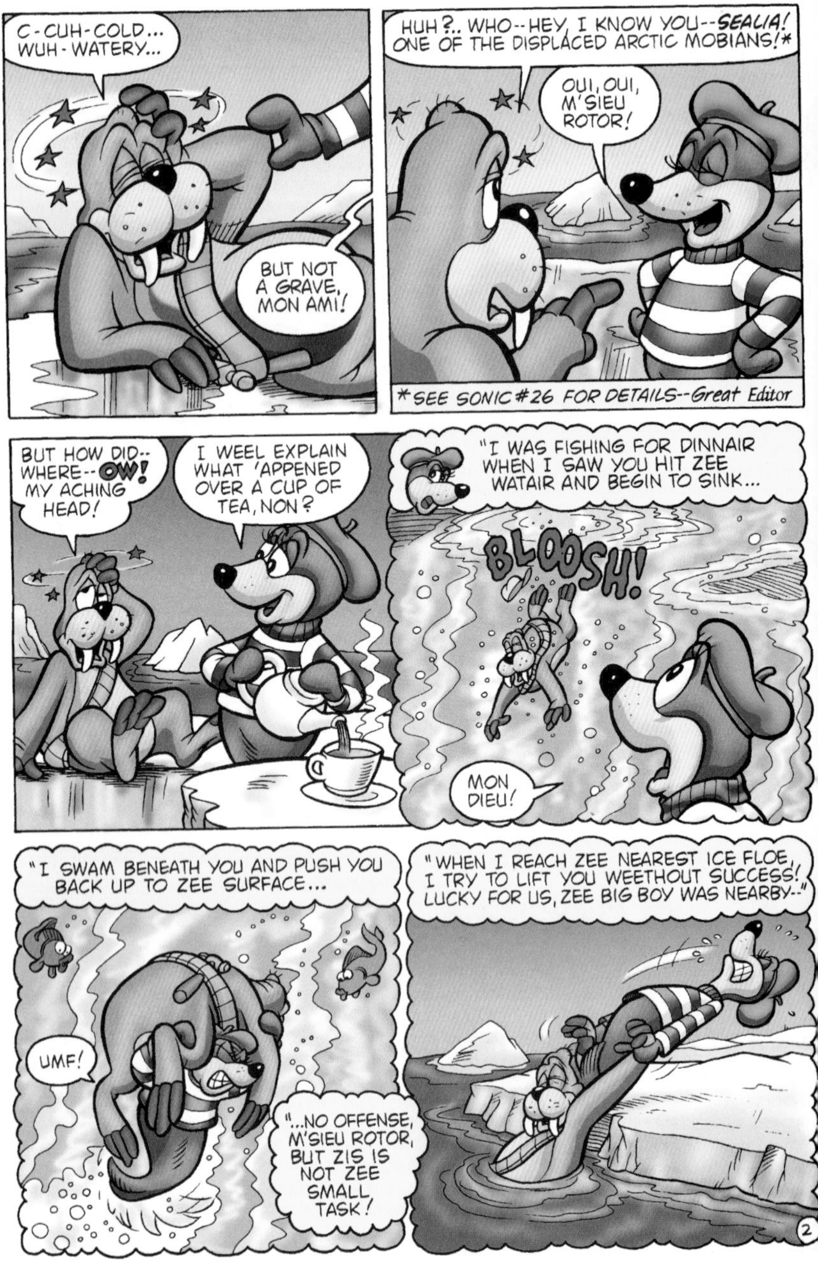
C-CUH-COLD... WUH-WATERY...
BUT NOT A GRAVE, MON AMI!
HUH?.. WHO--HEY, I KNOW YOU--SEALIA! ONE OF THE DISPLACED ARCTIC MOBIANS!*
OUI, OUI, M'SIEU ROTOR!
*SEE SONIC #26 FOR DETAILS--Great Editor
BUT HOW DID-- WHERE--OW! MY ACHING HEAD!
I WEEL EXPLAIN WHAT 'APPENED OVER A CUP OF TEA, NON?
"I WAS FISHING FOR DINNAIR WHEN I SAW YOU HIT ZEE WATAIR AND BEGIN TO SINK...
BLOOSH!
MON DIEU!
"I SWAM BENEATH YOU AND PUSH YOU BACK UP TO ZEE SURFACE...
UMF!
"...NO OFFENSE, M'SIEU ROTOR, BUT ZIS IS NOT ZEE SMALL TASK!
"WHEN I REACH ZEE NEAREST ICE FLOE, I TRY TO LIFT YOU WEETHOUT SUCCESS! LUCKY FOR US, ZEE BIG BOY WAS NEARBY--"

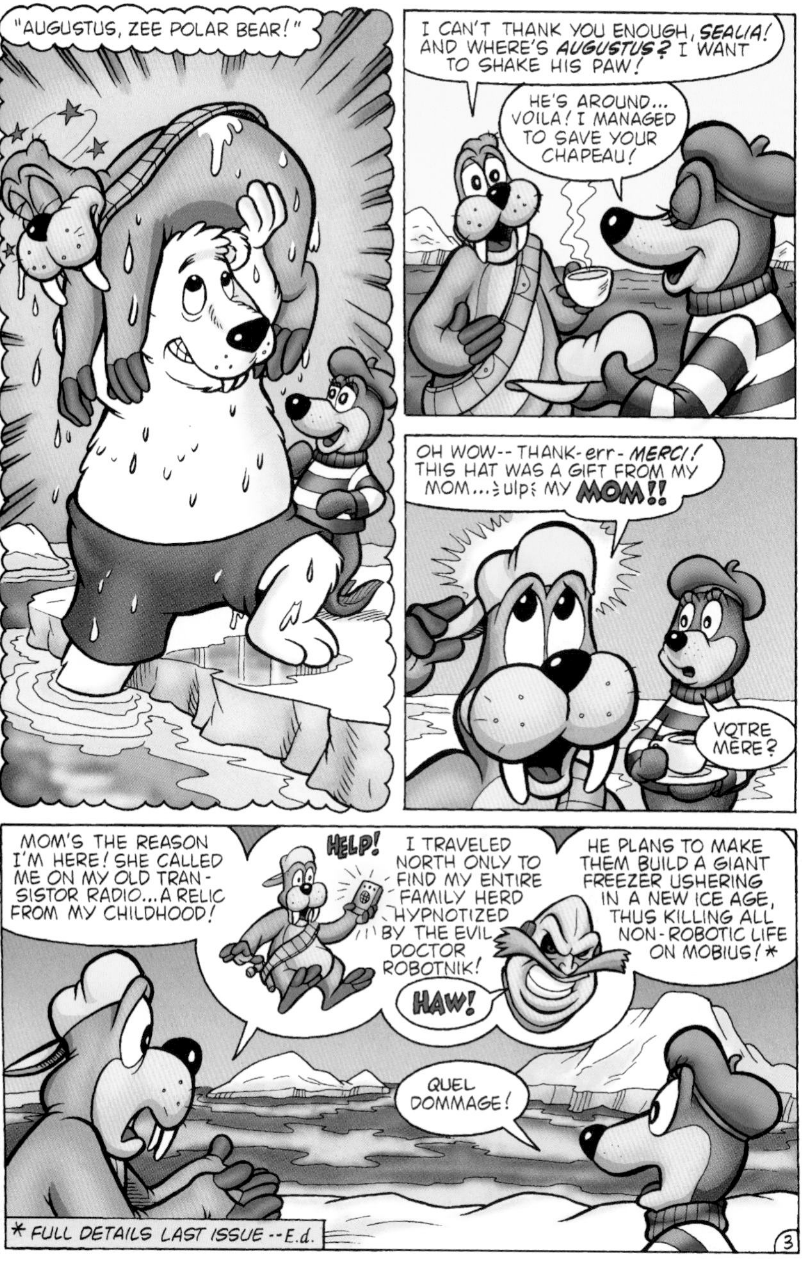
"AUGUSTUS, ZEE POLAR BEAR!"
I CAN'T THANK YOU ENOUGH, SEALIA! AND WHERE'S AUGUSTUS? I WANT TO SHAKE HIS PAW!
HE'S AROUND... VOILA! I MANAGED TO SAVE YOUR CHAPEAU!
OH WOW-- THANK-err-MERCI! THIS HAT WAS A GIFT FROM MY MOM... ≷ulp≶ MY MOM!!
VOTRE MÈRE?
MOM'S THE REASON I'M HERE! SHE CALLED ME ON MY OLD TRAN-SISTOR RADIO...A RELIC FROM MY CHILDHOOD!
HELP!
I TRAVELED NORTH ONLY TO FIND MY ENTIRE FAMILY HERD HYPNOTIZED BY THE EVIL DOCTOR ROBOTNIK!
HE PLANS TO MAKE THEM BUILD A GIANT FREEZER USHERING IN A NEW ICE AGE, THUS KILLING ALL NON-ROBOTIC LIFE ON MOBIUS! *
HAW!
QUEL DOMMAGE!
* FULL DETAILS LAST ISSUE -- E.d.
3

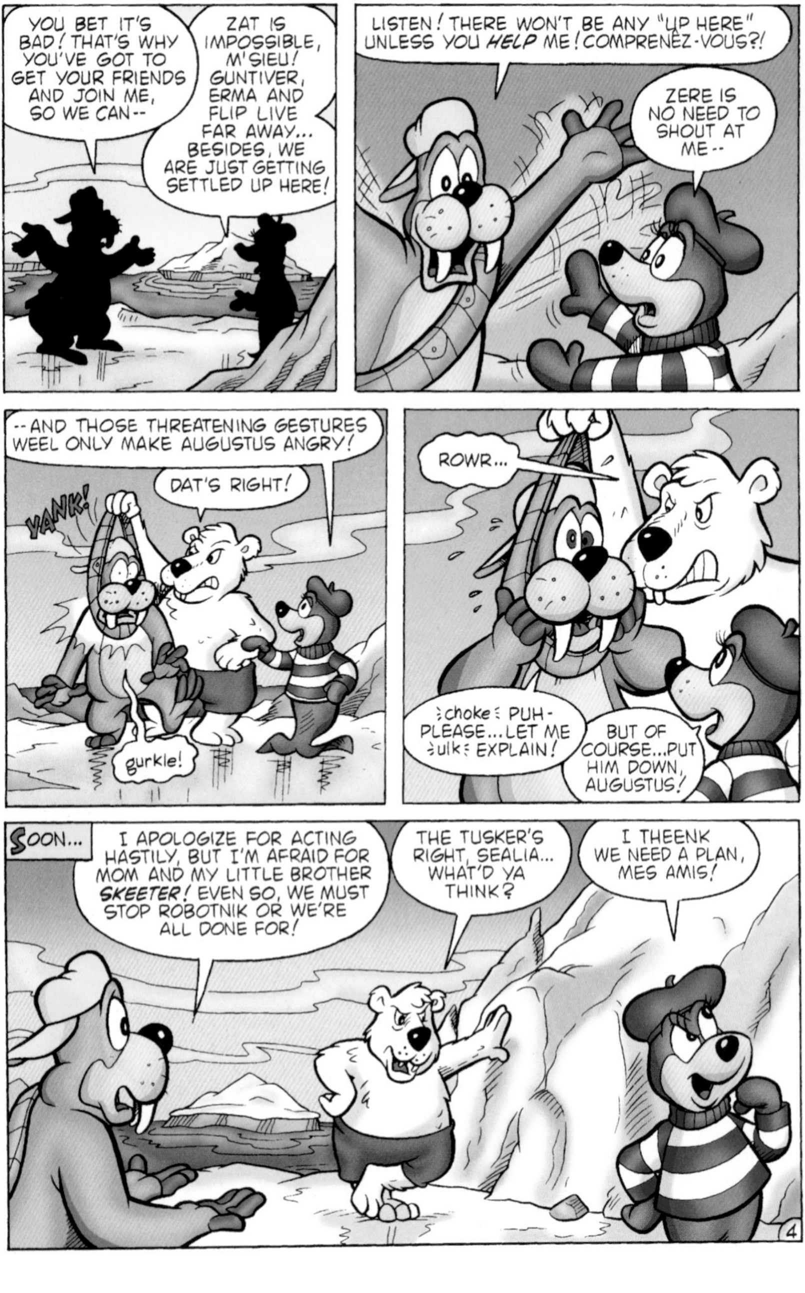
YOU BET IT'S BAD! THAT'S WHY YOU'VE GOT TO GET YOUR FRIENDS AND JOIN ME, SO WE CAN--
ZAT IS IMPOSSIBLE, M'SIEU! GUNTIVER, ERMA AND FLIP LIVE FAR AWAY... BESIDES, WE ARE JUST GETTING SETTLED UP HERE!
LISTEN! THERE WON'T BE ANY "UP HERE" UNLESS YOU *HELP* ME! COMPRENÉZ-VOUS?!
ZERE IS NO NEED TO SHOUT AT ME--
--AND THOSE THREATENING GESTURES WEEL ONLY MAKE AUGUSTUS ANGRY!
DAT'S RIGHT!
YANK!
gurkle!
ROWR...
choke PUH-PLEASE...LET ME ulk EXPLAIN!
BUT OF COURSE...PUT HIM DOWN, AUGUSTUS!
SOON...
I APOLOGIZE FOR ACTING HASTILY, BUT I'M AFRAID FOR MOM AND MY LITTLE BROTHER *SKEETER*! EVEN SO, WE MUST STOP ROBOTNIK OR WE'RE ALL DONE FOR!
THE TUSKER'S RIGHT, SEALIA... WHAT'D YA THINK?
I THEENK WE NEED A PLAN, MES AMIS!
4

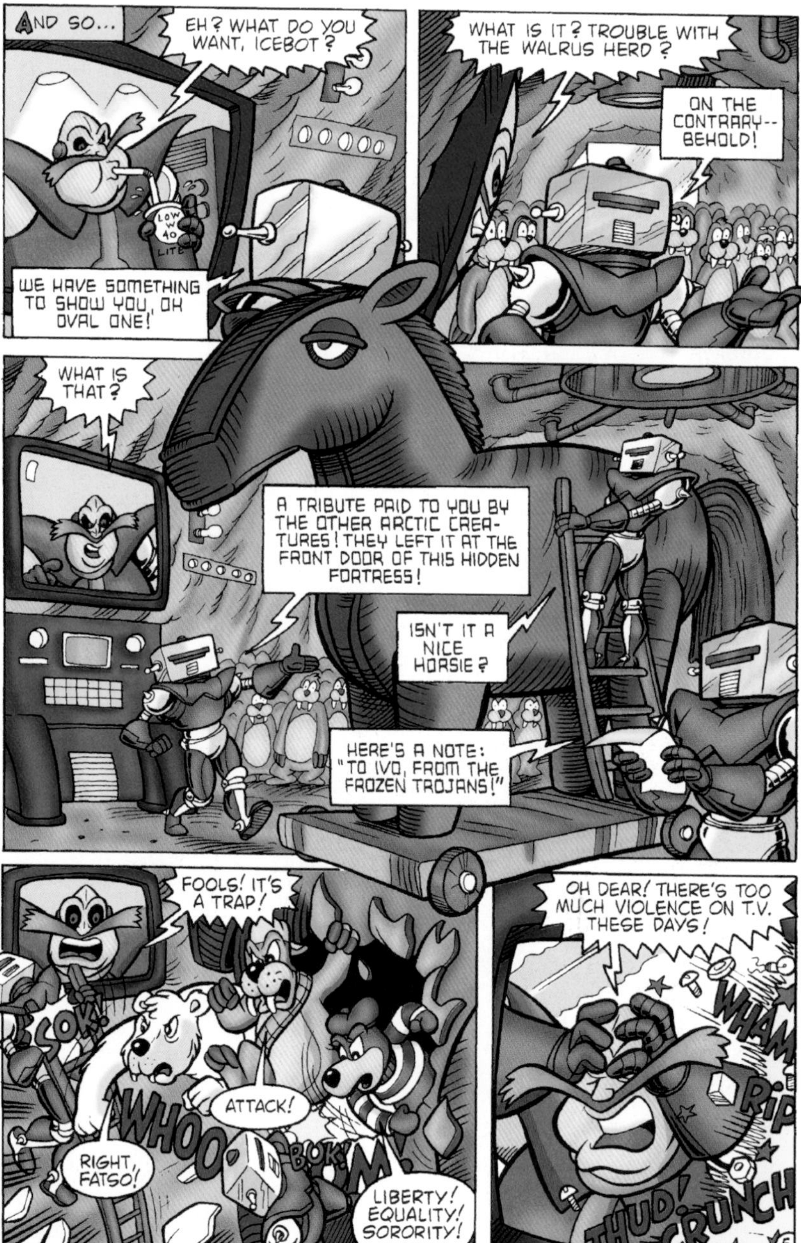
AND SO...
EH? WHAT DO YOU WANT, ICEBOT?
LOW W 40 LITE
WE HAVE SOMETHING TO SHOW YOU, OH OVAL ONE!
WHAT IS IT? TROUBLE WITH THE WALRUS HERD?
ON THE CONTRARY-- BEHOLD!
WHAT IS THAT?
A TRIBUTE PAID TO YOU BY THE OTHER ARCTIC CREATURES! THEY LEFT IT AT THE FRONT DOOR OF THIS HIDDEN FORTRESS!
ISN'T IT A NICE HORSIE?
HERE'S A NOTE: "TO IVO, FROM THE FROZEN TROJANS!"
FOOLS! IT'S A TRAP!
SOK!
ATTACK!
WHOOM
BOK!
RIGHT, FATSO!
LIBERTY! EQUALITY! SORORITY!
OH DEAR! THERE'S TOO MUCH VIOLENCE ON T.V. THESE DAYS!
WHAM
RIP
THUD!
CRUNCH

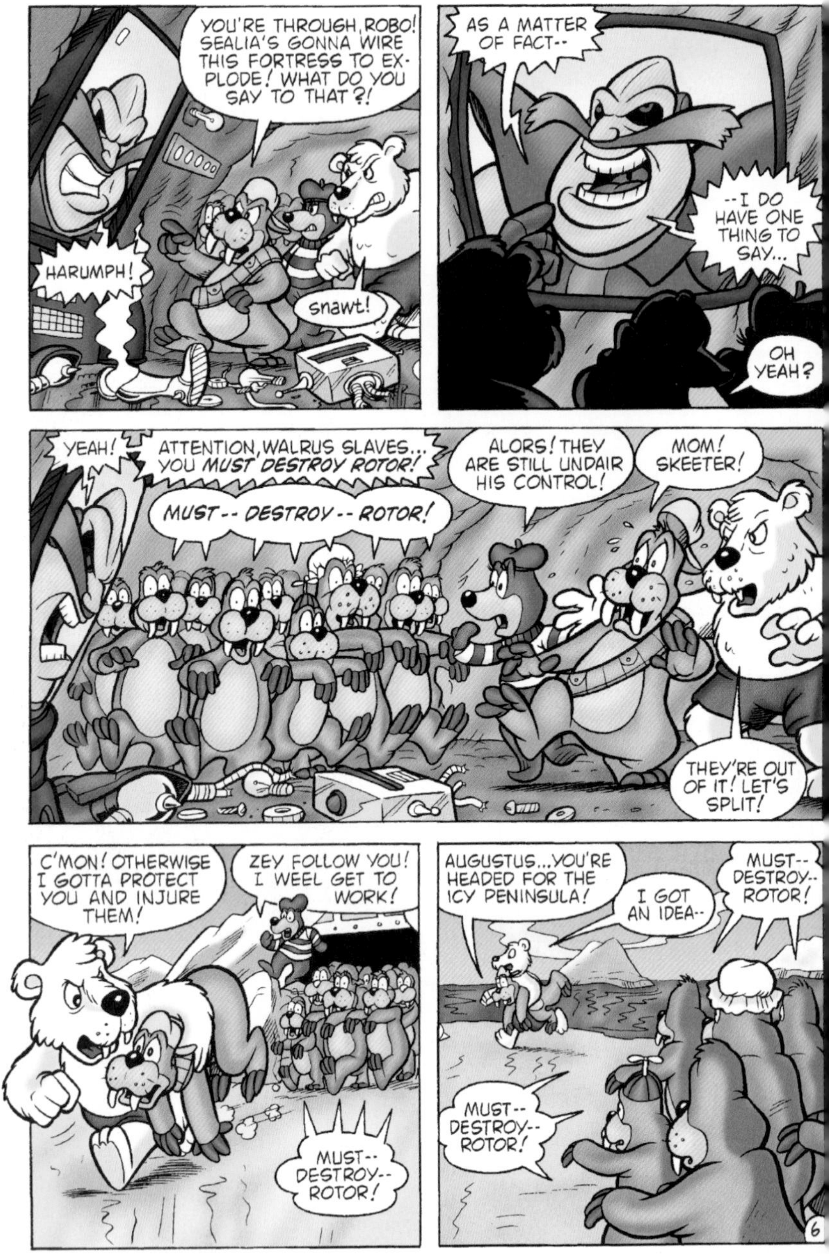
YOU'RE THROUGH, ROBO! SEALIA'S GONNA WIRE THIS FORTRESS TO EXPLODE! WHAT DO YOU SAY TO THAT?!
HARUMPH!
snawt!
AS A MATTER OF FACT--
--I DO HAVE ONE THING TO SAY...
OH YEAH?
YEAH!
ATTENTION, WALRUS SLAVES... YOU MUST DESTROY ROTOR!
MUST--DESTROY--ROTOR!
ALORS! THEY ARE STILL UNDAIR HIS CONTROL!
MOM! SKEETER!
THEY'RE OUT OF IT! LET'S SPLIT!
C'MON! OTHERWISE I GOTTA PROTECT YOU AND INJURE THEM!
ZEY FOLLOW YOU! I WEEL GET TO WORK!
MUST--DESTROY--ROTOR!
AUGUSTUS...YOU'RE HEADED FOR THE ICY PENINSULA!
I GOT AN IDEA--
MUST--DESTROY--ROTOR!
MUST--DESTROY--ROTOR!
6

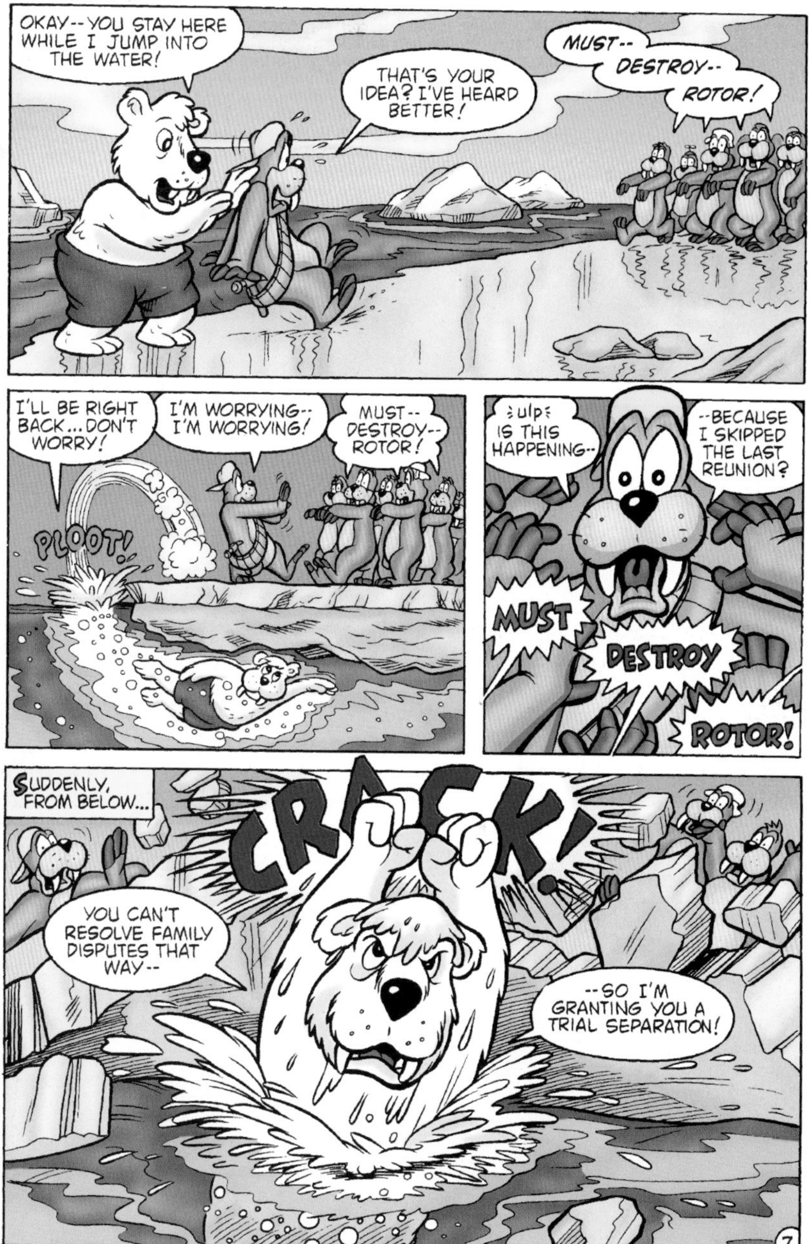
OKAY--YOU STAY HERE WHILE I JUMP INTO THE WATER!
THAT'S YOUR IDEA? I'VE HEARD BETTER!
MUST--
DESTROY--
ROTOR!
I'LL BE RIGHT BACK...DON'T WORRY!
I'M WORRYING-- I'M WORRYING!
MUST-- DESTROY-- ROTOR!
PLOOT!
gulp
IS THIS HAPPENING--
--BECAUSE I SKIPPED THE LAST REUNION?
MUST
DESTROY
ROTOR!
SUDDENLY, FROM BELOW...
CRACK!
YOU CAN'T RESOLVE FAMILY DISPUTES THAT WAY--
--SO I'M GRANTING YOU A TRIAL SEPARATION!

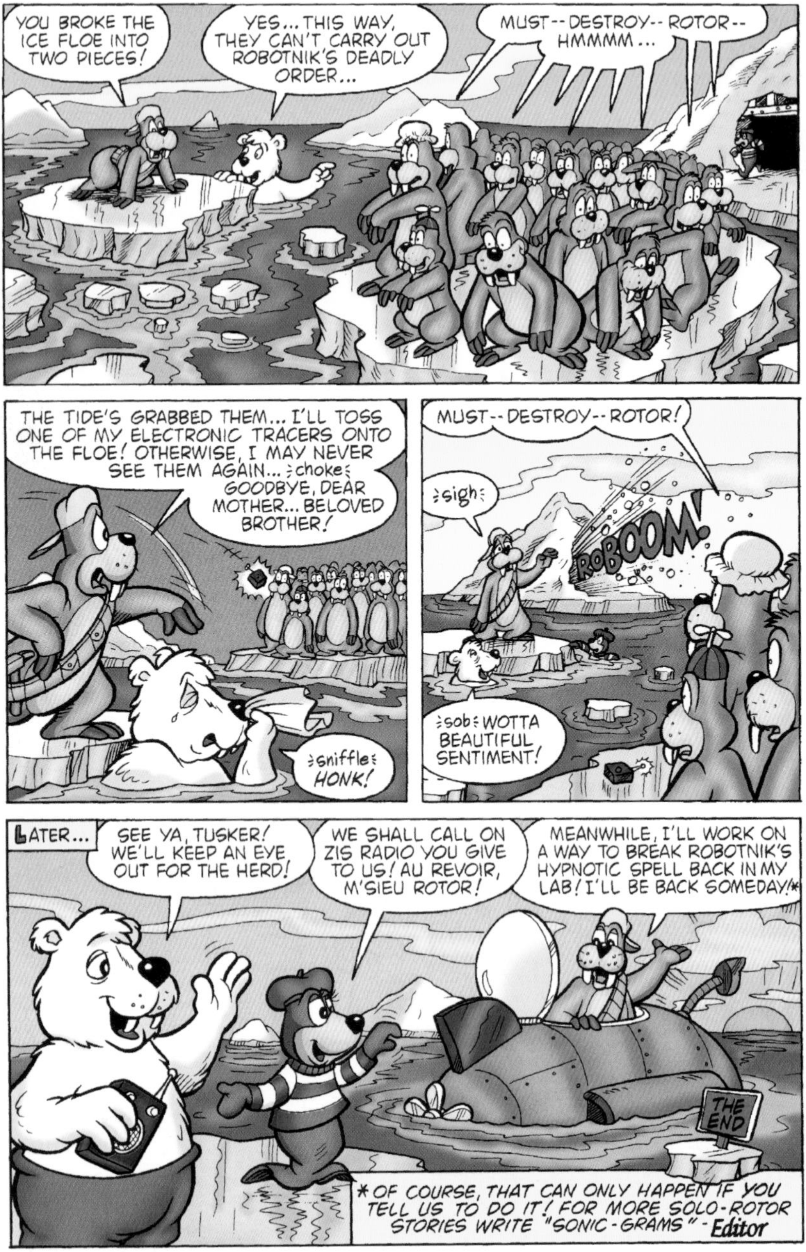
YOU BROKE THE ICE FLOE INTO TWO PIECES!
YES... THIS WAY, THEY CAN'T CARRY OUT ROBOTNIK'S DEADLY ORDER...
MUST--DESTROY--ROTOR--HMMMM...
THE TIDE'S GRABBED THEM... I'LL TOSS ONE OF MY ELECTRONIC TRACERS ONTO THE FLOE! OTHERWISE, I MAY NEVER SEE THEM AGAIN... choke GOODBYE, DEAR MOTHER... BELOVED BROTHER!
sniffle HONK!
MUST--DESTROY--ROTOR!
sigh
ROBOOM!
sob WOTTA BEAUTIFUL SENTIMENT!
LATER...
SEE YA, TUSKER! WE'LL KEEP AN EYE OUT FOR THE HERD!
WE SHALL CALL ON ZIS RADIO YOU GIVE TO US! AU REVOIR, M'SIEU ROTOR!
MEANWHILE, I'LL WORK ON A WAY TO BREAK ROBOTNIK'S HYPNOTIC SPELL BACK IN MY LAB! I'LL BE BACK SOMEDAY!*
THE END
* OF COURSE, THAT CAN ONLY HAPPEN IF YOU TELL US TO DO IT! FOR MORE SOLO-ROTOR STORIES WRITE "SONIC-GRAMS" - Editor

SONIC
THE HEDGEHOG™

Welcome to a brief who's who
of the Sonic universe.
You have just read some
of the earliest
and most loved stories from the
Sonic comic. We thought
you'd like to learn a little extra
about a few of your
favorite Sonic characters.

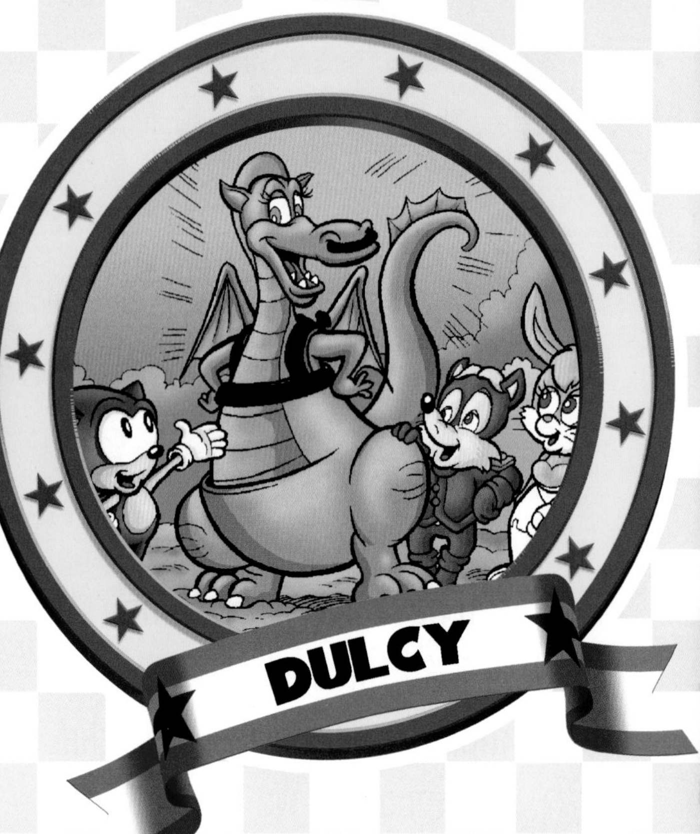
DULCY

Dulcy

The newest member of the Freedom Fighters, Dulcy the Dragon is one of the last of her people. Ever on the lookout for more of her kind, Dulcy spends her time helping the Freedom Fighters both as a transport from place to place and as a heavy-hitting fighter with a penchant for fire-breathing!

Robo-Chuck

Due to a freak accident in Dr. Robotnik's lab, Uncle Chuck has regained his free will! Now he can act as a double-agent for Sonic and the crew, as long as evil Dr. R doesn't find out!

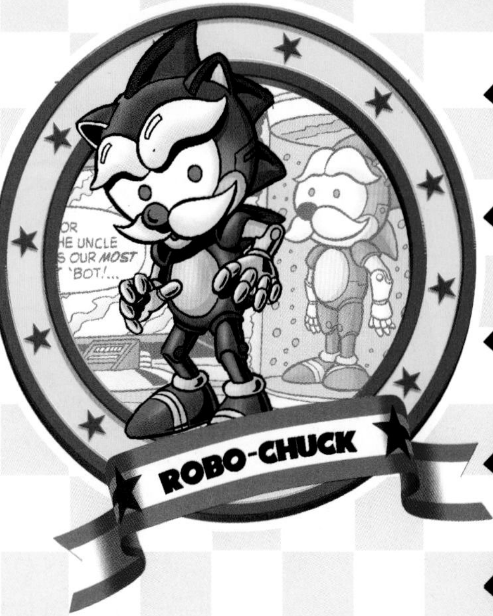

ROBO-CHUCK

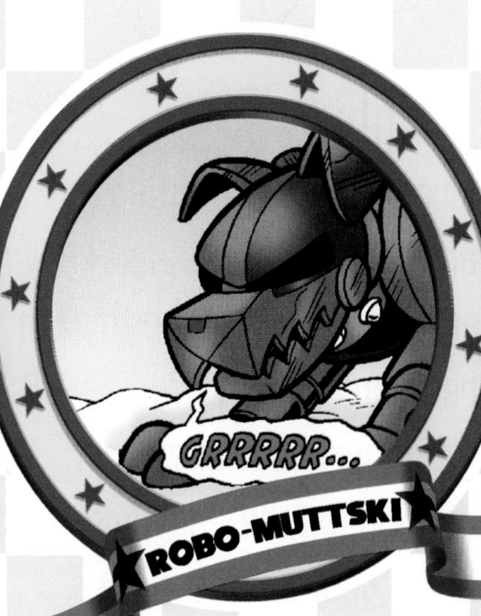

GRRRRR...
ROBO-MUTTSKI

Robo-Muttski

Man's best friend...not! Poor Sonic has to face off against his own pet, Muttski, after the cuddly canine was transformed into a monstrous metallic mutt! Can our hero reverse the effects?

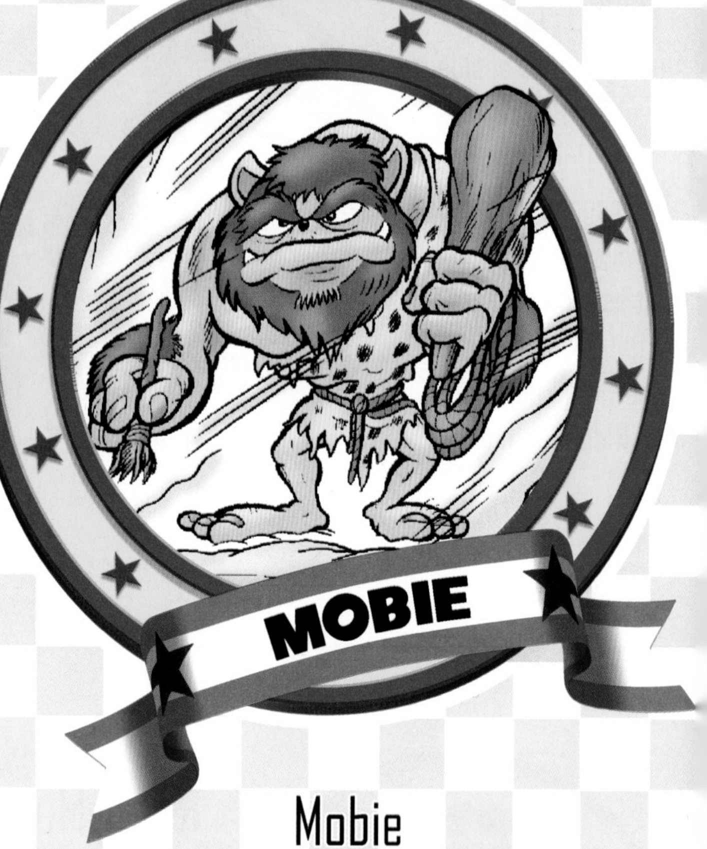
MOBIE

Mobie

Frozen underground for countless centuries, the giant bear from the past known as Mobie has been uncovered and unfrozen thanks to the Freedom Fighters! While a bit confused and temperamental at first, this club-wielding Neanderthal may prove to be one of the biggest assets in the battle against Robotnik.

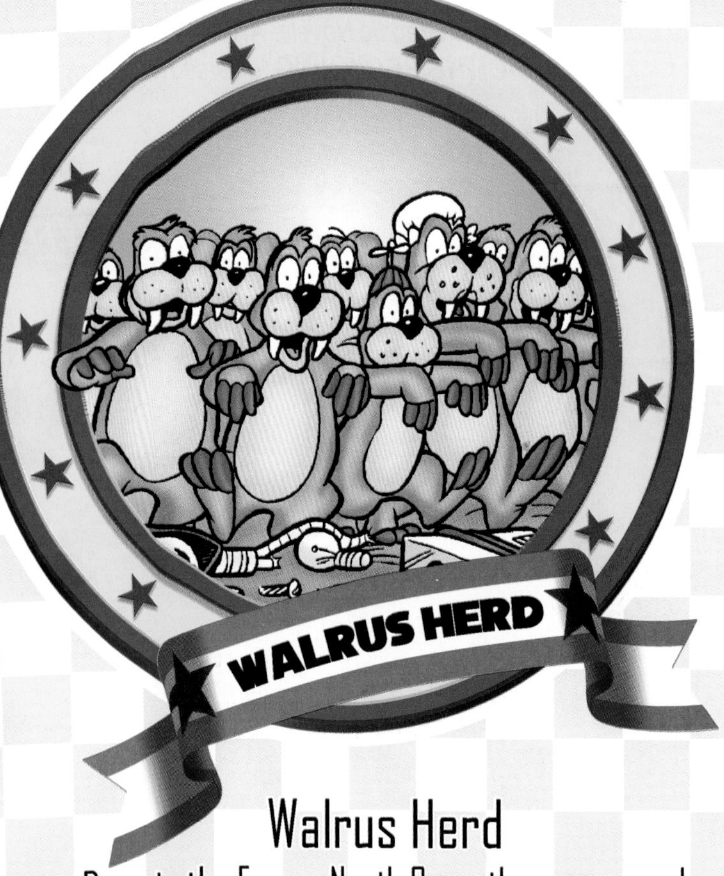
WALRUS HERD

Walrus Herd

Deep in the Frozen North Seas, the once-proud Walrus Herd has been brainwashed by evil Dr. Robotnik to help him in his latest schemes. And since few people ever visit this area of the world, he is free to scheme all he likes! At least he was, until a certain Freedom Fighter journeyed up to find his family and discovered the truth. Will Rotor be able to save the Walrus Herd, or will he need some help?

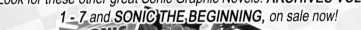